CW01011356

TO FIND OUT MORE ABOUT OUR READERS' CLUB WRITE TO;

SILVER MOON READER SERVICES;
Hexgreave Hall
Farnsfield
Nottinghamshire NG22 8LS
Tel: 01157 141616

YOU WILL RECEIVE A FREE MAGAZINE OF EXTRACTS FROM OUR EXTENSIVE RANGE OF EROTIC FICTION ABSOLUTELY FREE. YOU WILL ALSO HAVE THE CHANCE TO PURCHASE BOOKS WHICH ARE EXCLUSIVE TO OUR READERS' CLUB

***

NEW AUTHORS ARE WELCOME

Please send submissions to;
The Editor; Silver Moon Books
Hexgreave Hall
Farnsfield N22 8LS

This edition published 2010

ISBN 978-1-907475-71-9

Also by Sean O'Kane in Silver Moon

Church of Chains
Taming the Brat
The Story of Emma
Tales from the Lodge (with Falconer Bridges)
Bad Blood (with Francine Whittaker)
Slavemaker

The Arena Series

Into the Arena
The Gladiator
The Prize
Slave's Honour
Last Slave Standing
Girl Squad
Naked Ambition

Thanks to Falconer for the loan of ‘Dandy’,
and many thanks to Caroline as well.

Lost Property

by

Sean O'Kane

PROLOGUE

Marcel's chauffeur swung the hired limo off the highway when the sat nav told him he had reached his destination. It didn't really need to, the garish pink and purple, clap board house with the ten foot high letters above its roof were quite adequate to alert him.

The letters spelt out 'Mister B's' and underneath them, in slightly smaller letters was the legend; 'Finest whores in the state'.

Marcel told the man to wait once he had parked and walked up onto the porch, then in through the screen door and rang the front door bell. A woman who was all lipstick, teeth and bouffant blonde hair answered it. She looked him up and down, then gave him a wide lascivious grin, taking in the superbly tailored, lightweight suit, hand made shoes and the wrist watch that could have paid for a street of houses in this part of Louisiana.

"Honey, I'll do you a special price right here and now!"

"Thank you," he replied with a slight bow and a polite smile. "However I regret that my business is of a different nature. Is Mister Brubaker available please?"

Her smile faded and she shrugged, then stood aside to let him in. He squeezed past her massive breasts, held in a bright pink corset and waited while she sashayed off into the house's interior. Presently there was the sound of male footsteps and a large man in denim shirt and jeans came into the hall.

"You the Frenchie, yeah?" he said, holding out his hand.

Marcel smiled and took it. It was the ID he had adopted on the net for this particular quest. "Yes, and you are Mr Bee."

"That I am! Harrison Brubaker at your service. Got the merchandise all ready if you'd like to take a look before we get down to dickerin'"

"I would like that very much."

Brubaker led the way out the back of the house and through a large yard, into a stand of trees. In the middle of this was an aged barn. He unlocked the door and ushered Marcel into the dusk within.

What he had spent two years searching for and come thousands of miles to see and maybe buy, was standing in the middle of the floor. She was naked and was restrained, with her hands raised and tied to a rope that descended from a beam above her. Her head was completely enclosed in a black leather hood. Stray beams of sunlight, striking through gaps in the roof, illuminated her skin and made her glow in the dusk. Marcel noted her body was in good condition, her legs were long and the thighs smooth but powerful. The buttocks were high and tight, not too big but big enough to flatten and rebound pleasantly under beating. Her waist was trim and the stomach flat above a shaven crotch. Her raised arms gave her breasts some extra lift, but they didn't look as though they needed it.

He walked around her a few times, noting that the hood had breathing holes for her nostrils alone. That would enforce calmness on her in the confines of the leather scented darkness. Her breathing was quiet and steady.

"She certainly looks like arena stock. Athletic, well trained."

"Oh, she is. I can confirm that! I got a ring set up out in another barn back in the woods. Sometimes one of the punters brings his girl along and we bet on how long she'll last against this little darling. And she can take the whip all night long. With all the paperwork I got, she's the real deal ok. Wanna see her take down one of the bitches indoors?" He cocked his head back towards the house.

"Maybe later. Now I need to see her face." Marcel took some folded papers out of his pocket as Brubaker unlaced the hood and eased it off the woman.

Her dark hair was tousled and sweat-slicked and she shook it out, taking in mouthfuls of air now the stopple had been removed from her mouth, and running her tongue round her lips.

Marcel looked at the pictures he held. They were stills from videos which had deteriorated somewhat and been restored to the best of a very expensive studio's ability but were still a little grainy. One showed a dark haired girl, naked and armed with a whip combating another girl on the sand floor of an arena. Both girls were attractively welted as well as being sand-caked and sweat-lathered. In another picture the same dark haired girl was in some sort of cage and dressed in a leather corset with rounded metal studs all over it. Her fists were enclosed in thick leather straps and her opponent was reeling from a jab to the stomach. Marcel knew the rounded studs on the outsides of the corsets hid pointed studs on the insides and the straps at the knuckles were weighted.

The girl in the pictures was younger than the one standing in front of him but there was no mistaking her; the lithe figure, the large, dark eyes and the thick black hair. Besides, he had some marks to identify her by.

The woman stared at him as he approached, calm and unafraid; confident in her ability to serve in whatever way was required. She was experienced all right. He consulted the printout of an e mail and bent down slightly to examine her stomach. Sure enough there was the slight scar of a navel piercing still evident to someone prepared to look. He straightened up and moved closer, reaching out and grasping her right breast. She made no move to try and shrink away. He squeezed it hard and she simply looked down at the way her flesh spilled out from between his fingers. He twisted his hand slightly and saw what he was looking for; an inch long, shallow scar up by her shoulder – a memento of some accident long ago. The first agent to trade her had noted it, as well as removing the navel piercing.

He moved behind her and tapped her left calf. Obediently she raised it and he took her foot as though he were a blacksmith about to shoe a horse, but what he was looking for was on the inside of her thigh, right up at the junction with her buttock. He smoothed the skin of the buttock cheek up a little and found another scar; a semi circular one this time and only a couple of centimetres long. That one was from a crash in a chariot race. It had taken him months to track down her old trainer and then he had had to lubricate him with Scotch for a week before he would talk.

"It's her alright," he said, letting the slave's leg drop and straightening up.

"She was sold off before they chipped and branded them, so it makes identifying them harder don't it," Brubaker agreed.

"What I can't understand is why she was sold on at all!" Marcel ran a hand down her back, feeling the muscle tone and the smooth skin.

"Back then there was no way they coulda known what was going to happen. And once she'd gone, I guess it was outa sight, outa mind. Until I began to put two and two together when I saw her come up at auction."

"Thank God you did, M'sieur! She would've been a sad loss. And now perhaps we can check out a couple of details on paper and then reach agreement on a price."

Back at the house and in Brubaker's office they drank fiery local whisky while Marcel shuffled through the bills of sale and auctioneers' spiels that had followed the woman from dealer to dealer before Brubaker had spotted her real identity, bought her and begun to stir up interest on the net.

"You want a percentage of her?" Marcel asked eventually.

"No Sir! You got a mess of borders to get her across, then there's a lot of folk who'll do their damnedest to stop you doing what you're planning. No, I just want a good price paid up front and she's all yours."

Marcel didn't blame Brubaker, there was a long way to go before he could bring all his plans to fruition, and in any case it would be cheaper not to pay a percentage, if all went according to those plans.

"A million, here and now," he said.

"Add a half to that and she's yours."

"Done!"

The two men shook hands and went online to have their respective people make the transfer.

"Soon as I get confirmation it's landed, she'll be ready to go. Wanna see her whipped?" Brubaker asked once the various transactions had been started.

Marcel shrugged. "Why not? Although I have no doubt that she is genuine and will take whatever she is given. I still cannot believe that her stable sold her to buy a faster runner!"

"Wisdom of hindsight. The guy who signed her over to the auctioneer's been crying in his beer ever since! I think I told you that I tracked him down," Brubaker said with a smile and picked a tightly coiled single tail, braided whip up from behind his desk.

The two men walked back out to the barn. The slave was hooded once more and made no response to the door opening, clearly the hood was keeping her in complete isolation. Brubaker made to approach her and take it off but Marcel held him back and pointed to the whip. Brubaker smiled again and shook out the lash. Marcel stood back and watched as the American swept the lash forwards in a long arc. It wrapped itself around the slave's lower back, the tasselled end biting in just beneath her breasts. She leapt and twisted like a hooked salmon, and Marcel could well understand why. Locked in her silent and dark world, the lash would have come as a scarlet lightning bolt of shocking pain from nowhere. Brubaker landed another across her buttocks with the end biting at her delta. A muffled yelp and a doomed attempt to lift her thigh to protect herself greeted it and then Marcel suggested the hood be removed. With her breathing free, she would give better sport.

He stayed and watched long enough to see that despite her gyrations at the end of the rope the woman could absorb the kind of punishment an arena slave had to be able to and then left Brubaker to it.

"Don't damage her M'sieur, if you please, but by all means bid her a fond farewell," he said as he left. He had a friend arriving soon at his hotel, a young heiress with some interesting toys she had acquired recently in the Far East.

Soon after breakfast the next morning he got a call from Brubaker confirming receipt of the money and by mid morning he was standing in the brothel's hall as Brubaker handed the woman over, complete with her passport and all the papers that pertained to her.

"I'll follow your progress with interest, Marcel," Brubaker said as he shook hands and followed them out to the car.

Marcel gallantly gestured the woman should go first into the car and then made his farewells before joining her. With the heavy clunk of the door closing, they were alone, the chauffeur safely behind a closed glass panel. He looked across at his new acquisition, she was dressed simply in a cheap cotton shift dress, with a tasteless floral pattern on it, that stopped mid thigh. Sitting down, her long legs were naked almost to the buttocks as she had made no attempt to pull it down as she sat, Marcel noted the fading welts that striped them. She was regarding him with unabashed interest. Like any woman with a truly good figure, she transcended the tawdry dress and Marcel found his cock beginning to stir as he looked at her flat stomach and her breasts nearly spilling from its bodice.

"You are my new owner, yes?" Her accent was heavily Eastern European.

"The fifth Baron Sagemont at your service," he said, inclining his head and giving her a wry smile.

She looked around the limo, her eyes wide with interest.

"I do not wish to restrain you," he told her, "although I can if necessary. I have your passport and if you promise to behave yourself, I can promise you a comfortable journey to your new home."

Her full lips curled up into a smile and Marcel caught a glimpse of even, white teeth. His cock responded again.

"You have my passport, you have me, I think." she said. "But if you buy me, why you let Brubaker whip the fuck out of me last night? And then have all his friends fuck me afterwards?" She smiled again and leaned forwards to scratch at something on her ankle, moving with all the unconscious grace of someone accustomed to nudity. Or perhaps, Marcel found himself thinking, it was to show off the generous, quivering swells of breastflesh to her new owner.

"I will make no trouble, but I am one sore girl now," she added.

"You're used to plenty of whip."

"Not recently. It is two years now since I was in a stable. Since then I have been just a whore with some whip, time to time."

Marcel grinned across at her. "Time you got back into practice then… Annette from…Lithuania," he said, flicking through her passport.

"I used to be schoolteacher," she said and gave him a flagrantly flirtatious look from under her eyelashes.

When they reached the airport and climbed out of the car, Annette's eyes widened again as she took in the private jet with the famous logo emblazoned on it, a logo known wherever in the world lovers of fine brandy congregated.

Once they were airborne and the seatbelt light had gone out, Marcel's butler, Guillaume, served him with a glass of crisp white wine as an aperitif to lunch. Annette looked on with longing in her eyes for a moment and then in one simple movement, reached up and behind her, wriggled and lifted her dress off. She was entirely naked underneath and her tanned skin was laced with fading, dusky pink lines from Brubaker's whip. They encircled her entire torso from shoulders to crotch. When she stood up, Marcel saw that they embraced her thighs right to her knees.

She licked her lips and advanced on Guillaume.

"I think I have to pay my way, no?" she said and reached for Guillaume's trousers, running her palm up his flies and pouting her lips.

"Feel free, Guillaume," Marcel said. "It's what she's for."

He watched her sink to her knees and take his butler's cock deeply into her mouth before it was fully erect and begin to suck ardently.

He added mentally that whoring was only a part of what he wanted her for, but another look at her strong, whip-scored back, flexing as she worked on her knees, made him feel that he had spent his money wisely. If he got her into France without a fuss, then he could set about making his plans in earnest.

CHAPTER ONE

Kath looked up as her office door opened. He never knocked; just walked in as if he owned the place. And seeing as this was government property, then most certainly he didn't. It never stopped him however.

She stopped filling in the spreadsheet on screen and sat back, waiting until he decided to tell her what had brought him here. Her boss was a large man, well built, with a thick head of greying hair, he was dressed in a light grey suit that was expensively well tailored. Her eyes were drawn to his broad, muscular shoulders as he walked over to the window, hands in trouser pockets, his back to her and the room, almost silhouetted against the view over the Thames far below.

"It's not good enough," he said at length, turning and facing her, legs planted apart, full of confidence and self possession. Clive Mostyn was tipped for high political rank one day in the not too distant future and Kath had always been able to see why. He never entertained a single second's doubt about himself. But for now he was a junior minister tasked with statistical analysis of inter-departmental data; with special responsibility for youth affairs. He would brief his seniors when they had to face select committees. She knew he was irked by the rank of 'junior', and she had to agree that the title didn't sit easily with his six foot plus stature, and rugby forward physique.

"Sloppy spelling and syntax, careless research and on top of that your time keeping is appalling."

Kath knew the trains had let her down a couple of times over the past couple of weeks but had hoped that she might have sneaked past the Wicked Witch of the West on Reception. Obviously not. As for the standard of her report writing, well, first class honours level English hadn't been mentioned in the job specs or in the interview. But she sat nervously apprehensive and waited to see where this was leading. There was too much at stake to allow a rebellious outburst to jeopardise things. Mister Mostyn seemed to be considering her perceived shortcomings deeply.

He sighed, as though regretfully having to discipline a favoured child for its own good.

"Report to my office at five thirty." He turned abruptly and left the room as suddenly as he had entered it.

She checked her watch. Damn him! He had left her two hours to stew in. How serious was this going to be? She sighed in her turn and tried her best to concentrate on her work for the rest of the afternoon, reluctant to incur any more black marks before her carpeting with Mostyn.

What made it worse was that making her stay behind for half an hour made it feel like he was a strict headteacher giving a naughty girl detention. But there was nothing for it but to humour him and she worked on until quarter past five and then adjourned to the Ladies to try and freshen up.

She took her pale green shirt off and splashed some cool water over her face and underarms then patted herself dry and repaired her make up – she used some lash thickener to emphasise her large dark eyes; one of her better features she felt, although she was also well aware that the breasts straining against her lacy white bra would have got quite a few votes from various males about the place. She shrugged her shirt back on and then brushed out her thick black hair until it shone as it hung straight down onto her shoulders. She surveyed herself critically and stepped back from the mirror a little to check her grey pencil skirt wasn't too creased – although if it had been there wasn't a lot she could do about it now. She leaned back in and decided some blusher wouldn't go amiss. Tension had made her a bit pale.

At five thirty precisely she knocked on Clive Mostyn's door, feeling confident in looking the best she could under the circumstances and deriving some comfort from that fact. She pulled her shoulders back and straightened up then marched in confidently when she heard him tell her to come in.

His office was much bigger than hers of course, dark blue carpet stretched like a sea away in front of her to where he was sitting on a grey settee behind a dark wood coffee table. His desk was over to her right and his computer station was built under the bookshelves beyond that. The wall on her left was occupied entirely by a plate glass window that overlooked the Thames, leaden and grey under a cloudy sky as it twisted its way out towards the Channel. The towers and the sprawl of London seemed to go on for ever on either bank. On this visit however, she had no time for the view. Mister Mostyn was sitting forward in his shirt sleeves, his arms resting on his thickly muscled thighs. He was glowering at her.

And under his gaze she seemed to shrink as she walked with rapidly waning self confidence towards him. The carpet went on and on and the table and her boss seemed to get bigger and bigger until finally she came to a halt in front of the low table, her feet together and her hands held, little-girl like, clasped together in front of her.

He stood up and she almost took a step back but was so rooted to the spot that all she could do was blink up at him, frightened and rabbit-like, caught in the headlights of his blue-eyed gaze.

"If there's one thing that really irritates me Miss Knowles, it's pretty girls thinking they can get away with murder just by batting the lashes of their big, sad, soulful eyes."

"I…I'm sorry, Sir," Kath stammered, not sure how to react to being told she was batting her eyelashes at him at the same time as he had told her she was pretty.

"But are you sorry enough?" he rumbled, his resonant voice stirring the same odd heat inside her that it always did, even when he was just talking to people in the office. She flinched nervously as he suddenly reached up and loosened his tie, pulling it free of his collar and holding it tight between his big fists across the fronts of his thighs. Kath's throat went dry and her heart began to pound.

"You know I'm a stickler for discipline don't you." It wasn't a question.

The government was being tough on law and order just now and Clive Mostyn was prominent amongst those striving for a more disciplined and orderly society. Kath nodded.

Extending the forefinger of one hand her boss pointed to the table. A single key attached to a plain key ring lay there.

"Take it. Open the bottom right hand drawer of my desk and bring me what you find. Do it now!" His voice wasn't raised, it didn't need to be. Kath could feel the force of his personality and his will almost like a gale blowing into her face. She was helpless to stop herself from doing exactly what he told her to. Orders were something she had never been able to resist.

His desk was a classic boss's one in richly polished mahogany with an inlaid green leather top. As she went behind it and bent to open the drawer the scent of leather hit her and lit the fires inside her all the more fiercely. She adored leather, its scent and feel and the way her favourite leather mini skirt caressed her thighs. Biting her lip against the excitement, she pulled the drawer open and saw what it contained. The scent of leather became stronger and her heart raced even faster. She swallowed nervously and glanced up to see that he hadn't moved and was still standing with his tie held as before, almost as if it were some kind of strap he had some diabolical plans for. Not that he needed it, she thought, now that she had seen what was in his desk.

"Come on, quickly!" Mostyn told her.

With shaking hands, but with contradictory feelings of terror and fire in her stomach – and lower down now; much lower – she did as he told her, returned to the table and set down on it a tightly coiled leather belt about two inches wide and a curiously shaped broad strap with tongues cut in it.

"Do you know what that is?" he asked, seeing where she was looking. She shook her head. "It's a tawse. Been used to discipline unruly girls and boys in Scotland for years. And unruly is what you are Miss Knowles. Unruly." He rolled the 'r' with relish as she stood meekly, hands in front of her, eyes downcast, fixed on the instruments of chastisement. He surely wasn't seriously intending to use them on her was he? Not in this day and age? Surely not!

"Take off your shirt and bra please."

"But Mister Mostyn! I mean....Sir! That's not...... you can't......!"

"I can! And what's more I just have! I have ordered you to remove your shirt and bra as I intend to punish you. Now you may obey or you may leave, get fired, and then try reporting me to whichever lily livered, PC ridden quango exists to protect miscreants like you!"

He still wasn't shouting but his voice and his anger seemed to cut right through her and heap coals on the fire within her. He was so attractive and anger suited him somehow. And….well she had been late a couple of times…..and perhaps she hadn't been as conscientious as she might have been recently.

And she had to face it; she liked being given orders.

Her fingers went to her shirt buttons.

She lowered her eyes as she undid the shirt, she couldn't bear to see whether or not he was smirking at his victory over her but he stood quite still and she couldn't take her eyes off the stretched taut tie between his big fists which lay against his powerful thighs. She didn't really know what to do with the shirt once it was off and Mostyn obviously wasn't inclined to help her, in the end she just dropped it at her feet and reached behind her to unclasp her bra and then when that was dropped at her feet she crossed her arms over her breasts, standing huddled and humiliated before her boss.

She was confidently expecting to have to remove the skirt next when instead he marched straight past her towards the door. She half turned, wondering what on earth he had in mind.

He stopped by the door and turned to her.

"Come here!" he said curtly.

She went to him; there didn't seem much alternative. As she neared him he reached up to the lintel and threaded the tie through a small eye bolt that she hadn't seen, screwed into the top of it.

"Put your hands together and raise them please," he ordered brusquely and once again she found herself obeying, although it meant finally baring her breasts.

He ignored them completely however and set about tying her wrists together so that her forearms were raised and flat against the wood of the door and her nipples were pressed against it too. Fear had hardened them and an odd little thrill ran through her as they were touched.

Once she was secured, Mostyn stepped back and Kath looked over her shoulder to see that he had returned to the table and picked up the belt. God! He was actually going to beat her! He had no right to! He was going to though. What was the belt going to feel like when a big man like Mostyn swung it against her naked flesh? Would it feel good?

She was aghast at the treacherous thought. But it was real nonetheless. The thought of leather smacking down onto her unprotected flesh was deeply and disturbingly exciting. When it came, the answer to her question was that it felt as though someone had punched her and then it felt as though that part of her back was on fire. The first blow had landed high up towards her left shoulder with a shockingly loud smacking noise. A soft cry had been wrung from her and she instinctively twisted away from the pain, the movement rasped her nipples against the grain of the wood and by the time the second lash hit, her head was already throwing back in shock at the intensity of the excitement. Again there was the heavy impact and the burning and again she twisted. This time she was pressed a little harder against the wood and the thrill from her nipples lanced through her so vividly that her eyes were wide and staring at her bound hands above her, they looked so small and vulnerable, as the third lash smacked across her middle back. She cried out again and flung her head back, thrusting her breasts hard against the door and growling as the shards of excitement in her nipples lanced through her again.

There was a pause and Kath craned her head round to see Mostyn rolling up the shirt sleeve of the arm he was using to beat her. She saw that he had doubled the belt over to make a flexible sort of club – and that must be why it was making that shocking impact on her skin – she also saw the thick ropes of muscle across his forearm and quickly turned her face away, burying her head against her own forearms. Deep inside her now and undeniable in its ferocity was a fire that burned in her sex. Under the tailored smartness of her skirt and the pretty, lace-edged panties, her cunt was hot and moist, and what had cranked up the level of excitement was the fact that Mr. Mostyn was frowning in concentration as he turned up his sleeve and prepared to resume the punishment, completely ignoring the half naked woman he was beating. To him she was merely the job in hand. For some reason that thought alone almost brought her to a minor orgasm.

Then another blow landed and she squirmed against the door and gasped as a tremor of climax finally did spiral through her. From then on the blows landed hard and regular until he finally stopped when her whole back felt raw and burning, her nipples were throbbing and her insides were in such a turmoil that she was panting and groaning and drowning in sensations so powerful she had no name for them. But they were strangely and darkly pleasurable.

For a second she continued to lean her head against her arms and listen to her ragged breathing as the thunder in her body subsided. But then she jumped as she felt his hard, heavy hands run up her back and reach over her to release her own hands. Slowly she pushed herself away from the door and turned around, carefully avoiding rubbing her sore back against the door.

Mostyn was now beside his desk and he had the tawse in his hand. Wordlessly he beckoned to her. Again for reasons she couldn't explain she tottered forward and for a few steps forgot that her breasts were naked and in full view. Instinctively one hand came up to cover them but then she saw his eyes fix on them as they swayed with her movement and she could read the excitement in them. It was a small victory, but a victory of sorts, at least he had enjoyed punishing her and found her attractive – he had called her pretty after all – she dropped her hand and tried to straighten up as she approached him.

Once again she stood submissively in front of him, hands clasped in front of her, naked breasts still heaving as she regained her breath. He was holding the tawse as he had held the tie and she kept her eyes lowered to it, suddenly realising that what she would really like would be for him to reach out and touch her breasts.

But that wasn't on his menu just yet.

"Skirt, pants," he said simply.

Before she knew it her hands were fumbling with the zip at her hip but at the same time she was grimly determined that he was going to touch her this time. Even he wasn't going to be able to remain unmoved in the face of her complete nudity while he thrashed her.

The word 'thrash' went through her mind and echoed in it as she pushed the skirt down and stepped free of it, then did the same with the deep maroon and white lace knickers. Her back stung again as she moved and the word 'thrash' wouldn't go away. It was a good word; she liked the sound of it.

As she straightened up fully naked apart from her black court shoes, he jerked his head towards the desk.

"Over you go!"

She advanced and prepared to lay herself across it, pressing her breasts and face into the leather inlay.

"No! I don't want you sweating and dribbling over it!" he snapped. "Just stretch your arms out to the sides, rest your face on the wood at the front and hang on."

She did as he said, bereft of the chance to experience that magical feeling in her nipples and instead resting her cheek on the hard wood and feeling her breasts hang beneath her. It was more comfortable if she shuffled her feet apart and lowered herself a little, she found. The fact that Mr Mostyn standing behind her now had a grandstand view of everything between her legs, perversely only added to her desire to settle herself comfortably. She gripped the ends of the desk and readied herself to undergo further punishment.

She felt cold leather come to rest gently against the skin of her buttocks.

"This is for the poor time keeping," he told her. "Ten."

Whack!

The impact was much more fierce and the sting excruciating, but the noise was wonderful and even as she drew in a long shuddering gasp of shock and almost rose off the desk, she registered another eruption of molten heat in her loins.

Whack!

A scream was cut off by choking as the second lash made her breath catch and she gulped helplessly until the third landed, making no allowances for her ability or otherwise to cope with it.

From there on she endured the punishment in a mist of wriggling, stinging, coughing, excitement and yelping until finally it stopped and she lay sobbing and undone on the wood of the desk. Slowly, as her mind began to clear, she began to realise that his hand was inside her. As the numbing fires of the tawse subsided, they were overtaken by fires of bright pleasure as his fingers swirled and twisted inside her, his other hand suddenly reached under her and gripped a breast - hard. She lifted her head and moaned.

"Slut!" he hissed beside her ear. "How can I punish a slut who enjoys her own degradation so much?"

"Sorry, Sir!" she whispered hopelessly, limp with the pleasure of what he was doing to her.

Suddenly, terribly, he stopped what he was doing and she gave a despairing cry as she felt herself emptied with brutal speed.

"Stand up and admit to what a whore you really are, Mizz Knowles! Show me and the whole world…" he gestured behind himself to the view, "what a shameless creature you are. Admit to what your punishment has made you desire!" His voice rose enough to achieve a resonance that Kath, already excited, dazed and bewildered, was utterly unable to resist.

She slowly stood up, gripping the desk for a moment until she got her balance then turned to face the room, spread her legs and with her mouth still hanging half open, her hair tousled, she reached both hands between her legs and began to masturbate.

With one hand she began a merciless assault on her clitoris, rubbing and grinding it while with her other hand she reached as deep inside her vagina as she could and thrust with her fingers, desperately trying to imitate the action of a thick hard cock fucking her. And a thick hard cock was what she focussed her eyes on. Hands on hips, Mostyn stood sneering at her, but in his trousers Kath could see that he wasn't immune to her. He was as turned on as she was.

She felt the first waves of climax build inside her and tried to steady her feet – almost fell but managed to keep on masturbating.

"Go on, you cock hungry slapper!" he urged her. "Show me how shameless you really are!"

"Yess! Yess!" The fires inside her and on her skin were all joined now and if she had to undergo it all again she would gladly do so, just so long as she reached the peak that she knew was coming.

When it broke she put her head back and her trembling fingers administered the coup de grace which blinded her and unbalanced her so that she staggered back against the desk, igniting the bitter fires in her bottom.

When the spasms and tremors finally stopped and her hands dropped away from the hot morass between her thighs, she saw that Mostyn was leaning back against an arm of the settee, just in front of her. His hands were unbuckling his belt and as she watched he slowly slid the zip of his flies down. She brushed some errant hair out of her eyes and staggered forwards. There was only one way this was going to end.

Mostyn caught a handful of her hair as she tottered towards him and pulled her head back to make her look at his cruelly curled lip and the triumph in his blue eyes.

"Whore!" he whispered.

"Yes, Sir." She sank to her knees and watched as he pulled his trousers and pants down until a furiously thick and urgent cock sprang free. With one hand bracing herself against his thigh, she used the other to ease the foreskin back off the enormous head. It was every bit as angry, hard and demanding as Mostyn himself had been earlier, and those emotions somehow suited it just as well as they had him. Furling her lips carefully over her teeth, she leaned in and opening her mouth until she was sure her jaw would crack, she gently engulfed him, letting her tongue rasp softly along the underside of the helm as it pushed through into her mouth and lodged at her throat.

Above her she heard him sigh in pleasure, then she felt his hands on her head. She began to nod back and forth, feeling the ribbed harness of the shaft pass out from and back into her mouth, tasting the salty pre-come. She parted her knees a bit farther to lower herself so that she could allow him more travel into and out of her mouth and he began to speed up. His hands gripped either side of her head and she readied herself for the eruption of thick, slimy spend that would need swallowing.

When it came he rammed her face onto him, fucking it as he would her cunt and she had to use all her skill to contain him. Even so she did manage to furtively rub at her clit while he came into her.

They dressed hurriedly and without speaking. Now the storms of desire, anger, pain and pleasure had passed, there was no need to speak and Kath didn't know what words could be said.

Eventually, when she was fully dressed again, she faced him and he regarded her seriously but quite calmly – as if she couldn't just march out of the room and have him fired and possibly prosecuted – instead she took his hand after a few moments and held it to her face, nuzzling the palm with her cheek and brushing it with her lips.

"Please, Sir. Next time, could we do it a bit earlier? I'm late for a dinner date," she whispered.

CHAPTER TWO

Kath took a minute to get her breath before she entered the bar. Once she had left Mostyn she had had to go straight back to the Ladies and repair the damage. A quick look to regret the fading belt marks on her back hadn't been originally intended but had been indulged in anyway. Then she had had a rush to the tube and a crowded carriage to stand in across town, then a scrum to push through on the platform where she alighted and a brisk two hundred yard walk to the bar where Angie, her editor was meeting her. It was pointless trying to hide anything from Angie, she knew her too well, so she didn't bother with brushing her hair again or anything, just waited till she felt a bit more settled and then entered.

The bar was high-ceilinged and fashionably beige and cool inside, it wasn't yet crowded so it didn't take long for her to pick out Angie, sitting on a bar stool and earnestly trying to seduce a barman. Smiling, she went over and took the stool next to her. As she took it, her knees brushed Angie's and she felt the soft rasp of nylon. So Angie was wearing stockings, that always meant she was up for a good night. Kath's heart sank a little but rallied at the smile of pure pleasure Angie turned on her.

"Oh my!" she said quietly. "There's only one thing that'll bring a sparkle like that to a girl's eye. James! Bring a large G and T here will you! Ice no slice!"

James who looked as though he spent every waking hour on a surf board when he wasn't waiting bar, grinned across and began to prepare it.

Kath relaxed against the textured aluminium of the bar. "Tell you later?"

"Sure. You want dinner here, or rustle up something at my place?" Angie's voice was ruined by years of cigarettes, although now she no longer indulged, and it had a dark brown quality that Kath found highly attractive. The two women looked at each other for a moment, then Angie reached out and touched Kath's knee.

"He mention Proteus yet?"

Kath shook her head as James delivered her drink and she took a long and much-needed swig as Angie paid and told him that he could shag her lights out any time he was at a loose end. James said he would certainly bear that in mind and laughed. It was a well practised camouflage that Angie had perfected over the years, but it still irked Kath that she felt it was necessary in these days of improved tolerance and equality.

"Better eat at your place. Safer," Kath said once the gin had hit home and she felt the day begin to drain away.

"Okay, babe. Let's drink up and get a taxi."

The taxi dropped them a few yards from Angie's front door so that Kath could pick up an Indian takeaway while Angie went ahead.

By the time Kath let herself in to the apartment with her key, Angie had laid the table and added candles and lit them. They were the only light in the dining room and the lights in the lounge were low. It was definitely going to be a stockings night, Kath told herself ruefully, still feeling some traces of stinging from her bottom.

"What do you want me as, Mistress?" she asked, putting the meal down on the kitchen work surface. Angie was magnificent in a red leather bustier and matching thong with red thigh boots that accentuated the long, pale thighs. Her blonde hair hung in thick waves about her strong, handsome face and Kath felt herself begin to respond all over again. She was a sucker for dominants. That was all there was to it!

Angie was in her early forties and was supple and fit, her stomach was flat and her hips curved out smoothly from her trim waist. Beneath the strictures of her bustier, her breasts were full and firm. Kath was suddenly eager to be ordered to suck on the thick, red nipples, hard with desire and standing proud of the lust-swollen areolas.

As Kath watched she poured herself a glass of wine.

"Maid, tonight. You can serve me."

"Yes, Mistress." It was such a relief to be able to call her by her proper title when they were in private. Kath hated having to call her Angie or Mrs. Hepple when they were together in public, not that that occurred very much since she had been sent to work undercover at the Home Office's offshoot that Clive Mostyn ran.

In the main bedroom, Kath sorted through her costumes; the nurse, the nun, the school girl, the whore until she found the little black satin number and laid it on the bed while she stripped, and then she pulled it on and went to her stockings and knicker drawer to find a pair of black hold ups, there was absolutely no point in bothering with knickers. She slipped her black court shoes back on and gave her hair yet another quick brush through, tugged the minute satin skirt more squarely over the net skirts underneath it, checked there was a reasonable amount of cleavage on view; Mistress was partial to a casual breast and nipple fondle whenever the mood took her, turned sideways to admire the way the skirt stuck out over her bottom invitingly and trotted back to the kitchen.

Angie looked her over critically.

"Left stocking seam's a bit skewed," she opined.

"Sorry, Mistress," Kath said contritely as she bent to straighten it.

Her Mistress gave a 'Hmph' noise that usually meant a caning later and swept out. Kath busied herself with the meal and brought it to the table, where, over the gentle candlelight, she was brought up to date with all the office gossip from The Journal, the paper that Angie edited.

At last they sat back and Kath was allowed a glass of wine herself.

"So tell me what the old goat did this time," Angie asked.

"It was a belt and a tawse – I've not had one of those, can we get one please?"

"You'll get what you're given. Now concentrate on telling me exactly what Mostyn said and did," her Mistress growled. "And you can have the pegs while you do it, you cheeky little madam!"

Kath's heart began to pound again, just as it had done with Mostyn earlier. As her Mistress sauntered into the lounge, Kath started the next ritual. She fetched a footstool from the spare bedroom – where she slept when she had been very naughty – and set it in front of where Angie now sat on the sofa. Then she went to a kitchen cupboard and took out a box that rattled as she carried it back to the lounge. Finally she took a clean white handkerchief from the airing cupboard and spread it on the stool then she carefully sat on it, making sure her thighs were parted and her labia were in full contact with the handkerchief. Only when she was properly settled did she reach for the box, take off the lid and place it on her Mistress' lap.

"Pop them out for me, girl!" she commanded.

Kath reached into her bodice and squeezed her breasts out, so that the neckline of the little costume now stretched tightly across her chest under the breasts, pushing them together and thrusting them forwards. With that done, Kath put her hands behind her, straightened her back and leaned towards her Mistress.

Trying to concentrate on getting each detail precisely right, Kath told her editor and adored Mistress all that had happened during the day. While she did so, Angie took pinch after pinch of soft breast flesh and clamped a clothes peg over it.

From time to time Kath glanced down to admire the multi-coloured spiky mounds that her poor breasts had become. She would lose her way in a sentence as she watched Mistress' hand close over another piece of skin and pull it, whilst with her other hand she lowered a cheerfully coloured plastic peg over it and then let it close, adding a shrill descant to the overall throbbing that was her entire breast area. She would stumble over her account and Mistress would slap her thigh irritably to bring her attention back to where it belonged. What Mistress did with Kath's tits was none of Kath's business after all.

"Hmm." Angie sat back and surveyed her handiwork when Kath had ended her account. "But you're still finding evidence of Proteus?"

"Oh yes, Mistress. I've seen it mentioned in several documents and sometimes one or other of the senior staff refer to it if they think they won't be overheard."

"We're running out of time. The big boss man wants results and if Mostyn doesn't make his move soon, we'll just have to run with another 'Minister found with his leg over' scandal. And they're two a penny."

The Proteus project had been why Kath had been sent undercover to apply for a job with Mostyn's department. Rumours had been circulating for some time about a hush-hush project that he had been tasked with by someone very high up in government. From what could be picked up, there seemed to be a salacious element to whatever it was and The Journal was always alert to the circulation boosting possibilities of good sex stories.

To begin with Angie had been delighted with how quickly Mostyn had responded to Kath's charms and when he had stumbled across her submissiveness when she had allowed herself to be put over his knee and spanked for talking at the water station for too long, hopes were high that he would drop hints about Proteus during a night at a hotel or something. But so far he had limited himself to punishing her in the office and had only used her orally.

They had hoped for pillow talk but Mostyn seemed to be resisting the temptation.

Mistress stood up and gestured to Kath to do the same, together they surveyed the state of the handkerchief on which Kath had been sitting. It was sodden in a long, wet mark in the centre.

"Hopeless slut! Into the bedroom for caning!" Mistress ordered cheerfully, ignoring the soft whimper from Kath at the lack of permission to remove the pegs first. They always hurt more in the coming off than in the putting on, so that meant all the havoc a cane could cause, followed by a fresh burst of breast pain…..The trouble was that the cruelty just meant that she was getting even wetter.

Bent over the wrought iron foot of the bed with her miniscule skirt pushed up onto her lower back, Kath received a slow and excruciating caning that left her bruised, ecstatic and so turned on that Angie's hand was almost sucked in to the wrist by her cunt. After a good feeling around, Angie had Kath stand with hands on head while the pegs were slowly removed from her tits and then she was sent to shower while Angie undressed and selected her biggest strap-on, put it on, made sure the lube was close to hand and climbed into bed.

The room was dark when Kath returned and she slipped under the duvet to find her Mistress' body, soft and warm, waiting for her. She groaned in pleasure as her questing fingers found the strap-on and further investigation revealed it to be the biggest one they possessed. In the dark she heard the lid of the lube pot open and giggling huskily she turned onto her front and got her knees under her so that her bottom was in the air.

The lube was cold and the strap-on hurt to start with but then Mistress drove her fingernails into the cane weals on her buttocks and all was well.

CHAPTER THREE.

The first part of the following week passed uneventfully but on the Wednesday, Kath's office door opened without warning and Mostyn entered again. This time he strode straight over to Kath and planted his fists on the front of her desk, leaning across so that he loomed over her.

"Rather than punishing you in the office for mistakes I just know I'm going to find when I start looking again, I'm going to suggest – your dinner dates permitting of course! – that I take rather more time about it. I have to go somewhere at the end of the week and I'd like you to accompany me. It'll be overnight, we'll leave here mid-afternoon. I've cleared it with your team leader."

He didn't wait for a reply.

Kath sat staring stupidly at the door after he had closed it. It just hadn't entered his head that she might not be able – might not want – to go with him. But then she had played the compliant subby for all she was worth and if she was honest, she could feel herself moistening as she replayed the scene in her mind... the way he had towered over her at her desk, the way his will had almost formed a bow wave in front of him when he entered. And there was the possibility of getting what her Mistress wanted, which opened up the prospect of being on the receiving end of two dominants' pleasures.

That night saw some controlled panic at Angie's apartment. Stripped in front of the cheval mirror in the bedroom Kath examined her backside by twisting around as best she could while Angie lathered on Witch Hazel and anything else they could think of to try and make the bruising from the cane dissipate before the night of the trip. By applying all the various lotions morning and night – and Kath putting some on during the day – her bottom was more or less clear by the day in question.

"Ready to take plenty more!" Mistress declared before Kath set off for work, then she suddenly went serious and came close to Kath to kiss her gently on the lips.

"You know how much I enjoy sharing you around," she said and Kath nodded. Many had been the time that Mistress had stood and passed humorous comments while other Mistresses' playthings had fucked her. "But this time is different. It's work and I won't be happy till you're back safe and sound. Then by God I'll flay you, so make sure you come back with something juicy about Proteus!" She favoured Kath with a smile that set her heart thumping and she left walking on air, looking forward to serving her Mistress and getting her just desserts.

John Carpenter's office at The Lodge, the most select and secretive SM club in the land was, at first sight, not where a lot of people expected. It wasn't above the main entrance overlooking the sweeping parkland and woods beyond, instead it was tucked away at the end of the massive frontage with windows on two aspects. It did overlook part of the views to the front but also it had three windows on the side of the main building that overlooked the stableyard. It also meant that he could see over the trees to where the equestrian arena now stood and the new CSL stables beyond that. In The Lodge's own stableyard, directly below him, the Housegirls who were required to serve as ponies by their owners or by members of The Lodge were stabled and catered for. Farther away, the fighting girls of the CSL stable trained in the arena and were housed in the new stableyard, which was even now being extended; meaning that the members were having to do without ponies as the CSL slaves were being housed in the old stables temporarily. No one was complaining because he and Carlo – who jointly owned the CSL stable – were offering out the CSL slaves at greatly reduced rates while the work was finished. From over at the new stables the sounds of angle grinders and drills at work drifted up.

Soon there would be twenty slaves housed by CSL, the only stable on the arena circuit that didn't have its own full-sized arena but which specialised instead in training up slaves who could be hired in to strengthen other stables' squads. It was a far bigger stable now than Carlo had ever envisaged, but change was everywhere. CSL was changing, the whole arena landscape was changing and one of the main agents of that change was the other occupant of the room. There was a third person present but as she was a Housegirl who was currently receiving a vigorous beating with a crop, she didn't really count.

John turned from contemplating the view as Clive Mostyn paused in his beating for a moment.

"We should be ready to go in about a fortnight," he said without taking his eyes off the quivering buttocks of the girl in front of him. Having delivered a salvo of full blooded lashes he made her jump by delivering a few light flicks at various targets. The girl cast an anxious glance at John, who, as owner of The Lodge, was her owner as well, and settled again. "What can you let us have?" Mostyn asked, placing the crop against her bottom and settling his feet so that the girl knew hard strokes were coming. Then he made her wait.

John was impressed. Mostyn couldn't have afforded a day's membership of The Lodge but he understood how to play on a submissive's fear and excitement, so he was clearly experienced at handling submissive girlflesh.

"I can let you have Jet and Cherry with Helga as groom for a fortnight in the South."

Mostyn nodded thoughtfully and then let fly with a hard lash. The girl let out a stifled scream and arched her back, pushing her face up from her crossed arms and frantically wriggling her stern. Mostyn quietened her by laying the crop against her skin once more.

"They're docile enough to cope with the change in routine and personnel," John went on.

"Indeed," Mostyn agreed and treated the girl to another hard whack.

"You can have Brian as instructor. Carlo will be away with Blondie, Ox, Trouble and a couple of the others at the N'Benga arena. I'll need Tony to keep an eye on things here."

"Ok. That sounds fine. What are your thoughts about the other place?"

The crop blurred once more as it scythed into the prominent and inviting buttocks. The girl's back humped and her feet jigged about as she fought to contain the pain. Mostyn smiled and inserted three fingers between her spread legs. He worked her until she was squelching shamelessly then withdrew them and tapped her bottom with the crop again.

"I'll send Blackie and Legs with Anne Marie as groom. They're relatively new but they're docile too."

Whack! The girl's long legs bent and her breath hissed as she absorbed the strike, which John had to admit was a stern one. The new uniform suited the tall girl's build well he thought.

The new uniform.

Suddenly it seemed as if change was everywhere. Even Madame Stalevsky was talking about early retirement, the formidable ex-ballerina who had schooled The Lodge's Housegirls to a standard that made them world famous was in her late fifties now. She had redesigned the uniforms almost as if it was a kind of swansong, giving in at last to the members' desire to have the girls' bodies more easily available.

She had started with superbly tailored and boned corsets and had had the skirts sewn onto a broad waistband that could be removed by two simple clips at the back. The skirts themselves were split front and back but with ample overlap so the front one only revealed itself when the girl walked and even then – owing to the underskirts sewn in – they only hinted at the length and shapeliness of the limbs beneath. The result was that any member, or even this comparative upstart, Mostyn, could easily have a girl bare herself below the waist and beat her while enjoying the length of her stockinged legs and the quivering fullness of her smooth buttocks.

"Who can you get to instruct the first students if you need Tony here?" Mostyn asked, tapping at the girl's bottom repeatedly.

"I'll provide you with Peter Lang."

Whack!

Mostyn looked up, impressed, while the girl's arse gyrated desperately.

"You can get him?"

"With what the government's paying, it wasn't easy. But, yes, I've got him."

"Welcome to the public sector!" Mostyn gave him a cheeky grin and whacked in another lash, fetching a pretty, warbling cry from the girl.

John turned back to contemplating the view again as Mostyn gestured the girl to rise. He would need a blow job, and as far as John was concerned, the quicker the girl could see to him and bring the meeting to a successful close, the better. Another truck was roaring away from the building site at the CSL stableyard. The builders worked for a company owned by one of the members and the men's silence about anything they might see had been bought by the use of the Housegirls.

It was all change, he reflected again. Even governments were moving in on the arenas, it wasn't just here in the UK but all over the world. And it wasn't as if they were trying to stifle them and outlaw them any more. They had tried that and failed. Now they wanted to be involved – and share in the revenue of course - and in the UK one of The Lodge's oldest members was the moving force behind it in the corridors of power. MacIntyre – he of the eccentric waistcoats that the tabloids seldom saw beyond and who was content with the nickname of 'Dandy'– was manoeuvring towards the ultimate goal of making the arenas street legal.

John knew he meant well but both he and Carlo were anxious. Then again Carlo had never really seen beyond his slaves' performance out on the sands of the arena floors. That was what had made him great in the past, but was it enough in these changing times? John had always tried to see the bigger picture, the trouble was now that the picture could get almost too big!

A grunt of pleasure drew John's attention back to the room and he turned to see Mostyn face fucking the girl who was kneeling before him, his hands gripped tightly in her thick, wavy, chestnut hair.

He pushed her away as he finished spending, not bothering to let her clean him properly, pulled his trousers up and zipped his flies. She stood up, daintily wiping her chin with a finger and licking it clean, waiting to see if she was required for anything else. He noticed that she couldn't resist a quick rub at her bottom and a twist to see if she could see any of her welts.

If Madame had seen her she would have been in solitary for a fortnight, Madame held that no girl had any business being interested in what had been done to her as long as there was the possibility that she might need to serve again. John didn't object however, he liked seeing girls take an intelligent interest in their use.

"The agreed amount will be transferred at the end of this week," Mostyn said, gathering up his briefcase.

"Do you really think this will work?" John asked.

"It will. Part of society's got too fat and too safe and too cosseted. Part's got too feral. The arenas will act as safety valves for both. It's not a case of it might work, it's a case of it must work. Our research shows inner cities in particular are going to become wastelands if we don't do something. Now, I've got a prime candidate for Proteus waiting in my hotel room, so I'll be off and call you later in the week."

John rang down to reception for a girl to come and show Mostyn out while he went back to the window and looked out over the changing CSL stable. If this all went as the government wanted – what would the stock be like? Where would the girls come from? How would they be trained for life in the arenas? Could they be trained at all?

They were all questions that he wasn't sure he or Carlo had the answers to any more. He glanced back at the girl who was still standing quietly, legs neatly together, hands behind her back. Well, there were at least still some well trained girls bought from auction as they had always been……he clicked his fingers and she came to stand beside him.

Her corset mounded her pale, smooth skinned breasts up to perfection, coyly hiding the areolas and the nipples but nothing above them. It nipped her waist in so that her hips flared out spectacularly and at her neatly shaven delta an equally neat vulva just afforded a glimpse of the cleft between its lips. John felt his cock begin to unfurl and thicken as he contemplated the delights this recent purchase was offering. She kept her eyes respectfully lowered but he could see from the rise and fall of her breast that she was fully aware of the fact that none other than John Carpenter, owner of The Lodge was thinking about using her.

It occurred to him that in the midst of all this change through which he would have to navigate, there were still plenty of things that were changeless. One of them was the way that his body never failed to respond to the carnal smorgasbord The Lodge offered. He reached out a hand and ran his fingers over the ripe swells of breastflesh, the girl's breath caught in her throat in excitement. John looked past her to where the CCTV monitors showed the dungeons currently in use far below where he currently stood.

"Go down to Dungeon Five," he told her. "Tell whoever's on duty I want you mounted for….." He paused to consider, her backside was already well marked, and her back was best left for the guests later on. "Breastwork. Have them put out all the implements."

"Yes, Sir." With a waft of perfume she went from his side, put her skirt on and glided out to do his bidding. Mostyn had had her mouth, but when he was ready he would sample her cunt. The responsiveness of a well trained woman after an hour or two in a dungeon with skilled breastwork thrown in was assured. He would enjoy her womanhood – eventually – and she would be properly grateful. That was another changeless certainty; and he needed those just now.

Kath had been expecting one of those anonymous roadside stopover hotels, which seemed appropriate for a workplace affair. However, Mr Mostyn had driven them to a substantial market town with a wide thoroughfare through its centre and booked them into a hotel that presented a stately Georgian front to the prosperous boutiques and organic food emporia that lined the old market place.

He had taken off on his business and left her to wander about and explore for a couple of hours. She had phoned Angie and told her the name of the town and the hotel, just to be on the safe side. Then after a pleasant meander and window shop, she had noticed that time was getting on and decided to take a shower in plenty of time before dinner was served.

The en suite was spacious and the shower cabinet was as well. Kath relaxed as the hot water cascaded over her, she let it hit the back of her neck and felt herself relax under its massage. She was in no doubt that Mostyn would want to play and she was reasonably happy with that idea, he had shown himself to be an adept dominant in his office, progressing her from spanking to light flogging and then to belting and beating with a tawse in three self-controlled sessions. Kath had been a submissive long enough to know that were plenty of doms who betrayed themselves by their haste to get into a submissive's knickers or who were simply vicious instead of excitingly in control. She had thought she was a straight submissive until she had met Angie and experienced true, calm authoritative domination from a woman for the first time. And she could still recall the first time she had tasted another woman's breasts and cunt juice........Kath realised with a start that her thoughts had been rambling and taken her hand with them. It was now just starting to delve between her lips and rouse her clitoris. Suddenly she heard someone moving about in the bedroom and the door to the bathroom opened to reveal Mostyn, who was in the process of removing his shirt.

"Don't go away!" he told her with a smile and disappeared for a second, only to re-appear stark naked.

Kath looked at him with genuine interest as he pulled open the shower cabinet door and joined her. Mistress knew she still found men attractive and played on it for her own amusement so Kath knew she was at liberty to find Mostyn's body appealing. He was barrel chested and with a mat of slightly greying hair across it, his belly still had a six pack reasonably visible and his thighs were every bit as thick and muscular as her glimpses of them before had suggested.

Even though the cabinet was a reasonable size, with him in it, Kath was pushed against the tiles at the back of it. Without any preamble he reached between her legs and she opened for him, feeling his thick fingers find their way up into her vagina. She arched her back a little and felt her nipples graze his chest hair. His fingers found their way deeper inside her and began to stretch her and stimulate her in earnest. He pressed himself even harder against her and she could feel the growing hardness at his groin. Her hand slid down between their wet bodies and closed around the smooth, bulbous head of his cock which grew harder and bigger in response.

He took his hand out of her and then used both of them to grasp her waist and slide her up the tiled wall, Kath kept hold of his cock and as he lowered her she expertly fed him into her vagina, groaning as she felt herself spread wide and filled to the neck. The water continued to drum across them, plastering her wet hair across her face.

As this almost complete stranger began to thrust up into her and she tried her hardest to grip him with her pelvic floor, she threw her arms round his neck, buried her face in his shoulder and wrapped her legs around him. For some reason she could never fathom she always found the most basely physical of sexual contacts the most fulfilling – especially those with her Mistress – the simplicity of being enjoyed with a minimum of foreplay - being penetrated, giving pleasure with her body and only her body, always excited her and made her feel at her most feminine. And it was Angie who had given her the context in which she could indulge this. Angie decided who and how she would serve, Angie took responsibility and permitted her to be the submissive slut she so enjoyed being. It was part of why Kath worshipped her.

Inside her now, she could feel Mostyn begin to thrust for his climax, she could do no more than ride him however as her feet slid off his wet back when she tried to push herself up. She tried grinding and wriggling against him and managed a reasonable climax of her own by the time he froze against her and made small rapid pushes as his spunk jetted out into her.

When he let her down, panting but smiling, she slid further down until she was squatting and took his softening cock into her mouth, licking the final drops of his spend off him. He allowed her to soap him and in the curt way she was becoming used to he told her to wash and dress in her own time. He would meet her downstairs in the bar.

"I will expect stockings – with suspenders if you've brought them. There is absolutely no point in wearing knickers of course. And unpack everything you find in the portfolio case and leave what you find on the bed."

A shower was always better for being enjoyed with post orgasm lethargy and Kath took her time. If she was later than he wanted, then he would punish her, it didn't matter. And anyway, the more he enjoyed himself with her, the more he might let his guard down and mention something about Proteus.

She dressed carefully as Mistress had taught her to when preparing herself for use. Over the stockings and suspenders she slipped a halter neck dress in dark blue whose skirt finished two inches above the knee, her breasts were good enough to be left bra-less on these occasions. She and Mistress had chosen the dress to be attractive without being too tarty. It also left most of her back naked and her nipples did rather peak the material at the front, but it was a woman's dress, not a girl's or a tart's.

"If I've had to deprive myself of the pleasure of marking that," Mistress had observed, stroking her back, "let's at least see if beating it'll persuade him to let slip something useful."

When she was presentable she went over to the tall plastic tube that Mostyn had carried up from the car and unscrewed the lid. Inside she was not entirely surprised to see a variety of implements for sadistic pleasure.

Calmly she laid them on the bed. There was a riding crop, the leather tailed whip he had used on her in the second session, a leather belt and a type of whip she had not come across before. It consisted of a metre long, slender rod with a length of whipcord knotted at its end, attached to it. She ran the whipcord through her fingers and felt herself begin to heat at the prospect of being subjected to it; it looked interesting. There were also cuffs and a collar and a length of rope with a pocket knife – for cutting shorter lengths of rope, she assumed. There was also lube, a butt plug and a dildo. Plenty to keep him busy, she thought, and while he was busy working on her, there might be time for indiscretions. When she had laid the implements out tidily on the bed, she checked her appearance once more and then went downstairs.

If she had been too long, Mostyn didn't seem inclined to make an issue of it. She just had time to examine the menu and have a glass of wine before they moved into the dining room.

The meal was adequate and the house wine good. The staff clearly recognised Mostyn but were not overly obsequious or intrusive and he was able to relax. To Kath's delight the talk revolved around the goings-on at the office. Who did Kath like and dislike; who did she think was good at their job and who wasn't…… careful on that one, she told herself!

Once they had reached the coffee stage, Kath felt his shoe brush against her left calf and she gave him her best 'come on' smile and was rewarded by a rare smile in return.

"Kath, you've done very well in the sessions we've had to date," he told her. She hadn't realised she was being examined – unless job interviews had changed out of all recognition! – she was suddenly aware she had had a glass too much of wine and concentrated sternly on keeping Mostyn under close scrutiny.

"Thank you, Sir. I do like to please."

"Good, and as a result, I think I'm going to be able to offer you a place on a course that could make you for life."

"Really, Sir? I'd love that!" she tried to suck her mint in as suggestive a fashion as she could.

Mostyn leaned across the table and fixed her with his blue eyes.

"When we go back to our room, I'm going to tie you and whip you with a carriage whip," his voice was low and fervent. He clearly wanted to do what he was describing right here and now, but was putting off the pleasure to savour it all the more. "Then I'll stuff a butt plug up your arse and fuck you in the front door." He sat back. "What do you say to that?"

"It sounds wonderful!" she managed, leaving out the 'Sir' as a waitress came to clear the table. It did sound pretty good and she hoped Mistress would make her tell her everything so she could get punished severely and assuage the guilt she felt at looking forward to the rest of the evening.

"I think Proteus could be just the place for you!" he said as he stood and offered her his arm.

Kath struggled to keep her cool. Proteus at last! She managed a smile and linked her arm with his as he led her towards the bedroom and the whip. As it turned out he was in too much of a hurry to bother with the butt plug once he had finished whipping her. He just fucked her.

Kath had to admit that he did inflict a highly satisfactory beating however. Once she was naked apart from suspenders, stockings and heels, her feet were tied apart as she stood facing the mirror on the dressing table. Mostyn ran the rope around one of the feet of the bed on one side and around the TV unit on the other. Then he clipped her wrists to the ring at the back of her collar and she was able to watch herself being whipped.

The carriage whip stung in a way that she found she enjoyed instantly. It was a light sting and one that faded quickly, only to be replaced by the next, and the next and Mostyn was able to vary his target lash by lash so that her whole body soon sang to its tune.

She especially enjoyed seeing her reactions, in the mirror, as the lash landed. There was a flicker in the air as the tail sped towards her and then a soft thump as the knot bit, followed by the sting. And she loved the narrow, dusky pink welts it left behind it, criss crossing and overlapping on her breasts, making them tremble in their wake. Then steadily he began to increase the force of the blows and to wrap them further around her, making the knot land on her stomach with a strange, hollow thump, then aiming it down so that the knot bit at her delta, making her bend and twist her legs and try to shelter her womanhood. But it found that too and Kath orgasmed after a succession of sensual impacts. Mostyn kept lashing her until the spasms passed and then he was onto her.

He freed her wrists and pushed her roughly forwards so that she was able to support herself on the dressing table, able to see him standing directly behind her and to feel his hard cock pressing urgently against her anus. But he wasn't after that entrance, he bent his legs slightly and thrust straight into her burning and stinging vagina. Then, as she watched in the mirror, he leaned forwards and took a handful of her hair with one hand and raised the other. She saw he held a doubled over belt in it.

He beat her in time with his thrusts and despite her recent orgasm, Kath watched her mouth open in ecstasy as behind her Mostyn slammed his pelvis against her and smacked the belt down across her shoulders, sending shards of bright fire right through her until she broke.

For a long time she remained motionless, gasping for breath as she returned to earth but slowly her brain cleared and she realised she was still half lying across the dressing table.

"Come here," Mostyn said and she turned, discovering that her feet had been freed. He was lying back on the bed, propping himself up on his elbows, his powerful thighs were parted and his thick cock languished across one of them, still partly tumescent and glistening with discharge. She went to him and gently ran her hands up his rough, hairy thighs, feeling the muscles beneath the skin, until they encountered the soft wrinkled skin of the ball sac. Then she dropped her head forward and licked at it, fetching an appreciative groan from him. She tucked her hair behind one ear and licked again, more eagerly, letting her tongue run up the length of him, savouring the delicious mixture of essences that slicked it. As she reached the helm she felt it break free of the foreskin and one light touch from her hand completed the job.

She bent further and took him into her mouth.

"After that he told me a bit more about Proteus. Ow! Mmph!"

Kath was tied down on her Mistress' bed. She was on her back and her cuffs were linked through the wrought iron bars of the bedhead. Her legs were widely parted and tied with a rope that ran right under the bed, back up onto its top and was knotted in the middle of the duvet. Angie was kneeling astride her face, her thigh boots either side of Kath's breasts. She was naked otherwise and all Kath could see of her was her vulva and her anus and her glorious buttocks. She was also slowly adding to the tally of clothes pegs sprouting from Kath's breasts and labia. She added another one as Kath finished telling her about how she had swallowed every morsel of spunk that Mostyn had bestowed on her eager tongue. Then she had sat on her slave's face.

Angie wriggled a bit and chuckled as she felt Kath's tongue tickle her bottom.

"Alright you slut. What did he say?" She eased herself forwards enough to clear Kath's face and picked up another peg.

"He said it was a course I'd be going on. Oh!" The peg added its spite to the other five adorning Kath's left labium. "He….he said it would be good for me….. for my….Ow!"

Angie sat back on her slave's face again. "I didn't tell you to make stupid noises, girl! I want to know what he said!"

"Sorry, Mistress! He…um…..he said it would be soon…..oh not my clit, pleeease! Aaah! Mmmph!"

Angie relaxed and let Kath wriggle, gripping her hands in the jolly, multi-coloured, porcupine-like mounds of her breasts, making her arch her back and allowing her tongue to do beautiful things to her anus. But eventually she relented.

"Oh thank you, Mistress!" Kath panted as she was allowed to surface. "He said I'd passed the practical exam with flying colours, so he wouldn't bother with a theoretical exam."

"Meaning?"

"I don't know, Mistress."

"Hmm." Angie climbed off the bed. "Well it's enough to buy us a bit more time with the big boss. So we know it's got to be something to do with you being a good lay. Are they training up some kind of civil service elite band of whores?"

Kath craned her head up and surveyed her throbbing tits. "Don't know, Mistress."

Angie sauntered over to her toy cupboard and took something from it that made Kath whimper and try to dig herself deeper into the bed. She grinned evilly and went to stand over the helpless girl, running the tails of the whip through her fingers.

"Lie still, there's a good slut. You don't want me to take longer than necessary to whip those pegs off you, do you?"

Kath shook her head and bit her lip. Pegs always hurt more coming off than going on but the whip frequently made them slip a bit but still hang on, quadrupling their venom before they finally relinquished their grip.

It was going to be a long and painful afternoon. She couldn't wait for it to start.

CHAPTER FOUR.

Brian Holden surveyed his charges. They were four men in their early twenties and Mostyn had assured him that they had been winnowed from exhaustive personality tests which had rejected hundreds of hopefuls. Alex was a rather gangly black guy, Steve and John were both blond and stocky and Mike was shaven headed with the physique of a body builder.

But he was assured they all had very high sex drives but found straight sex unfulfilling. In conditions of what they believed to be complete privacy they had admitted to wanting to experiment with SM.

You shall go to the ball, Cinders! Brian thought. In trumps!

"Welcome to Proteus," he said as he approached them, standing outside the farm that had been rented in Sussex. The gentle hills and thick woods would provide perfect cover and it had even been the subject of a 'no fly' order. That was one advantage of being legitimate; you had real clout. He just hoped that the selection procedure hadn't been a cock up, after all governments weren't renowned for their ability to tread lightly and correctly.

Still they looked okay; excited and alert as they looked around them having had time, after the coach with the blacked out windows had dropped them, to unpack and look around the house they had to themselves. At his voice the men looked up and he was pleased to note that there was recognition in each face. At least that meant they all followed the arenas on the net. Maybe the government had got it right for once.

"You've been picked because.....well one reason is that you know who I am, don't you?"

There was a shy chorus of assent. They knew he was assistant slave trainer to Carlo Suarez at the legendary CSL stable, out of which the equally legendary Blondie fought.

"We're going to see if we can make trainers out of you," he announced and laughed at the looks of astonished delight on his audience's faces. "I've got two weeks to knock you guys into shape and then you're going to be doing it for real! So listen up and concentrate…you can have fun later."

He half turned and whistled, then turned back to watch his students. From around the corner of the farm house, where the yard was, with old, crumbling red brick walled and sagging roofed stables, came the sound of shoes scraping and a rumbling noise on the old cobbles. Then round the corner from behind him came Helga leading Jet and Cherry, both of whom were harnessed to traps.

Brian reckoned the first few seconds would tell him a lot. He watched his students carefully as they took in the reality of the near naked females they had previously only seen on screen, being displayed, used and enjoyed in pretty well every single way a female could be.

He was impressed. There was an only-to-be-expected instant of pure lust but then he could see that curiosity took over.

He stepped forwards as Helga came up to him, standing between the ponies, holding them by their bridles. He ran a hand affectionately over Jet's satin smooth flank and patted her deliciously prominent buttocks.

"I'm sure you'll know that this is Jet and that's Cherry over there. They've been around for a few years now and nothing much fazes them – that's why we're letting you guys loose on them. Proteus is all about training up more like you and more like these beauties here.

"Now as you can see the tack they've got on today is basic hacking stuff. We'll come to dressage and racing in later lessons. Now come close and see how it works."

The four men came closer and Brian was pleased to note that their faces only betrayed keen interest rather than any salacious intent.

He pointed out how the crupper strap was pulled tightly down between the labia and tightly up between the buttocks and then split into two slenderer straps, rejoining the girth at two buckles set in the thicker girth strap at angles just above each buttock. The girth itself was buckled in the small of the back.

"That way all the fastenings are kept out of sight and the slave presents a smooth and tidy appearance to the onlooker. For dressage and racing of course there are a few more adornments."

"Yeah!" Alex said with a broad grin. "I seen 'em! This really big plug up their arse and a dildo up their…" He suddenly realised that Helga was there and for a second paused in confusion.

"Cunt," Brian finished for him. "It's alright, Helga's a slave too. And you'll learn how to mix up Carlo's special jollop to coat the butt plug too! If you pass the exam, that is."

"What exam, Mr Holden?" Mike asked nervously.

"The one you're taking this very minute and will be sitting every minute of every day until I say otherwise. Now take a look at the tit straps please and note the thin strap that buckles at the back. Don't yank it too hard when you tack up or you'll break it and Carlo will take payment directly from your scrotum!"

There was nervous laughter but the ice was broken and the lads crowded round to check the tightness of the titstraps while Brian explained the need for them to be tight but not too constricting.

"We want them steadied, but not tightly bound so they look small. I'll cover tit bondage properly when we get to dungeon work. Tomorrow we'll get these beauties tacked up for a bit of racing and you'll see how the studded tack works."

There were whoops of glee and high fives at that prospect which Brian deflated immediately.

"CSL isn't going to let you lot just dig spikes any old how into these two!" he raised his voice enough to calm them down. "If I see one spot of blood, I'll send the whole lot of you packing!"

The students' faces fell and silence descended. It wasn't true of course, there were nearly always a few spots of blood after a slave had been run in full studded tack, but it didn't do any harm to dampen youthful high spirits before they got out of control. He noticed that Steve's hand withdrew swiftly from where it had been resting on Cherry's left buttock. He drove home his lesson by telling them how much the latest CSL slave had been bought in for. There were respectful whistles and he felt he could continue.

He took them through the complicated bridle and bit assembly, and of course showed them the famous tongue rings that the bits passed through – a piece of harnessing that Carlo and CSL had pioneered.

"You'll find in just a few minutes," Brian told them and noted the stir as it dawned on the young men that they might very soon be actually driving a CSL rig with an actual, real CSL slave between the shafts. "That the result is very positive steering. She can feel exactly where you want her to go and how sharply you want her to turn. When she's in blinkers that's very important."

"How do you decide when to use blinkers, and on which slaves to put them?" John asked.

"Good question. Any ideas?"

He stood beside Jet's head and put his fingers through her cheek strap, gently tugging her head sideways so she could nuzzle his sleeve. Neither she nor Cherry were blinkered on this occasion.

"Keep them calm?" Steve suggested.

"Yeah, but how do you know when they'll get distracted?" Alex asked.

"If there's crowds I suppose," Mike put in.

"You got to know your slave. And you got to know what you're putting them through," Brian told them. "Don't forget you're responsible for everything that happens to them. Get it wrong and you could devalue them by thousands of pounds, so you need to know your slaves. And you will do! You're responsible for every single bodily function, they belong utterly to you. So it's not all fuck and fun, guys!" He grinned at them as they registered the fact that every single bodily function went a lot farther than they'd ever seriously considered before.

"Helga will take you through the delights of stable craft," he said cheerfully. "Now the reason these two aren't blinkered is because I know they're experienced and don't get spooked too easily – so I reckon even you won't make 'em too frisky!"

There were nervous smiles again followed by relaxed and eager whoops when he told them they would get to drive for a bit right then and there. He and Helga showed them how to mount and ensure that their weight was squarely over the rig's axle as they sat.

"If you lean too far forward as you drive her, she'll end up carrying you instead of pulling you!" Brian told Mike and Alex, the first pair. "Try it now before you move off and watch what happens."

Both men leaned forwards and immediately the slaves had to grip the shafts harder and take more strain as more weight came onto the fronts of the rigs

"So you've always got to remember that as you drive – even if you whip them up to full speed - you can bring your own pony down in a race if you suddenly shift the load behind her. Now, let's try the whips."

Helga stood in front of the ponies and held their bridles firmly, pushing them backwards if they tried to prance forwards while their new drivers learned the range and the effect of the whips. But both were experienced and took it calmly enough, even when badly judged lashes wrapped their waists or ribs and the cord snapped at their breasts or deltas.

"Those are the lashes you need for racing!" Brian called as John managed two in a row right onto Jet's vulva, making her lunge and Helga have to snap her reins hard to bring her back under control. "If you can do it that accurately then all well and good. But for now I just want to you to work up to a trot and do a few circuits of the lawn."

By late afternoon the four men had mastered the basics of pony driving. On the smooth green turf in front of the old house, Cherry and Jet patiently described circuits while they were plied with lashes that sometimes conveyed contradictory messages, urging them to the right when their reins were pulling to the left and which sometimes were hard enough to urge them into a gallop despite the reins urging them to slow down. Alex at one point came close to driving through a rose bed because he flicked Cherry hard and misjudged the distance so that the length of cord snapped over her right shoulder and bit directly onto one of her famous nipples that had given her her name. She reared and twisted to the right and only some calm work on the reins prevented her from scratching herself badly by careering through the bushes.

"Okay!" Brian called as Steve and John pulled in from the last circuits, both ponies beginning to foam around their bits and champ. "That's enough for the first day. Well done everybody. Steve, John, you go with Helga and she'll show you the ropes about rubbing down, washing, grooming, feeding and all the rest of it. Once that's all done then you can start claiming the perks of the job! And Helga's as much on the menu as the other two. Mike and Alex you come with me and help get their evening feed ready – and our supper!"

The two reluctant chefs only stopped grumbling when Brian pointed out that they would take turns and tomorrow, they would have all the fun of rubbing down the slaves, fucking Helga and then overseeing feeding time.

CHAPTER FIVE

Two days later, Brian had to admit that it looked as though the government's Proteus scheme had come up with the goods. Alex was proving to be a dab hand at catering and grooming, displaying a surprising talent for getting Jet and Cherry looking their very best. As a result he and Helga were often in close consultation as she initiated him further into the mysteries of femininity, as it applied to getting a slave looking her best to serve her masters.

At first there were some ribald comments about getting in touch with his feminine side. However, on the second night, the sight of Jet and Cherry, dressed in black basques with fishnet, hold up stockings and four inch-heeled, court shoes, coming towards the dungeons silenced them all; even Brian. Their hair had been beautifully styled; Cherry's into a complex chignon, Jet's into corn rows, which together with the way Alex had made up her eyes and lashes, rendered her almost unrecognisable.

But what really surprised Brian was that the slaves themselves had responded. They moved with proud, exaggerated, catwalk, 'fuck me' sways of the hips, he felt his body respond immediately to the invitation, even though both he and they knew that there was nothing he couldn't do with them anyway. He laughed in delight as Cherry was brought to a stop beside him, her eyes were lowered and her cleverly blushed cheeks emphasised an attractiveness he had never seen in her before, it was as if he was going to enjoy her for the very first time.

"Brilliant, Alex!" he said. "You'll have punters queuing up to pay through the nose for beauties like these!"

Alex beamed at the compliment and Helga assured him that it had indeed been all Alex's work.

"Me mum kept a hairdressing salon," he finally volunteered. "I looked and learned but never thought I'd get to use what I picked up!"

The evening had gone on to be as successful as its beginning had been. The students learned how to handle stock whips and other varieties of single tail, as well as all the different ways a cat could be employed – and all the different places. Jet and Cherry's experience and fortitude were fully tested as they endured four sets of inexperienced floggings which gradually increased in skill and therefore in severity. With four men experimenting on two slaves, Helga was kept busy administering relief. By midnight however, Brian called a halt. Both slaves were on X crosses, Cherry's body was striped and welted almost to a consistent pink colour, while even Jet's gleaming chocolate skin was showing plenty of purple lines.

"Tomorrow night we'll do clamping, pegging and waxing. But we've got a full day's work before then!"

Mike and Steve slung the exhausted girls over their shoulders and took them back to their stalls while Helga cleaned up the dungeon.

John rubbed the crotch of his jeans ruefully as he coiled up a whip and watched Helga's breasts sway as she mopped the stone floor.

"My balls ache from coming so much!" he said. "They are so hot when they're all marked like that and so wet and open for you!"

Helga grinned at him.

"Oh no! Tomorrow, babe. No more tonight!" he said hurriedly.

The following day, Brian found that Mike, despite his muscular physique, was a very sensitive handler of harness and was able to put a pony into studded tack quickly and efficiently without making her cavil or rear, saving time and energy all round. Brian felt that was a talent which would come in very useful when their first intake of new livestock arrived.

Even more pleasing was the aptitude that Steve and John brought to driving. By the afternoon they were competently steering their rigs through the obstacle courses demanded by dressage events, as well as weaving their charges through specially constructed straw bale chicanes at a full gallop.

By the end of the third day, their work with the slaves in the dungeons was professional and calm and Helga's work on her knees was not as much in demand as it had been. Each of the students put a ring through a labium and a nipple and Brian had to admit they didn't do too badly. The raised and spread legs of the slaves only tensed and twisted sporadically as the soft flesh was pierced and the ungagged gasps as the nipples were done would not have disturbed a paying customer. Arena slaves had to pay for their keep in their owners' dungeons as well as out on the floor of his arena. And these lads were obviously going to be very capable at handling their boss's livestock at the same time as pleasing his customers.

The only quibble Brian had was that Helga dropped into bed with him so exhausted from having ministered to all four students that she was asleep before he could get any use out of her.

No arena slave could carry any rings anywhere on her body, it would give an opponent far too easy a target, so the following morning Brian removed the rings the students had threaded through Jet and Cherry and declared a day of rest, to allow the two slaves to recover and to allow him to widen the students' acquaintance with arena equipment.

In one of the old barns at the back of the yard, they found a hayloft supported by reasonably substantial wooden pillars and one of these served as a whipping post to tie Helga to. She was a slightly chubby girl of medium height but with no cellulite on her sturdy thighs and breasts that rode invitingly high on her chest. As Mike pointed out, her back was an excellent one for whipping as she had quite broad shoulders but a reasonably trim waist.

Brian dug out the heavy strap-type whips that arena slaves duelled with and for a couple of hours they got used to the weight and the range of them, as well as practising a few strokes that Brian would expect them to teach the new intake. The men took their time and broke for coffee a couple of times during the morning, leaving a panting and gasping Helga to recover at the post before her next session began. He was pleased to note that although she presented a deliciously tempting sight, with her legs planted wide apart to brace herself, her back a network of pink stripes and her breasts bulging out on either side of the post, none of the students suggested using her. She had come several times but was there purely as target practise and not for their fun. Jet and Cherry served that function for the day and while Brian brewed up, the stables echoed to the laughs of the students as they casually took their pleasure with Cherry's mouth or with Jet's backside.

A good spirit was developing amongst them, Brian felt, as he sipped his coffee, leaning against the side of a stall and watched Steve hold Jet by her tongue lead as she was bent forwards for Alex to bugger.

From then until lunch, with one more break, they practised uppercuts to Helga's crotch. They needed to know how best to land them so that they could teach their pupils. Brian felt it best to gag her after a while, the noise was becoming a distraction.

"She'll come like a bloody banshee when she's fucked tonight," Steve said as John succeeded in landing a sequence of excruciatingly accurate lashes and Helga collapsed to hang by her wrists for a while in the aftermath.

In the afternoon they polished and oiled the tack and whips. It was going to be studded whip practice the next day and Helga needed a rest before she underwent that; although with a day's rest from the driving whips, Jet and Cherry would share the burden. With Helga taken down and allowed to dress again, Brian took his little troop into the nearby village for a drink while she cooked the supper and fed the slaves.

The pub was a typical home counties one with plenty of beams and horse brasses on display, it was fairly crowded as it was towards the end of the week and Brian left the lads to find seats while he went to buy the first round. While he was there he noted another customer staring at him from the opposite side of the U shaped counter. She was a black haired girl, tall – about five feet eight, Brian estimated. With the practised ease of a professional surveyor of girlflesh, he took in her pert and not-too-big-breasts, pushing against the light fabric of a tunic top and the well proportioned swell of her hips – as far as he could see them with the counter in the way. She saw him returning her glance, blushed and gathered her drinks hurriedly before turning away. Brian watched her go with some amusement. She had on tight leggings which suited her length of limb rather well, he thought. They were nicely shaped too. But then the barmaid served him and Steve came to help him carry the pints back to the table. He thought no more about it, as it was happening increasingly often these days. More and more people were joining the websites and the CSL site frequently had footage of him and Carlo and the slaves and grooms. The arenas were existing more and more on the very cusp of – if not acceptability – then at least an uneasy acknowledgement of their existence.

At their table the conversation rambled easily across what they had learned – the ambient noise level was high enough to disguise the content of what they were discussing – and they asked him many questions about 'backstage' at shows. Brian was pleased at how much more calm they were about considering their naked female charges; already they were relaxing in the sure and certain knowledge that they could do whatever they chose to with them, whenever they chose to do it. Therefore there was no rush and the slaves' all round health and well being came more into prominence as they appreciated the cash value of the livestock in the long term, rather than their own immediate need for pleasure.

Alex eventually got up and went to get the next round in and Steve went to help shortly after. They returned with broad grins on their faces.

"Hey, Brian!" Alex said. "There's a girl over there who says she knows who you are and wants to talk to you…outside!"

Brian looked around and caught sight of the black haired girl from the bar earlier. She was looking at him and this time didn't look away but smiled a little nervously.

"Go on, boss! You can't keep a lady waiting!" Alex concluded to a rousing cheer from the others.

"Alright! Keep it down you lot!" Brian grumbled good-naturedly as he stood up.

The night air was refreshingly sharp as he stepped out into the car park. A few smokers stood close by and he looked beyond them to see the girl standing under the pub sign out by the front. He was curious now that he was away from the lads. He had been getting used to being recognised, but to be asked for a meeting was new. He walked over to her and appreciated her lithe figure again, noting that she stood nervously, her handbag held down in front of her in both hands. She watched him approach and tossed a few strands of hair back over one shoulder as he came up to her.

"You're Brian Holden, aren't you," she said.

"Yes. And you are?"

"Carol. Carol Harper."

Now he was close, he could see she was very attractive, with high cheekbones and large, lustrous eyes. Her lips were full and soft, he took a second glance a little further down and revised his opinion about the breasts. They were not that small considering she was fairly tall. She seemed to be struggling to find the next thing to say, although he could see she desperately wanted to say something.

"How do you know my name?" he asked. He was pretty sure he knew the answer but it gave the girl a chance to move the conversation along and she gave him a grateful smile.

"We're members of the CSL site."

"We?"

"Some friends. We met on the net and found we all liked the arenas. Now we meet most weekends, get a few bottles of wine in and catch up. Jenny likes the Blues, Chris and Tanya and me though, we all like CSL."

"And?"

Carol's hands twisted in the straps of her handbag.

"Well, we always said how great it'd be if we could… well if we were…involved in a stable. Turns out we all either kept ponies or worked in stables when we were younger!" She tried a light hearted laugh but her throat was dry with nerves and she coughed instead.

"So what you're telling me is you think you might want to be grooms."

"Yeah! I don't think we'd hack it as slaves, though they are gorgeous! But we reckon grooming looks really cool! I mean you get to work with Blondie, and Ox and Trouble and take them into dungeons and playrooms, and work inside the arenas at shows. Then you make them look good for whoever's paid for them…it's really hot!"

"Grooms get played with and fucked too, you know," Brian interrupted sharply, her reaction would tell him all he needed to know.

"Yes. We know." She looked down quickly. "I know."

"So you want to be fucked by the trainers and fuck the slaves." It was brutal but there was no point in being anything else.

Still looking down she nodded. He reached out and touched her cheek with the back of his hand.

"That took some guts, Carol," he said. "Come and meet the guys, when are your friends round again?"

Carol looked up at him with delight etched plainly all over her face.

"We said we'd meet on Saturday!"

Brian began to walk back towards the pub, Carol fell into step beside him.

"Well, if I tell you where I've got Jet and Cherry stabled, only a mile or so from here; reckon they'd want to meet there?"

Carol nearly squeaked with delight.

"God! You've actually got them here! Jet's one of my favourites! But why?"

Brian shushed her as they approached the bar. They made their way over to where the boys were sitting and he introduced them to her.

"Why are you all in this little dump of a place?" she asked as she took a seat and Steve went for another round. "I mean you guys have got the whole world to choose from!"

Brian could sense the anxiety almost steaming off the students. He smiled.

"These guys are helping me start a new stable." He felt the tension drain out of the atmosphere around him as it became plain to them that he wasn't going to spill the beans about them being trainees. "Now, tell me about your friends."

By the end of the evening it had been arranged that Carol would bring the girls to the stable on Saturday evening and they would be put through their paces.

"We won't hold back, mind," he had told Carol. "We trainers work hard and play hard, so make sure you tell the others that, yes, I can find them jobs, but this is going to be a job interview like no other."

"Oh yes, Sir!" Carol breathed, her eyes alight and her cheeks flushed. "It's what I know we've all talked about and...well I don't think there'll be any problem!"

For the next stage in their training, Brian worked his students hard on combat training. They learned to spar with the two slaves, holding pads in front of them for the slaves to use as target practice with their whips. They themselves were equipped with similar straps to the ones the slaves had, except these had weights at their ends to add real venom to a strike.

"When you're training raw recruits, that'll give 'em some incentive to keep moving, and in the arena that can mean the difference between winning and losing!" he called out as they dodged, and then lashed at the naked girls. “We’ll put ‘em on the whipping posts soon as they come in and ginger them up with a taste of the punishment whips! Then you buggers’ll really have to run to keep up with them!”

All four of the students were amazed at the speed and strength of the slaves to begin with but adapted quickly – fitness having been part of the profiling process – and within a couple of days, Jet and Cherry had been put back firmly in their places.

By the time Saturday evening came round, Brian had been able to e mail John Carpenter that so far had definitely been so good. It was to be hoped that it might get even better.

The four girls turned up promptly. Brian had been half expecting a no-show – by at least two of them – but all four came.

Tanya had something of the Slav in her rather thin face and green eyes, and her blonde hair and slim figure contrasted with Jenny’s slightly chubby good looks and buxom figure, while Chris was a brunette, like Jenny, but with small breasts and a pretty face. Brian noticed they all wore skirts, none of them below mid thigh.

They knew what this evening was about. But just in case they didn’t he called everyone together in the yard for introductions. His lads kept their composure well, he felt, and remained polite and self-contained, standing a few feet away, looking at the girls appraisingly but with no obvious signs of undignified lust. All four girls had very shapely legs, so that was a feat Brian was proud of.

Carol introduced the girls and Brian noticed she kept her eyes fixed firmly on him at all opportunities. He filed that for attention later and got straight down to business.

"Right. Carol tells me you're keen on the arenas and want to join a stable as grooms."

There were nods of assent.

"Any of you had any experience of being dominated? Because as grooms, if you make it that far, you'll be just as available as the slaves. Ask Helga."

Helga smiled and curtsied. All the girls' hands went up. He hadn't expected that.

"My ex used to put me over his knee," Tanya volunteered shyly. "But he didn't do anything else." She was blushing furiously but standing her ground.

"Did you ask him to?" Brian asked her.

"Oh yes!" Tanya joined in the laughter this provoked and the ice was broken.

Carol said she had had a boyfriend who had once used a belt on her before making love to her and she had never forgotten it. Jenny had been caned at school and it had taken her years to come to terms with the contradictory feelings it had aroused in her. Chris admitted to having been spanked, having her nipples pegged and fantasising about going much farther.

"We met online and the chats sort of just grew and we realised we all felt the same," Carol concluded.

"Well these gentlemen are capable of taking you where you think you want to go. The purpose of this evening is to see if it really is where you want to go. Now, first off, I suggest we go and take a look at Jet and Cherry. Helga can tell you what's involved in their care, and after that…well we'll see."

The group proceeded to the stables, Brian found himself with Helga on one side of him and Carol on the other, her hip occasionally touching his as they walked. The sight of the famous slaves bedded down on their straw, hands clipped behind backs, one ankle chained to the back of their stalls, fetched excited yelps from the girls, especially when they were allowed in and Helga began to explain where all the welts came from.

"Show them what you've taken too, Helga," Brian told her.

Obediently she unknotted the blouse she wore tied below her breasts and shrugged it off. The splays of small red dots left by the studded whip and fading long welts from the various other lashes criss crossing her breasts, back and shoulders, fetched only excited sighs from the girls and Brian began to have hopes. He noticed Carol took her eyes off Helga's body only to seek him out and give him a shy smile.

"We used Helga as target practice to save wear and tear on the slaves," Brian explained and went on to identify the different welts she carried. "Grooms serve wherever and however they're needed," he concluded.

Any doubts that Brian might have had about the girls' resolve, melted away the minute he showed them into the dungeon. The array of X frames, padded benches, caning stools, stocks, chains, weights and ropes provoked only more excited squeaks from the girls who were well aware that they were destined to experience most of them that very evening.

"Alright, ladies!" Brian addressed them once they had all looked around and none had made a break for the door. "Let's have you stripped. You too Helga."

There were a few moments of urgent fumbling with fasteners, buttons and knickers and then five naked girls stood in a line before the men.

"Make your choice, gentlemen. Remember I want them given as wide an introduction as possible, so do make full use of pegs, clamps, weights, whatever takes your fancy."

The four men moved forward and Brian beckoned Carol over, pushing Helga into the line. She gave him a knowing grin as she went but was immediately claimed by Mike whose eager pounce, Brian made a mental note of.

As for himself, since his last sub, Amelia, had spirited herself away from CSL and had become, after some adventures, the trainer for the Girl Squad in Eastern Europe, he felt he was owed some quality time with a girl who he might own. He missed the peace of mind that came with knowing there was always one female who could be utterly relied on to be pleasing no matter what she had been put through.

Carol was licking her lips nervously, holding her hands clasped in front of her, not knowing where else to put them. Brian took pity on her and ordered her to put them on her head. She obeyed and he could see the tension drain out of her as she came under the command of someone who knew exactly where she should put them. She had a submissive's need for the certainties that submission brought with it.

Stripped naked her body delivered on all the promises he had felt it make him in the pub car park.

Her dark eyes were wide with anxiety and all the prettier for that, nerves had made her cheeks a little more flushed and her slightly parted lips were full and wide, promising the gentlest of caresses as a man slid his cock between them. The breasts were a decent size, the areolas pleasantly dark and the nipples a nice shade of red as they stood partially erect. The breasts themselves were full and rounded, youthfully high and prominent. Her belly was flat and a jewelled piercing adorned the navel prettily. She was clean shaven at her delta and the divide of her labia was unusually high and visible – an attractive feature Brian felt. Her hips were smoothly flared and her thighs long and the skin flawless. He made a 'revolve' gesture with one hand and she shuffled around to allow him to inspect her from behind. As she was unable to see his face, Brian allowed himself a wide grin. Her backside was delicious, the buttocks were high, deep and wide, her back was long and perfect for the lash. He reached out and took a handful of her hair, making her turn back to face him with the other. She was still wide-eyed with anxiety but her face relaxed into a delighted smile when he told her she would do.

He led her over to a wall where the collars and cuffs were kept and fitted her with fleece lined cuffs and a deep, lined collar with three O rings. It suited her slender neck perfectly and Brian felt himself harden at the prospect of breaking this tasty morsel in.

He took her to a corner where a chain hung down from a steel ring in the ceiling and using the karabiners on her cuffs, fastened her wrists above her head, then he stripped off his shirt, selected a heavy leather flogger from a rack on the wall and went to stand behind her. Around him the session was getting into full swing, Tanya was over John's knee and her pert little bottom was getting the paddling its owner had been wishing for. Alex was already making Jenny twist and cry out on the X frame as his single tail wrapped her and bit at the sides of her breasts. Steve had Chris tied on her back on a table with her legs spread and raised and he was busily fucking her before he did anything else. Mike had Helga under the cane.

Having satisfied himself that all was progressing well, Brian moved forward and pressed himself against Carol's back. Immediately she pushed her bottom back against him and swayed her hips so that she rubbed against the erection she could feel through his trousers. He reached around her and fondled her breasts, the whip he held in his right hand making contact with her soft skin. She gasped as she felt it and as he started working on her nipples, he twisted and pinched them, then pulled them. He was gentle to begin with but gradually became rougher and more demanding. Carol made no complaint and her nipples achieved impressive sizes as they responded to their mistreatment. Brian smiled as she nuzzled her head against his shoulder as he began to slide his hands down across her stomach, the whip's tails stroking her sensuously. He ran his hands down to her delta and let his fingers explore the top of her cleft. She shuffled her feet as far apart as she could get them and as he sank his fingers further under her, he felt the physical expression of her need. Her sexflesh was warm and moist, her clitoris was a good sized nub and she groaned in appreciation as he rubbed it.

"That's a perfect size for pegs and needles," he told her.

Her only response was a breathless 'oh' of excitement. He reached further, the tails of the whip caressing her legs and put a couple of fingers up into her vagina which was surprisingly capacious and very wet. She began to work her hips against him urgently and he laughed softly as he stepped away and shook out the tails of the whip.

She gave a hoarse cry of shock as she felt a whip for the first time but from then on held her peace until Brian was working across her bottom, her back by then showing a fair covering of thick flares of reddened skin from the flogger. Her head fell back and she began making breathless little cries that signalled a climb towards orgasm. Brian laid the lash on harder and watched as she worked her hips back and forth, jerking them as though she was being fucked and eventually giving out a climactic shout before her head flopped forwards and Brian could see her ribs heaving in the aftermath.

He looked around again. The room was filled now with groans and sighs, interspersed with the thud and smack of whips, the swooshing of a cane and the more meaty slapping of a heavy paddle or tawse. All of the girls were serving with admirable determination and it wouldn't be long before the men gave in to the urge to satisfy the raging erections that were tenting every pair of trousers. Brian realised his were no exception and took them off before going to stand in front of Carol. Her head was lolling against one upraised arm, her eyes were heavy lidded and her mouth was open and softly inviting. Brian considered that she would be a fitting adornment to any man's bed but for the moment he was in a hurry and simply lifted her legs and moved in. She responded eagerly and gripped him around his waist so he could guide his cock safely into her. Her cunt suctioned open quickly and smoothly and he slid fully into her. Once he was safely lodged he reached behind her and took a bracing grip on her flogged buttocks as he began to fuck her. She looked him in the eye and gritted her teeth as he dug his nails into her bottom and she thrust back against him as he pounded into her.

When he finally came, he was pleased to note that she kept her attention on him, ensuring that he came fully and satisfactorily. Whether she came or not he couldn't tell but she understood that her pleasure was secondary to his.

A very pleasing beginning.

From there the evening progressed as well as it had promised to. He left Carol in Alex's capable hands as he passed an agreeable few minutes with Jenny's melons. He whipped them first and then pierced the nipples – just once through each and then left her energetically fucking Steve. Tanya gave him a superb blow job as he discussed her progress with John. A prolonged beating with a single tail was decided on as her next test. Mike had pretty little Chris on the medical bench and was dilating her rectum and vagina. The insides of her thighs bore the marks of an earlier beating and her hands were stroking them and feeling the steel implements that invaded her body, even as Mike opened her arse up even further. As Brian watched, he decided she was open enough and went round the bench to her head. He dropped the support so that her head fell back and he drove his cock deep into her mouth. After a few seconds a smile of purest delight lit up his features and Brian concluded that Chris could deep throat a man quite readily.

That left Helga. She was held against a wall, her back to it, her legs spread and her arms raised and spread too. Locking forceps had been attached to her labia and weights suspended from them. She smiled as she saw him approach.

"They're a talented bunch," she said.

"Which?" he asked.

"Both! But Patti will love knocking some new girls into shape."

"Yeah, I'll make arrangements tomorrow to send 'em along. Mike seems to have taken a liking to you. I'll have to see that doesn't cause any friction."

As he had been speaking he had dug his fingers into Helga's ample breastmeat, deliberately teasing the whip reddened skin again. She pushed against his hands, urging him on.

"Oooh! Thank you, Sir," she whispered, closing her eyes to savour the pain more intensely. He massaged her brutally hard for a while and then flogged her again before returning to Carol and claiming her.

She was on her knees before Steve and he waited until she had finished before he stood her up and clipped a lead to her collar.

"Last ones out, turn the lights off!" he called as he led her up to his bedroom.

In the dark she was compliance itself, her soft body sliding against his under the duvet, performing whatever service he required with no murmur of dissent or hesitation.

Having sampled her vagina before, he wanted to see how her oral skills were and was pleasantly surprised, her lips were even more gently passionate than they had looked to be. Originally he had intended merely using her mouth to lubricate his cock prior to sampling her bottom, but her eagerness to take as much of him down as she could, seduced him into staying and spilling himself into her throat. She purred with delight as he came and swallowed quickly and smoothly. To cap it all, she was in no hurry to finish sucking him and carried on until every last tremor had been wrung from him and every last inch of his cock and balls had been licked in case a drop of sperm had escaped her.

When she finally slid up to lie beside him again, he told her that she had disrupted his plan to bugger her. She giggled huskily and he felt her lips brush his cheek.

"Better punish me then, Sir," she whispered.

"Oh I will! But not just now," he said.

CHAPTER SIX.

At breakfast the next morning the girls slipped into role with no need for any instruction and served their men perfectly before joining them at the table. Brian glanced around in amusement at the dark circles under various eyes and the occasional wince of discomfort from one or other of the girls.

"Any complaints, gentlemen?" he asked.

The men all shook their heads but Brian pressed on. As grooms there would be no place for modesty in their lives and they might as well learn that straightaway.

"Any disobedience?"

Again there were no takers.

"Any holes not entirely satisfactory?" he went on, helping himself to more coffee.

There were some blushes from the girls who were now keeping their eyes firmly fixed on their plates.

"Jenny's pelvic floor muscles could do with some work. Ideally she could grip a cock a bit more firmly," Mike suggested.

Brian glanced across at Jenny to see her reaction. Her cheeks were scarlet with embarrassment but she held her tongue.

"True," Alex agreed. "But her mouth is terrific."

"And her arse, and that definitely doesn't want to be any tighter. You only just slip in comfortably as it is," Steve added.

"Chris could do with some widening to her arse," John put in. "But she's willing enough and took the stretching well. Made a bit of noise but nothing too serious."

Beside him, Brian felt Carol stir. He had tried buggering her in the night but she had admitted it was her first time and had been too tight to take him, even with lube. Still, she had to learn that she could have no secrets any more.

“Carol needs widening too,” he told the others and could practically feel the heat of her blush. “But she’s virgin there so that’s understandable.” Tanya and Chris looked up in surprise and Carol hid her face in her hands. Brian winked at the lads who had cottoned on to what he was doing.

“But are we agreed that all four are keen to learn and can take discipline?”

There were nods and murmurs of assent.

“Good. I’ll talk to The Lodge in a minute. You girls go back home and put your affairs in order, give notice to work and landlords.”

There were voices raised in complaint immediately. None of them wanted to leave.

Brian raised his hand for silence.

“We don’t want missing persons enquiries do we? You can come back next weekend or sooner if you’ve tidied up your affairs.”

There were happier noises at the news – as much from the males as from the girls. Brian put his hand down and gripped Carol’s thigh under the table.

“Not you,” he whispered. “You’re staying here and you can tie up loose ends as you move in. The rest are going to The Lodge but you’re serving me here and helping Helga.”

She turned a look of undiluted joy on him.

As farewells were said after breakfast, Brian phoned The Lodge and told a delighted John Carpenter that a fresh batch of grooms would be dispatched shortly for training under Patti Campbell. He also told Clive Mostyn that the new stable would have some staff trained up and ready to go as soon as the slaves themselves were ready.

Then while Helga and her new assistant went to sort out Jet and Cherry for their day, Brian got back to the business of developing his new trainers' skills. Time was getting short.

Kath knew that her Mistress was just not going to be able to resist it. They had spent the whole weekend preparing the sting for Clive Mostyn in a hotel bedroom. They had made sure that the cameras could follow Kath over every square inch of the four poster bed and that they could get a clear view of whoever sat on the chairs prior to moving to the bed.

After that promising night at the hotel in the market town in Berkshire, nothing further about Proteus had emerged and Angie's boss was now insisting that they move to a straightforward 'politician found with leg over' story. It wasn't as good a scoop as Proteus had seemed to be but it looked like it was all they were going to get.

It was Sunday night and Kath would have to go back to working for Mostyn in the morning. During the week she would try and lure him to the room for what the paper would call a depraved sado-masochistic orgy. It sounded good to her! And her Mistress was sure to want to use the facilities once all the technicians left.

"All right, you slut! Get your kit off," Angie growled almost immediately the last of the men had gone. "Don't think I haven't noticed you flaunting your arse and tits at me all afternoon!"

Of course it had been Angie who decreed that she wear the low necked T shirt and the tight skirt that ended three inches above the knee. And of course it had been Angie who had decreed that no underwear was allowed, but there was really no point in Kath bringing that up.

She stripped obediently and saw that Angie had unpacked some lengths of the bondage rope they used at home and a flogger from her shoulder bag.

Kath's hands were tied behind her back and she was made to lie on her back across the bed about half way down it. Then Angie had her raise her legs in turn and tied each ankle to a post, one to the foot of the bed and the other to the head, leaving her cunt very exposed between her widely spread thighs. Kath's heart was thundering in her chest as it always did when her Mistress prepared to enjoy her. And now she ratcheted up the excitement by laying the whip on her so that the leather tails trailed down along her cunt and the handle weighed heavily on her stomach. Kath craned her head up to watch her Mistress as she stood, framed in the V of her legs as she too stripped off for action. And as she looked closely at her Mistress' face, her excitement fizzled out instantly.

She was regarding Kath with a coldness that was almost contempt.

"I've been coming under real pressure because you haven't come up with the goods, Kath. So I think you need to understand just how I feel about that, I don't like my professional judgement being called into question by the incompetence of my slut! You have just one week to break open Proteus or to get Mostyn in here. Understand?"

"Yes, Mistress. I'm sorry, I have tried!"

"Can it! I've had enough excuses," Angie said curtly. "You'll certainly understand that by the time I finish with you today!"

There was a knock on the door and Angie called out for the person to enter. Kath panicked and tried to crane her head around to see who was coming in. Desperately she tried to close her legs, suddenly feeling hideously exposed and vulnerable. But the person who entered was a petite blonde that she had seen at some clubs and parties they had been to but couldn't recall having played with. The girl was wearing a simple, dark blue, shift dress and giggled excitedly when she saw the scene before her.

"Get that off," Angie ordered and leaned over to tie a blindfold onto Kath.

"Please, Mistress!" Kath began to protest, it wasn't unusual for her Mistress to introduce a third party into their sessions but there was something new about Angie's demeanour this time. She was being punished – and for real this time.

Isolated in the darkness, Kath wondered whether to continue to plead with her beloved Mistress, but in the end decided against it. With her being in this sombre mood, it was probably advisable just to ride out the storm.

She heard the rustle of clothing as the new girl stripped and then there was silence, followed by soft mews of pleasure, Angie was kissing and caressing her new toy. It was nothing that hadn't happened before, but never with Mistress in this mood.

Then Kath felt the whip taken up off her stomach and she tensed just in time as the heavy tails bludgeoned down onto the inside of her left thigh and then her right. The lashes were repeated, moving close to her defenceless cunt and then thudding home on it. Kath arched and twisted against the stinging that lanced into her and set her senses ablaze in the darkness. The lashes kept coming, moving from thigh to thigh, up and down and then hitting dead centre, making her light up with pain and desire. She couldn't tell who was wielding the whip but by the time it stopped her whole groin was a throbbing, hot mass of lustful excitement. She was panting for breath and could feel sweat running off her. Someone grabbed her breasts and gave her nipples the kind of treatment she craved and she arched upwards again, offering them shamelessly.

"Careful. She comes easily under tit pain."

It was her Mistress' voice, so at least she knew who was doing it, but the hands left her and Kath had a horrible feeling that at least part of her punishment was to be orgasm denial. She felt the mattress sink and move under her. There were the sounds of people positioning themselves and her Mistress' husky chuckle that turned Kath's knees to jelly normally, but now the breath was knocked from her as a body fell across her chest, squashing her breasts, soft skin brushed her face and automatically she licked and kissed it. More weight came onto her, the flesh against her face moved again and she realised it was a woman's thigh, the outside of it and suddenly in her mind's eye she pieced together the scene unfolding across her helpless body. One woman was lying on her back with her legs wide open and another was lying on top of her, between them. There was more movement and another husky laugh from her Mistress, followed by the unmistakable sounds of a tongue eagerly licking and probing a very moist cunt.

"Do me with the vibrator while you lick my clit," she heard her Mistress say, urgent and fierce in her desire.

Kath heard the buzzing start and then fade as the device was inserted. Almost immediately her Mistress began her climb to orgasm, crying out and shouting in the way that Kath knew so well. Her buttocks began to bounce up and down on Kath's chest, her thigh practically mashed itself against Kath's face as she spread her legs even farther. Then there was the frozen moment of climax before the weight collapsed back down onto Kath again and the buzzing stopped.

"Roll off me," she heard Angie say. "I want this slut to know what she's missing."

Some of the weight left her and she felt her Mistress shift so that her groin was directly above Kath's mouth and nose. She could catch its post orgasmic scent and helplessly stuck out her tongue to see if she was to be granted a taste. But she wasn't. Again there was movement and breath-expelling weight and then she felt her Mistress calmly sitting on her chest, legs apart on either side of her head, the scent of her cunt filled Kath's senses and she whimpered in her need.

"Stoke her up with the vibrator. I want the bitch to beg."

Kath felt the thing being plunged swiftly into her and switched on, she cried out in shock at the abrupt stimulation of her inner tissues after the peaks she had nearly achieved earlier had receded. And still the scent of her Mistress wafted over her face as she took pleasure from Kath's suffering. As far as she could, Kath moved herself on the metal shaft inside her as it was thrust back and forth. Slowly she began to hope that she might make it this time and decided on a desperate series of pelvic thrusts and rotations to try and reach it before anyone knew, but her Mistress wasn't fooled.

"Take it out!" she snapped and Kath cried out again in shock as she was emptied.

There was more movement on the mattress beside her and finally the weight came off her, but it was only so that the two women could lie in each other's arms beside her and pleasure themselves all over again. She could feel the hands and legs moving, brushing her own bound body. After the unmistakable sounds of orgasm there was more movement and she heard the blonde being whipped and being allowed to come again and then lick out Angie again.

Then they played with her some more. This time the blonde – her Mistress would never go down on a sub – licked her out while Mistress whipped Kath's tits but stopped short again before she was anywhere close to orgasm.

By the time the session ended, Kath was weeping and begging dementedly, tugging at her ankle bonds, desperate to close her legs and see if she couldn't bring herself off. But once her blindfold was removed and her legs lowered, her Mistress, still with that horribly cold expression told her that if she brought herself off she could start packing when they got home.

Then she turned to the blonde who was getting dressed and embraced her and thanked her for her help, patting her on the bottom fondly as she sent her on her way.

Miserable, frustrated and confused, Kath put back on the few garments she had been permitted.

"It's either Mostyn in here or Proteus by the end of this week or you're out," Angie told her once she was dressed and indeed she really did understand that she absolutely had to make progress, life without her Mistress was not to be considered.

She pulled out all the stops at work. She turned up late, she wore jeans, she even had a drink at lunch and returned late, breathing alcohol fumes over her supervisor. By Wednesday she was carpeted in Mostyn's office.

"Are you deliberately provoking me, Knowles?" he asked once the supervisor had gone, smiling triumphantly, Kath's list of offences duly read out.

"Yes, Sir," Kath confirmed.

"Why?"

"Since…since that night in the hotel, Sir, I haven't been able to think of anything else but doing it again! So

I saved up and I've got a room on Friday night…if that's ok, Sir." The lines had been carefully rehearsed and Kath felt she delivered them with heart-felt sincerity.

"No. It isn't," Mostyn said, getting to his feet and coming to stand beside her. One of his hands found its way to her bottom and cupped a buttock appreciatively. "And it won't be necessary. Trust me on this," and that was all she could get out of him.

She reported to her Mistress that night. Since the weekend she had been banished to the spare bedroom and was desperately hoping that this piece of news might allow her to return to her rightful place in her Mistress' bed.

"Did he actually say what was happening on Friday?"

"No, Mistress, but he knew what I meant alright and said it wouldn't be necessary, so it must be Proteus!"

"Why must it? We might suspect but we don't know for sure that Proteus has anything at all to do with SM. Maybe he wants to take you to another hotel that he's booked! It could mean anything, so you'd better just hope it means what you think it means."

And that was that.

Kath had to admit that Mostyn hadn't mentioned Proteus, and it could mean that he just wanted a dirty weekend on his own terms, but somehow she was sure it didn't. He had seemed pre-occupied and the touch to her bottom had been almost an afterthought. But in any case there was absolutely nothing more she could do. If she misbehaved any more, he might lose patience and sack her. She just had to wait and see if, by Friday night, she had a Mistress any more. And it really was all down to Proteus now, Angie had the technical staff at the hotel stand down and Kath was ordered to the spare bedroom even before bed time.

Thursday was a nightmare, she could hardly concentrate on work at all and the minutes dragged by interminably. The atmosphere at home continued to be cold and hostile so that by Friday morning, Kath was a nervous wreck.

She traipsed into work, listless and depressed and hardly bothered to react when one of the temporary staff stuck her head round her door.

"Kath Knowles?" she asked.

"Yes."

"Delivery at the main entrance for you."

Puzzled but still far too worried about Angie to bother with much else, Kath made her way down to the main hall, vaguely wondering who the delivery was actually for – it had to be some kind of mistake.

When she stepped out of the lift she saw Charlie the doorman talking to a smartly dressed pair of men who immediately came across to her. They were large men – and it wasn't fat.

"Miss Knowles?"

"Yes." Kath's voice was uncertain all of a sudden.

"Could you sign for something please, just out there." He pointed through the glass doors to where a minibus stood in the car park. "It won't take a moment, Miss." He leaned close. "You've been selected for Proteus, haven't you?"

Kath nodded, excited, relieved and scared all at the same time.

She followed the men outside and they ushered her to the sliding door on the side of the bus. She peered in and saw six or seven other young women.

"Don't worry, Miss. It's all very hush, hush. All your nearest and dearest will get letters telling them you're on a residential course."

Giving him a nervous smile she stepped up and into the bus, buckling herself in to a seat that was the nearest unoccupied one. The door slid shut and the driver, whose seat was partitioned off, steered the bus out into the London traffic. Suddenly, Kath realised that she was off at last. This was Proteus and she had no clothes other than those she stood up in and no bag, no money, no cards, no nothing. Frantically she slapped her skirt pocket and felt the thin shape of her mobile there. She pulled it out, desperate to tell Angie the good news but a girl sitting in one of the seats ahead turned round.

"Don't bother, hun. We think there's a signal suppresser on board, we all got diddly squat when we tried to call."

"Oh," Kath tried to hide her disappointment at not being able to restore herself to her Mistress' good books. "Well I expect it'll all be made clear eventually," she said and tried a bright smile.

"Yeah," the other girl sounded unconvinced but no one seemed inclined to talk and the bus wound its way out of London while its passengers tried to see the signs outside – or to see anything outside. The smoked glass was just as dark from the inside as from the outside. She tried to open a window at one point and found they were all sealed shut.

Someone wanted the girls taken onto the Proteus course to enjoy very high levels of privacy.

Kath fretted about not being able to let Angie know where she was and there was a core of unease that wouldn't go away. The journey went on for a long time and when someone tried to strike up a conversation an LED message scrolled across above the windscreen telling them that the course mentors at Proteus would immediately mark down anyone who talked. With no idea what advantage or damage Proteus could do to their future prospects, the girls held their peace as the journey wore on and more passengers were added until Kath counted ten of them.

Sharon was definitely of the opinion that that final vodka and whatever it was, had been one too many. Even for her. And besides it had taken the last of her cab fare home.

That was why she had decided to put out for those lads – to earn the cash for a taxi. And that was where she had been, in an alley just around the corner from the club when the police had found her with her skirt up round her waist, one lad going in from behind while she took another in her mouth.

There had been the usual scuffle as they were loaded into the wagon but with tazers it was one sided these days – especially when those on the receiving end were as paralytic as they had all been to start with.

Of course she had offered to do the same for the officers – it was a tactic that had got her out of some scrapes in the past – but there were no takers this time from Manchester's finest and now she languished in a cell awaiting the inevitable charge and remand. It'd be Community Service again, she was dead sure but it might just be a chat about changing her ways, for once she hadn't actually nicked anything or fought anyone. She'd just been shagging a bit too publicly.

Still they seemed to be taking a lot more time about things this than usual. She was sure she'd been there at least for a day, her stomach was rumbling and her hangover was fading fast. But at last she heard the hatch in the door slide open and saw a man peering in. Then a key turned and the door opened.

Two men entered. One was in the uniform of a prison officer, the other was in jeans and a plain shirt.

He was lean and sun tanned and he looked directly at her in a way no one else ever had. He was assessing her and whatever it was for, she reckoned she was failing. He wasn't sneering exactly, he didn't appear to think he even needed to do that. It was as if he knew he was superior to her in ways she couldn't even begin to understand. She felt the familiar heat of rage stir inside her. The rage that had won her so many fights, but which had also had her in and out of the nick for the last four of her nineteen years.

"Sharon Wilkins, Mr Lang. Got form as long as your arm."

Sharon was proud of that fact and decided to try it on a bit with this guy who was probably some kind of poncey social worker. She was still wearing just the short black skirt and pale blue shirt she had worn the night before. She let her left leg slide off the narrow cot she was sitting on, giving the stranger a direct view up to her knickerless crotch.

The man's eyes took in the view but not a flicker of expression registered on his face.

"Done last night for gross indecency. Shagging some guys in the city centre. She said she needed the taxi fare home, but had enough in her bag to buy a bloody taxi!"

That was news to Sharon. Christ! She must've been more hammered than she had known.

"The lads've been sent to a quarry for a year's hard labour. You want her?"

Sharon sat up straighter. This wasn't how it was supposed to go. She'd heard some rumours about a crackdown but it wouldn't apply to her. Not to her. They wouldn't dare! But there was something about this guy she didn't like.

"She's a slut alright," the man said with a posh, southern drawl, his eyes never leaving her for a second. "But is she the brainless scumbag she seems to be, I wonder?"

The rage that always seethed just below the surface inside her, erupted and Sharon was up off the bed and charging, hands outstretched, fingers clawed, ready to scratch and tear. It was a tactic that made her feared by all the other girls on her estate. She could punch above her weight with them and a lot of the guys too. Those she couldn't fight she could shag, and there were always plenty of guys who wanted to do that. It was why she had her own gang.

But on this occasion it went badly wrong. The man simply wasn't there. Instead she crashed heavily into the opposite wall. She spun round and found him standing in the middle of the floor with hands nonchalantly on hips.

She rushed him again, this time staying lower, aiming to get him around the waist and bear him down with the ferocity of her charge. But once again he wasn't there. What was there however was an arm that took one of hers and lifted it high above her back as she charged past, and a foot that took hers out from under her.

She somersaulted helplessly back onto the cot, landing flat on her back, winding herself and smashing both chains that held it horizontal from the wall, against which it could be folded.

The small room echoed with the crash and Sharon lay whooping and gasping for breath in the middle of the ruin. The man made no move towards her and as her wind returned, she found one of the chains that had held the cot and with a wordless snarl she rose again and charged. Pain exploded in her arm as she swung it at him, the chain swinging lethally behind it. Without seeing how he did it, Sharon found he had her hand twisted back under forearm in such a way that it had to drop the chain, she had been spun round and something that felt like a red hot poker was pressed against the side of her neck. She tried to kick back and free herself. Effortlessly, he lifted her off the ground and kept her there. All the time the pressure on her neck was growing and it didn't help to realise that all he was using was his fingers. The pain became such that she knew she had to make it stop. The only way was to go limp. She slumped and he let her down, pushing her away from him. She took a shuddering gasp of air and massaged the side of her neck where he had applied the grip.

"She's scum," the man said. "She'll do nicely. I'll take her."

The men turned and left. Sharon tried to scream imprecations at them but found that he had robbed her of her voice temporarily. And by the time it returned, she was on a truck, chained by her ankles in the dark, heading for somewhere she thought sounded like Preston, which was not far from Manchester. But then again she might have misheard and all of a sudden she was not certain of anything any more.

CHAPTER SEVEN.

On the second night of a three day show, Carlo Suarez always took things easy, especially if the outcome was as precariously balanced as this one was. Therefore he was sipping at a soft drink only as he walked along the walls of the great fortress that looked out across the Mediterranean. It was the base for the home team, the team that had hired in CSL livestock to strengthen its own squad against a stable from East Asia that fielded many diminutive but surprisingly tough slaves. Beside him paced the elegantly dressed owner, Johnson N'Benga; a man whose fortune had been made in commodity dealing and who was now dealing in slightly less legal commodities, which nevertheless afforded him much more pleasure than fruit and beans, as he happily admitted with an infectious grin whenever he was asked.

In the courtyard below them some of the spectators of the games had paid for the use of the slaves in the evening and were ensuring they got good value for money. It was standard procedure at games and whereas the squad members could be hired quite cheaply as there were at least a hundred in each stable these days, these punters had paid for the solo fighters; Carlo's hired-in ones amongst them and in the privacy of this closed area were sampling the delights of Blondie herself, Ox, Trouble, Purdy and El Tigre from CSL plus several more of Johnson's.

The two men paused in their promenade and looked down as Ox roared her way to another orgasm, nipples and labia pierced, her backside caned and now being energetically fucked. Carlo's eyes sought out Blondie, as they always did. She was the widely acknowledged 'Queen of the Arenas', capable of winning at everything from pony racing to chariot racing, pursuit running and studded whip duelling. She was Mistress of all trades within the arenas and currently there was a queue of men and women waiting to use her so they could have their photos taken with the spectacular blonde's body playing host to them at one end or the other, or both at the same time. Purdy was undergoing her usual breast torments – they were uncommonly big for an arena slave and she always attracted those who loved to ply the whips, pegs, needles and clamps the stables thoughtfully supplied for such purposes. As he watched, she threw her head back and joined Ox in wherever it was slaves went to when they orgasmed under punishment. Beside her, Trouble, the indefatigable lover of Ox and fellow whip specialist was taking yet more lashes and soaking them up stoically. Tigre was suspended by her ankles with her legs wide open and was clearly lost to this world as she sucked hard on one cock while another priapic man belaboured her back with a single tail whip.

All was as it should be, but Carlo would only be happy when they were all bedded down safely.

"Have you submitted the list of entrants for tomorrow's events?" Carlo asked Johnson.

"Yes, as agreed I've put Blondie in for the pony racing, but put Purdy in for the chariots with Tigre. That way we can field Blondie for the finale. I think we'll come through ok but they've been tough competitors," Johnson said.

"It's a long time since I saw Ox and Trouble have to work so hard for points in the log pulls," Carlo agreed.

"And even Blondie only tied for first place in the pursuit running. Mind you the girl who matched her was way ahead of the rest of her stable too."

"Yes."

Carlo looked thoughtfully as Blondie's exhausted body was hauled up off the table it had been tied down to and she was turned around and laid face down. Someone wanted to have their photo taken up to the hilt in the famous blonde's arse. A few years ago he would have happily put her in for the studded whip duelling and the pursuit running on the same day but this time he had held back and let Purdy take on the duelling. She had done well too, winning all three of her bouts, but whereas Blondie would normally have been a foregone conclusion for the pursuit running – where a naked girl was released ahead of a rider in the arena and had to make as many circuits before being caught as possible – she had been equalled this time by a delicate but superbly athletic Chinese girl. And only a few months ago in Asia she had barely won a studded whip duel and struggled in the pursuit running. Carlo knew everyone was watching him, waiting to see when he would call time on the girl who had almost invented the mystique of the female gladiator, who had suffered more and achieved more in the arenas than any other.

Johnson seemed to read his mind.

"You'll know when it's time, my friend. You and she know each other more closely than any two people I ever met."

"Thanks," Carlo said and they moved on.

Later that evening, Carlo considered having her brought to his room for a while but dismissed the thought. It was better that she get a full night's sleep after a day competing and then being used in the evening. He made do with one of Johnson's household girls, a demure looking African girl who nevertheless took him in her back passage with all the knowledge and competence he could have wanted. He allowed her to stay once she had cleaned him up and he woke refreshed and ready for the final day.

The N'Benga arena, like all the new ones that were springing up, had abandoned the original practice of naming themselves under colours – as the Roman teams had. There were simply not enough colours to go around and although The Girl Squad fought under yellow and black colours, it was simply referred to by everyone as The Girl Squad. Johnson's stable competed under a sort of deep maroon coloured flag but was known as the N'Benga stable. It sprawled along the North African coast and was kept reasonably cool by the breezes off the Mediterranean, so after a light breakfast, Carlo and the other drivers strolled under clear blue skies and with a salt wind in their faces along from the old fort that housed the majority of the N'Benga household, past the hotels and restaurants that catered for the guests and towards the pony racing course.

On their right as they walked was the actual arena, it was partly built from stones recovered from ruins that had been unearthed when Johnson had first started to develop the site. Around it were ranged the cages, surrounded by banks of terracing where the individual boxing and wrestling contests would take place quite shortly. Then just past them was the circus where the chariots would race before everyone returned to the arena proper for the climactic finale. The pony racing course was laid out around the dressage ground, starting and finishing within the stadium but leaving that arena and going across country for most of its length. Video screens would keep the crowds apprised of the rigs' progress as they went. It was a good course, Carlo had walked it carefully and he was looking forward to the day as he and the others walked into the tack room.

Blondie was standing against the rear wall of the long room, tethered by a lead running from her heavy tongue ring to a hook over the pegs that held her tack. Carlo greeted her fondly with a pat on the rump and was nuzzled in return, then he set about giving her a quick examination, running his hands up and down her legs and arms, seeing if there were any strains or any bruising. The vets would have done it anyway but old habits died hard. He parted her buttocks and peered at the whorled pit of her anus, checking that the previous night's usage hadn't left it reddened and sore. He would coat her butt plug with his usual secret brew and it would certainly be sore by the day's end, so he wanted to ensure it was in good condition to take what was coming its way.

As he straightened up from his examination the two vets entered accompanied by the Owners' Council Referee, one of a group of men who were now a common sight at events. After their lawless and piratical start, the arenas' owners had formed a body which now legislated for such things as the length and weight of whips to be given to slaves to fight with, the sort of tack that they should wear for racing and dressage. And in the arenas themselves they decided when a girl was down and out and oversaw the awarding of points. The owners had had the sense to see that as the scale of the investment they were making grew, so the need to ensure that that investment was protected by rules and regulations also grew. The introduction of vets to oversee the well being of the slaves had been grudgingly accepted by trainers and now the earning potential of the slaves was being considerably extended by more cautious treatment outside the arenas themselves, and even Carlo couldn't argue with that.

He stood back as the two women in white coats gave each girl a quick going over, each vet examining the opposition's slaves in their respective tack rooms, watched over by the stable's own vet, to ensure there was no fixing going on from either side. Pupil dilation and pulse were checked and later on a urine sample test would be run. Then the referee stepped forwards and scrupulously examined the sets of tack to make sure that the length of the tines on the inside of the leather strapping was within regulation and that the plugs' dimensions conformed to Council Rule No.1706 ii (c) and finally he checked that the whips all conformed too.

"Thank you, gentlemen, ladies," he said when the formalities were concluded. "See you in the paddock in twenty minutes please."

As soon as the door had closed behind him the day's work began. Carlo took out his trusty spirit stove, just as Johnson's drivers did and the air filled with the odours of the various spices the men employed to get the best out of their ponies. The materials had all been submitted in advance and examined by the Council, now the ingredients had been left on the central table in the room, in sealed plastic bags which only now were opened.

While the mixture was heated and the smell of ginger pervaded the room, Carlo began tacking Blondie up, settling the bridle over her head, passing the bit through her tongue ring and clipping the reins to its ends, then tightening the buckle at the back of the bridle that allowed a thick pony tail of blonde hair to escape and bounce at the nape of her neck, where she, like all arena slaves, bore her chip that contained her record. Lastly he settled the blinkers and made the final adjustments to the buckles that held the cheek and chin strap snug against her face. Then he turned back to the stove.

He gave the evil looking brew a quick stir, turned down the heat and went back to Blondie. He took down the tack and began to fit it, starting with the crupper and girth. As soon as she saw him take it down she spread her legs apart and he was able to buckle the girth on then leave the crupper hanging free for a moment. He returned to the stove, stirred and sniffed the pungent brew once more, turned off the heat and moved the small pan to cool down for a few moments. He returned to Blondie and, whistling happily between his teeth, buckled her tit straps in place. She stamped a couple of times as the tines on the insides bit into her, holding the straps firmly and thus ensuring her tits didn't bounce too much as she ran. He moved behind her to buckle the thin strap that helped brace the front ones. It was kept thin so as not to interfere with however much whip her driver felt it was necessary to apply during a race. He gave her nipples a couple of lighthearted twists as he passed back in front of her, returned to the pan and tested the brew for heat. Around him the room began to echo to the snorts and whinnies of the other ponies as they were plugged and began to register the effects of their drivers' concoctions.

Taking the pan over to Blondie, he dunked her butt plug deeply into the green brew, then he set the pan down and began to tighten the crupper, locating its dildo at her vaginal entrance and checking that the tines would lie nicely in between her labia then, once that had been achieved and the dildo easily inserted into her moist vagina, the butt plug was located at her anus. Despite her experience at anal penetration, her training kept her fairly tight and he had to screw and push the prong at first until it was accepted and sank into her. Then he wrenched the crupper up between her buttocks just as she began to stamp and cavil at the stinging that was beginning deep in her entrails.

"Whoa, there girl!" he chided. "Nothing you haven't had before. Now, let's get you buckled up nice and snug, then show you off to the punters!"

He tugged hard at the straps which came off the base of the plug and buckled each of them to the girth on either side of where it was buckled to itself.

There was none of the decorative detail of the dressage tack, no plumes atop the bridle, no flowing tail, no nipple piercing decorations and no decoration on the leather itself. This was simple working tack.

Hooking a finger through a cheek strap, Carlo led his pony out to where the rigs waited. He backed her between the shafts and unclipped her wrists from behind her before clipping them to rings on the shafts. Then he mounted the lightweight trap, stepping over the shaft carefully and lifted the carriage whip out of its holster once he had gathered the reins.

Between the shafts ahead of him he saw the most famous figure in the arenas, her shoulders were broad but her waist was trim and her hips swelled out enticingly to long, flawless thighs. And to his mind, the criss crossing welts and flares she bore from two days of competing and serving only made her more beautiful. Beside him the other N'Benga rigs pulled out towards the paddock and Carlo dragged his mind back to the job in hand.

There were to be two heats run between six rigs in each. The first two plus the two fastest losers from each heat went through to the final. He had tried to persuade Johnson to hire in Jet or Legs to strengthen the stable at this event but the owner had felt his side were strong enough. Carlo was not at all sure. In the first heat, the N'Benga stable were running a tall, beautiful girl whose skin was so dark it was almost true black but whose features were uncommonly delicate, and a Middle Eastern girl who was the colour of honey and who was hardly marked, having been held back for this event and the chariots. The tall black girl had fought in several melées and boxed in the pens as well but it was difficult to tell how marked she was. She moved very gracefully and Carlo knew a lot of punters would bet on her but he wasn't sure about her stamina.

Their drivers were wiry Africans who carried no excess weight. Carlo had been impressed with their expertise in practice runs, they didn't throw the lash unnecessarily but showed sound judgement in urging their mounts to perform rather than thrashing them into exhaustion.

As the rigs emerged into the paddock from the yard, there was applause from the crowds who leant over the railings, anxious to study form. The visiting team had the privilege of parading first and their three rigs were completing their circuit when Carlo and his fellow drivers emerged.

"Ladies and gentlemen!" the compere's voice boomed out over the PA. "Please welcome the N'Benga stable's entries for the first heat!"

One of the household girls darted forwards and applied a thin PVC number to the black girl's stomach and right thigh, then came towards Carlo and Blondie, putting a number five on the pony's stomach and thigh.

"I need hardly remind you of the identity of Number Five! Owned and trained by the CSL stable but running in the N'Benga colours today, the incomparable Blondie, driven by none other than Carlo Suarez himself! Number Four is Desert Night who's won three, been placed five times and pulled up once.

Number Six, Turkish Delight has been placed four times but has yet to win – but don't let that deter you from a flutter on her! I'm told she's been improving markedly in training."

As he had been speaking, Carlo had steered the rig over to the railings and was walking Blondie along it, letting hands reach out to trail across whatever parts of her body they could touch. She was used to it and didn't let it spook her, she even played to the gallery a bit these days. She arched her neck prettily and lifted her legs occasionally as if she was impatient to break into a trot. Carlo would haul back on the reins and she would champ at the bit and get a couple of touches from the driving whip. Carlo let her entertain the public while he glanced over to the bookies' pitches. Even as he watched the odds on Blondie were shortening, she was just as pert and spirited as ever, as far as the public could see. But Carlo was aware that nowadays more and more people came to watch her to see the mighty fall, whereas before they came to marvel at her prowess.

Well they would just see what happened today, he told himself grimly.

As the six rigs began to exit the paddock and head for the starting line, the crowd drifted towards the stands on either side of the track, a multi-coloured flock of spectators from all corners of the world, all enjoying the fine morning and looking forward to a good day's sport. And unlike the crowds who had elected to stay at the arena and watch the contests in the pens, the racegoers were more genuinely sporting. At the arena, the contests would form the backdrop for continual orgies on the terraces, the naked women grappling and struggling inflaming the crowd's passions. But here the focus was on the performances themselves and Carlo knew that across the world in private clubs and in houses and in some public places too, the images of the races would be being relayed live and heated debates would be taking place as bets were placed.

The track was wide enough for four rigs to line up abreast and the visitors had already taken their places, so, as had been agreed among the drivers the tall black girl took the lead position for the home team while Carlo and the driver who rejoiced in the given name of Holiday, lined up behind. Over a middle distance race like this one, it wouldn't make any difference.

As was a tradition by now, while the compere went through the runners' names and numbers again and gave the state of the odds, the drivers dismounted and checked their ponies' tack one last time. Carlo ensured the crupper was correctly settled between Blondie's labia so that the pain and pleasure would keep her focussed, just as the stinging in her rectum and the dildo in her vagina and the way the two shafts would rub against each other inside her would ensure she ran as fast as she could to get them all removed, and that in turn would serve her master.

"Number One; Orient, sixteen to one. Number Two; Sweet Dream, eight to one from ten to one. Number Three; Susie, twenty to one, drifting out from fifteen to one. Number Four; Desert Night, five to one from eight to one. Number Five, Blondie, three to two on. Number Six; Turkish Delight, thirty to one from twenty to one."

Carlo let the compere's voice drift over him as he stroked Blondie's nipples into even harder erection than the plugging and tines had. He would fancy an each way bet on Turkish Delight at those odds. She looked a sturdy little thing he thought as he took his seat again, wrapped the reins tight around his left hand and shook out the whip in his right.

The starter came to stand by the fence on their right, the crowd behind both fences fell silent in the stands. He raised his pistol and with a loud report and a small cloud of cordite, they were off. Immediately Desert Night was whipped up hard and the tall girl stretched her legs into long strides and took the lead. Turkish Delight stayed on Carlo's right shoulder as he let two of the opposition rigs settle in ahead of him. The strategy was to make Desert Night the target for the visitors, give them something other than Blondie to worry about. Meanwhile Turkish Delight who was not expected to do very much anyway, was to ride shotgun on Blondie to prevent any boring or barging. In a heat it was always possible that a team would sacrifice one entry to take out the opposition's strongest entrant – this was part of the arenas after all and definitely not the playing fields of Eton.

For one circuit of the track they settled into a steady canter, Carlo could hear Holiday holding station just by his right shoulder, Desert Night had opened up a significant lead and was holding it, forcing the two rigs ahead of him to concentrate on her.

"As they exit the stadium it's Desert Night by three or four lengths from Orient and Sweet Dream. Blondie is tucked in at fourth and looking comfortable with Turkish Delight half a length behind and Susie is the back marker!" The compere began his race commentary.

They veered off the grass track and onto a dirt road that led them out and round behind one of the stands.

"If you watch the screens ladies and gentlemen, you'll see how the race progresses. The rigs will take the big circuit twice and return to race twice around the stadium track to the finish line."

They were following the road that Carlo had walked down after breakfast, it sloped uphill in this direction and immediately he could feel Blondie begin to work. Her shoulders strained and her strides became more laboured as she pushed off with each foot against the gradient. It continued at a gentle slope for some two hundred yards before turning off to the left and climbing more steeply. Carlo began to ply the whip, stroking it across Blondie's upper back and shoulders, just encouraging her to keep on trying. Soon the course took another left hand corner and levelled out. Here it skirted the feet of the hills that stood behind Johnson's estate and looking to his left, Carlo could see out to sea over the stadium a little below him. Blondie began to speed up, relishing the level ground once more. Carlo reined her in slightly, the track was undulating and if a pony charged too quickly she could stumble on one of the down slopes.

"Desert Night is still well clear! Orient and Sweet Dream are holding station. Blondie has moved up a little and Turkish Delight and Susie are bunching behind her!"

After a straight that was nearly a quarter of a mile long, Carlo knew the track veered left once more and entered its most demanding stretch. It sloped downhill but went through a series of turns which meant that between turns the rigs were running almost across the face of the slope. Too much speed over the rough, hard earth could easily overturn a rig as they had no suspension. However, a bold and confident driver could possibly launch an overtaking manoeuvre there.

Blondie ran smoothly along the straight, needing no more than the occasional touch of the whip and tweak of the reins as the dips opened up before her and then Carlo pulled her back before she began the descent, then let her run on. The pull back would alert her to the danger, but it was imperative she had her head to watch where she trod on the downward slope, so pulling her head back the whole way down was out of the question.

"Steady, girl!" Carlo admonished as one foot slid a little in the dust, he touched her briefly on both shoulders and she leaned back against the weight as she turned right. Carlo leaned out to his right to help with balance and then they were turning left and Carlo leaned to his left, then it was right again, one more left and the slope eased off. Carlo whipped her up to let her know the way was good ahead and she sped off.

"Turkish Delight and Susie are losing Blondie! She's moving up on Sweet Dream but Carlo's not using much whip yet!"

Carlo knew there was still a long way to go as they pounded past the stadium and began the second lap. The gradient told straight away once more and this time, Turkish Delight and Susie closed right up. Susie's driver even attempted to come round the outside of Turkish Delight and for a while they ran three abreast, then when Carlo thought he had tired Susie enough, he lashed Blondie with some strength for the first time and as they began the steeper climb, the tall blonde really dug in and pulled clear. Her back began to shine with sweat. Turkish Delight dropped back but still stayed in touch. He was fairly sure they had lost Susie though. This time around Carlo began to let Blondie loose and whipped her along briskly. Once more he balanced the rig as it zig zagged across the slope with, surprisingly, Turkish Delight guarding his shoulder. He looked back at one turn and saw that Susie was far from finished and that Delight was performing her function very well and blocking her.

At the bottom of the slope the whips began to be plied in earnest. From here it was a sprint on level ground.

Carlo began to lay into Blondie's quivering buttocks, urging her onwards. As they entered the stadium once more, she at last began to pull clear of Susie but now she was closing on the fast tiring Sweet Dream. Carlo glanced round to check that Delight wasn't too close and pulled sharply out to overtake. As he had thought he would, Sweet Dream's driver also pulled out to block him, but Carlo reined Blondie in just enough, pulled her back, veered in the other direction and then wrapped the lash so it caught her breasts.

She knew what that meant and surged forwards, missing the back of Sweet Dream's rig by inches but pulling past on the inside. He managed a quick look behind before he concentrated on Orient and saw that Turkish Delight had charged past on the outside of Sweet Dream as she had belatedly been swung in to try and block Blondie. He was impressed.

"Brilliant passing manoeuvre by Blondie! And by Turkish Delight who's looking good value for a placing! Orient is closing on Desert Night as they enter the last lap but Blondie's closing on both of them!"

Carlo kept the whipping steady to her back and shoulders to keep her concentrating, the plugs and the tines would be tormenting her as she sweated. Steadily they closed on Orient, and by the time the final lap began, Blondie was on her shoulder. As Orient was the best prospect for a place in the final for her team, Carlo knew the driver wouldn't risk tangling his pony up in a blocking manoeuvre. It was a straight race to the line and Blondie was pulling steadily past. Suddenly Desert Night's wind went and it happened so quickly it took them both by surprise and they had to pull sharply around her to sweep past. Second place in a heat was fine with Carlo and he reined Blondie in as the line approached, crossing it at a comfortable canter while

Orient was driven needlessly hard for victory. Turkish Delight came in third, overtaking Desert Night on the final turn.

Back in the tack room, Carlo had Blondie kneel under a shower with her bottom in the air and sluiced her down. He didn't give her a full enema as she would be plugged again for the final but cooling her down from where the studs had bitten in and the plugs tormented her meant she would be more refreshed and ready to go. He towelled her down and led her around at a gentle walk to ease her muscles off before he left her tongue-tethered to her hook and went to watch the end of the second heat. It was not a very successful one for the N'Benga estate, they only got one through but Turkish Delight's time had been good enough to see her into the final so it was evenly balanced.

There was a half hour pause for the second heat ponies to cool down and to allow their drivers to administer some refreshment. Carlo let Blondie kneel in front of him and allowed her a blow job. He adored the feel of her heavy steel tongue ring flicking around his helm and held himself there for a few moments before letting himself feel her lips caress his full length as he sank deep into her throat and pushed to achieve release in the tight channel. The spurts of protein he gave her to swallow, followed by some tepid fruit juice would help keep her going. Holiday did the same for Turkish Delight, his teeth gleaming white as he grimaced at his climax, the black haired pony swallowing him down with well-practised ease. The third Johnson rig was a pony called simply Melon; and it was plain to see why. She was almost as well endowed as Purdy, was as dark skinned as Desert Night but was more compact and stronger looking.

All three ponies objected to the fresh butt plugs and having the studded tack re-applied and for a while the room was noisy with snorts, stamps and rattling of bits against teeth. But with a few snaps of the reins across stomachs and thighs, things settled down. Melon's driver took special care to ensure her tits were tightly bound.

While they paraded this time, pictures from the arena itself were relayed, Carlo was proud to see Ox applying a pinning hold to her wrestling opponent in one of the pens. Out on the floor of the arena itself, Tigre was slugging it out in a boxing match and the camera just caught Trouble applying the winning body slam in her match. But despite that, it was still close and all was to play for.

"For the final of the racing today ladies and gentlemen!" the compere announced as the rigs assembled at the starting line again. "Number One is Orient; sixteen to one. Number Two is Blondie holding at six to four on. Number Three is Dawn Light; drifting out to forty to one. Number Four is Turkish Delight shortening to six to one. Number Five is Melon; also at forty to one and Number Six is Ash; fifteen to two."

The last pony was a Scandinavian looking blonde who towered over her stable mates and was almost as tall as Blondie.

Anything could happen in a final, especially as the points in the arena were so close and Carlo and the two N'Benga team drivers had decided on a different strategy. As soon as the starting pistol fired, Carlo really let the whip loose on Blondie. The big blonde reared in shock as the lash wrapped her breasts, time after time, but she got the message and surged off up the straight and into the first turn, her feet throwing up the dust in small clouds behind her. After a few minutes Carlo eased off and glanced up a screen, he was well clear of the field and he intended to stay there. He knew Blondie was happier in the thick of the action but there was too much at stake where a stray foot or a lash from a rival driver could see her flat on her face. As he steered out onto the big circuit again he saw Blondie's back sweat-gleaming again and grimly promised she would sweat a lot more before he let the gathering vultures in the crowd see her fail.

"Coming to the first corner of the big circuit and Blondie looks to have an unassailable lead; maybe seven or eight lengths clear of Orient in second, Dawn Light in third, Melon in fourth with Ash and Turkish Delight bringing up the rear!"

Carlo didn't spare the whip up the hill and Blondie dug her feet into the dirt and managed to extend her lead by the time they made the level ground. Carlo let her coast for a while and then when they got to the downhill zig zags he took it steadily, hoping that one or more rigs might come to grief in their haste to try and catch up.

"Blondie is cruising the downhill section, Orient and Dawn Light are blocking Melon who's trying to force her way round the outside of the left hander! She's down! Melon's a faller at the zig zags! Ash and Turkish Delight are past her so it's down to two for the N'Benga stable!"

Carlo heard the commentary and looked up at a screen as they passed the stadium, in slow motion he saw the black girl's feet slide sideways from under her as her driver tried to force his way past on the outside and the slope was just too much for her. She skidded for some way and Carlo doubted that she would play any further part in the race, even if she hadn't been hurt, she would be too far adrift.

He let Blondie have a few swipes backhand and forehand to make her keep her mind on her work as the sweat would be beginning to torment her and they set off on the last of the big circuits. By the time they had climbed back up to the level ground, Blondie was beginning to blow, her head was rearing and Carlo could see her ribs heaving under her glistening skin that was now plainly running with sweat.

"Turkish Delight is making a move! She's left Ash in her wake and is up with Dawn Light. They're neck and neck as they turn into the uphill stretch with Orient still trying to make any impression on Blondie's lead!"

As far as he dared, Carlo took it easy but a look down at one of the screens above the stadium showed him Orient was grimly pounding up behind him and he hoped that the brief respite would help Blondie cope with what he had in store. He jerked her reins back as they turned into the downhill but then lashed her hard across her bottom. Instead of leaning back against the weight of the rig she was forced into running with it, letting it propel her downhill. Carlo gritted his teeth and concentrated on steering. His plan was to use the fact that he was out on his own to almost steer across the zig zag corners, cutting close to left and right barriers to minimise the time he spent going across the slope. If Blondie could keep her feet, it would be a race winner. If she lost her footing, it would be curtains. He shaved the first right hand barrier, brushing it with his shoulder as he leaned out and then charged almost straight downhill and shaved the left hand barrier with his other shoulder. Blondie was almost out of control, he could see she was just barely keeping her feet under her. If he reined her in now she'd be down in no time, all he could do was steer and hang on. Two more corners came and went, faces blurred past him, inches away, he heard screams and yells of encouragement and then Blondie was stumbling onto level ground. Now she needed him and he hauled her head back up. She skidded and reared but held her footing somehow as they tore out onto the level ground and pounded for the stadium. Up on a screen he saw Turkish Delight bumping and boring her way down the slope with Orient. Carlo grinned to himself, he could still spot talent hen he saw it. She had just needed a few good races to settle in before she showed her true form. But with her to worry about, Orient had her hands full so Blondie and he could relax.

Except they weren't going to.

Carlo wrapped her chest with every lash in time to her running steps, scorching her breasts and making her throw herself forwards. Neither he nor anyone knew when or if she might pass this way again, so a course record would be her legacy in case she didn't. For the two laps of the track he yelled her on and whipped her until saliva began to fly back from around her bit and sweat sprayed up as the lash snapped home. Dimly he heard the crowd cheering her on as the line came closer and closer and closer.

"A new course record! Not just broken but smashed! Ladies and gentlemen, we've just seen history made! No less than seventeen seconds taken off the previous best time!"

Carlo pulled up in a cloud of dust, wrenching Blondie's head round in a triumphant skid that sent spirals of dust up around them as the rig's wheels slid sideways. The he jumped down and strode round to her head before anybody else got there. Quickly he slid her bit out and loosened her girth, then let her rest her head on his shoulder as she gasped and sobbed her way back to normal. Only then did he lead her into the winner's enclosure to have a rosette pinned to her left breast. Orient took second and Turkish Delight came in a creditable third. Both proudly posed with their drivers for photos with their rosettes pinned neatly above their left nipples so that they hung over them.

After a shower and a thorough cleansing Carlo led Blondie back up to the arena and left her in a holding cell to rest while the chariots raced and lunch was taken. He made his way up to the owner's box in the circus just as the racing began. The chariots were the standard six slave ones. Across the front of the long central shaft ran a spar to which four slaves were tethered, the outside ones had steel guards on their forearms for fighting off rival teams. Behind them and nearer the chariot was a narrower transverse spar to which two slaves were tethered. These provided basic power and were lashed to their work by their driver, while the whipman kept the front rank gingered up and struck out at rival teams as well.

The races were close and provided some entertaining spills and clashes. Purdy's team won through safely but could only manage third place in the final. This meant that in the final melée the N'Benga stable needed to score ten 'falls' to clinch victory while the opposition needed to score twenty.

When the full heat had begun to go out of the day, the crowd reconvened for the final orgy of female combat and the fun that traditionally closed a three day show. The full squads of slaves were flung at each other and if the outcome had already been settled it was staged purely for the fun of it, and the real stars were not risked in the free for all. But, as on this occasion, where every 'fall' counted, all hands were set to the pumps. Hence Carlo was in the dressing room beneath the arena, taking off Blondie's cuffs and massaging some looseness back into tired muscles and doing the same for Purdy while Anne Marie catered for Tigre, Trouble and Ox. Around them the whole of the N'Benga squad swirled and herded, impatient to be let loose inside the arena. And even more impatient for what would follow.

Blondie knew the routine well and Carlo could feel the slight trembles of anticipation that ran through her as he worked on her.

"Randy bitch!" he whispered. "Can't wait can you?" He didn't talk directly to her, that would be unseemly but she stamped her feet and shook her thick mane of hair impatiently.

At long last, and just as the heat in the long, low room was becoming unbearable, they were called out and over a hundred naked, aroused and excited females squeezed and pushed and squealed their way through the door, out into the tunnel under the terraces and from there out onto the brightly sunlit arena floor itself.

Carlo watched his favourite slave's bottom jiggle deliciously as she trotted amongst the crowd, her mane of honey blonde hair bouncing above her team mates, and standing out even more than usual against the predominantly black haired girls. Just as her golden tanned skin was in stark contrast to the chocolate darkness of the skins around her, skins which shone as if they had been polished.

Some spectators who paid a fortune for the privilege – as they would see it – were allowed to stand at the sides of the tunnel and touch the girls as they ran out, some used handkerchiefs to wipe the sweat from them. These found their way onto the net for exorbitant sums in due course although others were kept as parts of private collections of arena memorabilia.

The same people would be there when the girls limped back or were carried back. Then the object would be to get a wipe of their cunts and any other bodily fluid, which would fetch even more or become an even more prized possession. It was a practice that went as far back as the Roman arenas.

Now the guards and owners referred to them simply as 'gropies' and tolerated their presence in the name of extra income for the stable.

Once the slaves burst out into the sunlight of the stadium and the crowd erupted, Carlo hurried up to the owners' box which was directly over the slaves' entrance into the arena and took his place beside Johnson.

"I think we've got it now," he told Carlo. "We'll make ten before they make twenty, especially with Blondie out there."

Carlo was inclined to agree but made a non committal response out of superstition. The compere was explaining the rules of this particular finale to the eager crowd.

The two squads of naked girls stood at either end of the arena and in the dead centre was a pile of the sort of weapons they were used to using; there were cat o'nine tails, single tail whips, studded whips, weighted boxing straps, nets and staves. But as the compere was telling everyone, there were only enough for half the slaves in the arena. The squads would have to fight for possession and then fight to win. But before then they had to reach the centre of the arena.

In front of each squad and stretching across the whole width of the arena, were lines of ten foot high pillars and at first their purpose was unclear but at a signal from one of the referees a switch was thrown and the pillars began to revolve. They turned slowly at first, but as they speeded up a delighted cheer erupted from the crowd.

Each pillar had leather straps mounted all round its circumference and up its entire height, as it revolved the straps flew out until they were overlapping the ones from the next pillar. The only way the naked girls could get to the weapons was to squeeze between the pillars.

"But we don't want these lazy sluts keeping us waiting for our fun do we?!" the compere enquired and got the response he wanted.

"So the opposing team's guards will encourage each squad to get a move on!"

Another cheer greeted the appearance of the men, already stripped down to shorts, ready for the fun later on and each wielding a braided lash.

Out in the centre of the arena a referee held up his hands with all fingers up and the compere began a countdown from ten.

The crowd joyfully yelled "Go!" at the end and the men sprang forwards to drive the hapless squads between the pillars. It soon became apparent that the designers had done a very good job. The gaps between were just big enough for a girl to get through sideways, thus making her slow down and have to take a longer, whole body, flogging on her way through. It also meant that the pile up behind her was exacerbated as there were almost ten girls for each gap, and that meant that those behind took a more prolonged flogging from the opposition's guards. And put together with the loving close ups from the ever present cameras, shown on the giant screens, it was a highly entertaining spectacle.

Carlo sat back and applauded as the squeals from the first girls to make the passage between the pillars began to filter upwards. Already welted and bruised from three days of use and competition, each girl was taking scores of mechanical lashes as she desperately tried to make a dash through a gap, but it was too narrow to be rushed through and they emerged staggering and striped before they had even faced their opponents.

The cameras showed close up after close up of breasts being mercilessly flattened under the barrage and buttocks rippling, but then the pile ups behind began to make girls trip over against those in front of them and soon the gaps were all full of girls crawling over each other, all desperate to escape the lashes behind and on either side of them.. Fights broke out between team members under the blizzards of leather.

"Brilliant, Johnson!" Carlo shouted above the din. "You kept that quiet!"

"It was Mister Su's idea and he developed the pillars. I suggested we use the guards to encourage the opposition squads!"

Down on the arena floor the finale was entering its next phase. The last of the girls had made their way by whatever means through the pillars and the two squads now tottered towards the weapons pile. There was hardly an inch of female skin anywhere that wasn't welted. Carlo watched one of the screens that was picking up on a camera behind the N'Benga squad. Most of the girls were staggering, their buttocks red, striped and bruised purple in some cases. Some of them helped each other along, any quarrels now forgotten, subsumed in the knowledge that bad though the opposition's guards had been, they were nothing compared to their owner's wrath if they went down without putting on a good show. He sat forward, suddenly serious. Now that the fun of the pillars was over he realised it had evened the teams out, both were exhausted and the N'Benga's team weight and strength advantage had gone. Beside him Johnson sat forward too, suddenly nervous as he took on board the implications too.

Slowly the pace of the two squads picked up as they began to recover and by the time they met at the weapons pile, some of them had even broken into a trot. Carlo noted with pride that Blondie was among the first to arrive.

Then the scrapping became serious and the excitement in the crowd grew. As punches were thrown and girls' bodies pinwheeled in front of cameras, breasts were mauled and kicks landed with eye watering accuracy, so the images from the terraces became more excited. Most of the women were screaming their team on, faces grimacing in ferocity, seemingly unaware of the fact they were being taken or buggered from behind. Others were being pressed into service by urgent masters and were down on their knees sucking cock but with eyes fixed on the screens.

There was no science to the combat out in the arena. Groups and couples of slaves tottered round, supporting each other as much as anything until one or the other could land the telling blow.

Carlo noticed that even Blondie was off balance when she swung the whip she had managed to grab from the pile. The camera followed her as she confronted a girl from the opposing team and the two exchanged lashes until Blondie managed to combine a punch to the ribs with a lash to the girl's back that threw her off her own feet, she put so much effort into it. Her opponent went down and a referee signalled a fall to the N'Benga team, but Blondie was on all fours, panting for breath and never saw the kick coming from behind.

An opposition squaddie caught the blonde full on and sent her rearing up off the ground, hands clutched between her legs. She rolled frantically away from another blow, and got under the feet of another pair of grappling slaves and brought them down on her.

The crowd had let out one huge "Ooooh!" of sympathy and now went quiet as they waited to see whether she was flagged as down and out. The camera stayed on the thrashing pile of bodies, another fell over backwards as she was retreating and the heap became bigger and more ferocious. Carlo was biting his nails. Somewhere under it was Blondie who had never gone down this early in a melée before.

On another screen a referee flagged a fall for the visitors as Purdy was thrown down and made no attempt to defend herself as she was whipped, spreadeagled and submissive on the ground. Her conqueror settled astride her face and accepted her surrender. It made a brief tableau before another group of struggling slaves tripped over them and again it was a free for all.

"The home team need five more falls! The visitors are catching up and need only seven more! Blondie seems to be down and out! Can they hold on?!"

Carlo knew that in the old days, his blonde superstar would have struggled clear and returned to the fray as an avenging fury. But not today.

He looked elsewhere and saw Ox bodyslam a girl down, then drop to her knees on her midriff. It was an immediate fall and the impassive Russian went to find more work but got caught by a blow from a stave from behind and went down like a sack of potatoes.

Suddenly a whistle blast sounded deafeningly loudly.

"Five! The Home Team's done it!" the compere roared.

Carlo looked around to see where the victory had come from and saw the girl who had run as Turkish Delight, stagger upright, grinning broadly and holding her whip aloft in victory. At her feet two of the opposition lay writhing on the sand. The crowd stood to applaud and to a fanfare the naked men of both stables were allowed in, plus a few lucky spectators whose ticket numbers had come up in the draw. Usually the girls put up an entertaining struggle before they went down to inevitable defeat at the hands of the men but on this occasion they were too exhausted to do much more than trade a few whip strikes before opening whichever entrance the man wanted.

In little more than half an hour it was all over. The very last of the slaves had been ravished one more time and made no attempt to rise again. The crowd was sated, its carnal appetites fed and now there was the after-storm calm as Carlo, Johnson and Mr Su were applauded down onto the arena floor. It was tradition that the owners were thanked for the display, and this time as some of the losing team were put to whipping posts for penalties earned earlier in the day, Carlo could not take his usual pleasure in it. He used his foot to move supine bodies and where some were stirring he helped them out of his way.

At last he found her. Blondie was lying at the bottom of the heap she had originally gone down under and her eyes only fluttered open when he spoke her name. It took several men spraying the ground with a cold water hose to get the girls back on their feet. The lashes were still falling over by the whipping posts, those who had lost earlier on were condemned by the crowd to take a penalty, the thumbs only going up when the tally the compere called matched the majority of the crowd's opinion.

The gropies had good pickings after that finale. As the battered participants limped and crawled away, Ox and Trouble carried Tigre between them and the gropies wiped the sperm from their thighs and backsides as it mingled with the slave's own juices.

Carlo had no taste for the celebrations that normally followed a victory. He and Anne Marie were kept busy, applying cold compresses and bandaging to the CSL contingent. Meanwhile the stable vet was working on all her charges. The two of them agreed that the Council should be told that the pillars were a step too far for a final day and should be found a place elsewhere in the games.

"Mind you," Carlo said as he stared at the groaning, welted bodies around him in the home stables. "It was quite a spectacle!"

CHAPTER EIGHT

Before the full heat of the following day had taken hold, Carlo was clipping water bottles to the travelling crates the CSL slaves were shipped in. Each slave was hog tied and slid into her crate, all neatly parcelled for the journey with water where she could reach it, just beside her face.

Johnson had promised him a truck to take them to the airfield and dead on time it drew to a halt beside him as he stood at the great gate to the fortress. Dust swirled and rose before drifting away on the breeze. A man jumped down with a clipboard and counted the crates.

"Could you sign here please?" he said with a brilliant smile as his colleague began to slide Purdy's crate round to the back of the truck. Carlo took the clipboard.

"Mister Suarez!" A voice distracted him and he turned away. "Could I have your autograph please?"

"Please Mister Suarez!"

"Me too!"

A crowd of excited women was approaching from one of the hotels. He signed without looking at the clipboard, handed it back and turned to the fans. He spent a few minutes signing programmes and answering questions about the slaves and their treatment – it was frequently female fans who wanted to know about that. Then when they were satisfied he and Anne Marie climbed into the taxi that Johnson had booked for them and followed the truck to the airfield.

As was usual there were no problems in shipping the slaves out. The N'Benga stable was a major foreign currency earner and Anne Marie was only required to offer herself to three of the customs staff before everything was stamped and they could return to the plane.

It was not their usual pilot and air crew. The co-pilot who greeted them at the top of the steps apologised for Captain Seymour but he had become entangled in some customs wrangle in France and they had been summoned instead.

"But everything's on board safely, Mr Suarez and I signed for the cargo."

"Thanks." Carlo took the copy he proffered and entered the plane, stowed his hand luggage and glanced down at the paper only as he was about to sit down.

He felt suddenly sick, his heart skipped a beat and his hand shook as he picked it up to take a closer look.

"Four! It says four crates were loaded!"

"Yes, Mr Suarez. I counted them in and you had signed for four when they were loaded."

Carlo looked again. The man was right. He replayed the scene at the fort again, the gaggle of women. He turned and ran for the bulkhead and threw open the door to the cargo area. There were four crates and without looking any further, although he forced himself to, he knew who was missing. There was Ox, Trouble, Tigre and Purdy. Blondie had gone.

"But what are we going to do?!" Anne Marie wailed as she too took stock. Carlo whirled back and ran down the steps, he turned full circle, looking for a trail of dust that would mark out where the truck was. But it had gone.

The co-pilot stood at the top of the steps, distraught. "But the truck was empty Mister Suarez! There were four crates in the truck - and only four, I'm sure!"

"I bet there were," Carlo said grimly. He reached for his mobile phone and rang a number.

"Johnson!" he said when it was answered. "Where did you hire that truck from? A local firm you've used before? Can you get some men down there now!

Blondie's been stolen. The truck might still be in the country and you've got clout with the police here! We've got to stop them!"

Blondie had been so tired that she had hardly registered the pinprick at her left elbow, as the truck had jolted away towards the airport. At least the discomfort of the hog tie meant that she was on the way home. With luck her master would do what he sometimes did when they came home from a show. A day or so after, when she was beginning to recover, he would lean on her stall door and smile at her and cluck his tongue, holding out her favourite shortbreads. She would feed from his hand and adore him with all her heart and soul, then when the others had gone out training, he would come into her stall as she lay dozing on her sheet-covered straw. He would open her legs gently and slip his fingers inside her with exquisite, slow movements and bring her gradually to a pitch of pleasure that made her groan and whimper. He would make her keep her legs wide apart as he went on working his fingers deeper and more vigorously inside her, her tongue ring would render her pleas and her cries inarticulate, as was only right and proper for a creature like her, the creation of her master. He would make her come, once, twice and then as she was descending from the clouds. She would at last feel his weight on her and in a spasm of delight that was almost orgasmic in itself, she would feel his cock suction her lips open and slip easily into her, filling her, inch by exquisite inch as his full weight descended onto her. Then he would begin to move in her and she would hear his pleasure as he breathed by her face and then his lips were on hers, his tongue was penetrating her mouth just as his cock was reaming her vagina and he was claiming her back as his own.

She rose and thrust back at his every lunge, snapping her hips at him, rotating her pelvis, seeking to employ every single way a woman can bring pleasure to the man inside her. No repeated ravishings in the arenas, no post-whipping fucks, no orgasms under the whip itself came close to the heaven she entered when her master took her and she heard him groan as he released himself into her.

She woke with a start as light flooded around her and she felt her crate being dragged backwards.

"She's awake," a male voice declared as she tried to come to terms with the loss of her dream. "The false bulkhead behind the van driver worked perfectly, M'sieur, and so did the distraction. It all went like clockwork."

"Good. Onto the plane and let's get her out of here!"

She was a little surprised by the urgency in the men's voices but the crate lurched as it was lifted and she saw the grass of the airfield beneath her, then there was the dusk of the plane's interior, the clanging of doors the thundering of the engines; all familiar sights and sounds on the journeys to and from the arenas. She yawned and settled herself to sleep again. She was going to be stiff and sore for several days, this time. Even her cunt hurt.

When she awoke again, she was in a stall but it wasn't hers. This one faced directly outdoors and the daylight was stronger and brighter than in England. She sleepily began to examine her surroundings. Her hands were clipped together behind her back, so that was normal. Her left ankle was chained to the wall beside her, normal, but at home she was chained to the back wall. She was lying on a sheet over some straw and there was an appetising smell coming from the trough just beside the half door, and that was normal too.

If there was one thing her life as a slave had taught her, it was never to try and work out the masters' plans and intentions. Carlo had his reasons for her being wherever it was she was now. It would all be made clear in his good time. She struggled to her knees, wincing at the various pains that exploded in her legs, her back and her groin. But she ate, drank from the water bottle and slept again.

Her master always had perfectly good reasons for what he did with her and it was none of her business that he seemed to have hired her out straight after a show for once.

John Carpenter put the phone down and rubbed his forehead wearily. Carlo sat opposite him and suddenly John saw how this had aged him. He looked gaunt and pale, his infectious good humour gone with the crate that held his beloved slave. He had arrived home the previous day with the other stock. Johnson's men and the local police had found the real courier's truck some miles from the town with its occupants bound and gagged. They had been unable to furnish any descriptions but at least it looked as though Johnson and his stable were in the clear, something the Owner's Council had been very concerned about.

"The Council is making sure every trainer and owner knows and they'll alert every dealer and auction house on the circuit. Whoever's got her won't be able to make a move without us knowing," he said.

Carlo shook his head. "They won't try and sell her. There's no auction house will take her, I reckon she's gone to a private collector." He gave a wry smile. "The trouble is we can't call on any law because we're all illegal!"

"And the only law that matters is the one that says possession is nine tenths of it!" John sighed and got up. He wandered over to his office window and looked down at The Lodge's stableyard. The extension to the CSL stable had been completed only the previous week and now the yard was busy with CSL stock being moved out and Lodge girls being moved back in. Patti Campbell, the red haired, head groom of the CSL stable was holding centre stage as Anne Marie and Raika led the slaves here and there on their tongue rings. Madame Stalevsky fussed around her girls, the naked and collared pony girls being led by the beautifully gowned Lodge girls. It was a colourful scene and order was emerging from the chaos. But beneath it all he knew everyone was conscious of the huge gap that Blondie had left behind her.

"Our only hope is that whoever's taken her has got some sort of stunt set up, or will want her to do some exhibition bout. They're bound to be cock-a-hoop at having her in their collection! And when they let on that she's part of whatever it is, there's no way it'll stay secret. That's when we'll have to move to get her back. Whatever it takes," John said.

Carlo nodded. "Whatever it takes."

CHAPTER NINE.

It was early evening before the bus finally pulled into some sort of farmyard out in the country and the door hissed open to signify their journey was at an end. The moving LED sign above the windscreen invited them to leave the vehicle. Stiff, nervous and excited the ten girls disembarked and looked around them.

With the earlier exoneration about talking still in their minds, the group remained uneasily silent. Then the bus's door sighed shut and it drove away, back down the unmade road it had lurched along on the final mile or so of its journey. As it disappeared, almost in unison the girls produced their mobiles and began to try and make calls.

"They won't work," a voice told them, just as Kath registered the total lack of signal on her handset. She looked up to see that a tall, slender girl had come out of the house and was standing in the centre of the yard. She had straight black hair and was wearing a knee length white coat, in her hand she held a clipboard.

"The whole estate has been suppressed, except for some devices, to which you do not have access," she said as she approached them, smiling in what Kath felt was an unpleasantly smug way, as if she knew something they didn't and it wasn't going to be pleasant.

"The estate was specially selected as it is extremely isolated. The nearest road is two miles away. The nearest village is three miles. The local police have been fully briefed about Proteus and will return any girl who tries to leave before the course is complete. All your partners and families have been informed that you are on a residential course that will last for at least a month."

There was a stir among the girls at the mention of the fact that they could be here for a month.

"At least a month!" the girl repeated, more loudly. "Now let's get started. Follow me please."

The girl turned on her heel and headed for a door at the back of the large red brick, house.

"Hang on!" one of the girls said, as they all began to trail along in her wake. "Can't you tell us a bit more!"

"All will be made very clear, very shortly," the girl said, without turning and entered the house.

They followed her along a stone flagged, echoing corridor painted in institutional green. At the end they entered a room that was simply a changing room. There were pegs set on a board above a long bench against one wall. Opposite, there were ten lockers.

"Strip, please and put all your possessions including phones and jewellery in the lockers provided."

Giving them no time for any queries or protests she vanished through another door at the far end of the room. Kath and the others exchanged looks and grimaces. For her part Kath couldn't help feeling a certain amount of relief that someone was giving her orders again. And at least there was no doubt that at long last Proteus was underway, so Mistress would be pleased when she received the letter. And suddenly Kath realised that now that the course was taking place, it was down to her to do well at it – how she would report to Mistress was going to be a problem but she would deal with it in due course. For now, she had to fit in with whatever these people wanted, and she was good at obeying orders.

It was almost as if ten similar debates had been raging and had reached the same conclusion. Ten pairs of hands reached for buttons and zips and in only a few minutes the room echoed to the sound of lockers being slammed shut and keys turning. Kath had to admit that whatever the criteria were that had been applied to recruitment for Proteus, they had resulted in a pretty good looking bunch of girls being selected. Kath knew that she wasn't bad looking herself, she had brown eyes which were attractively large and a round face with a full-lipped mouth and a dimpled smile. Her body was trim and she stood about five feet three tall, her breasts were thirty-two E and she knew from repeatedly wonderful experience that her buttocks were spankably rounded and tight. However, she was up against stiff competition in the complement of Proteus, the girl who sat down next to her and self-consciously held one arm across her breasts was a green eyed blonde who was about five foot four and who had breasts that – had they been hers – Kath would not have hidden. Far from it, she would have proudly displayed them at all opportunities, from the glimpse she had had they looked like Gs. There was a black girl whose legs and buttocks were simply a dream.

The girls exchanged nervous smiles as they all sat naked and waited. Kath wondered how important submissiveness had been in the selection as still no one dared break the silence. She also noticed that one or two sets of nipples were standing to attention and to her horror, as she noticed it, she realised her own were reacting. The sense of going into the unknown was arousing her, and just to reinforce that feeling of submitting to an unknown future, the black haired girl re-entered and imposed her authority once more.

"Place all locker keys in the bag being passed around. Remember your number."

A simple cloth bag began to make the rounds. "Rebecca Stone!" The girl read out a name from her clipboard and a dark haired girl with pale, freckled skin put her hand up.

"Follow me."

A few minutes later the black haired girl came back and called another girl. And one by one they were summoned to the next stage. Kath was nearly last and when she eventually followed the girl through into the next room, she urgently needed a toilet. Nervously she asked for the use of one and was gestured over to a toilet mounted against the clinic-type room's far wall. There were no curtains or any sort of privacy.

"Use it or don't, it's up to you. You will have no privacy while on this course so I suggest you get used to it," the black haired girl told her coldly when she protested. The girl's relaxed authority and remoteness seemed to go straight to the submissive core of Kath's nature and she meekly sat and passed water while the girl watched her. Once that was over she was stood on a weighing machine, her height was recorded and virtually every dimension was measured and recorded on the clipboard. Her biceps, her thighs, her calves, her stomach, her bust, her hips – it all went down and while the girl worked, Kath noticed that there was no hem of a skirt beneath the white coat and there was something about the way she moved – not entirely fluently - that reminded Kath of times when Mistress had made her do housework with a dildo or a plug inside her…but surely not! Surely this almost arrogantly assertive girl couldn't have been subjected to such humiliation by a dominant…could she? But then as she well knew, the one sure way to get a submissive to be assertive and confident was to make sure they knew they were doing their Master's or Mistress's will. She filed the thought away as she began to mentally compile her first bulletin from Proteus.

Her mind was jerked back to the here and now by the sound of a surgical glove being snapped on.

"Over here and lie on your back! Legs spread."

Kath turned and saw the girl had lowered a spreader bar over one end of the couch she had seen opposite the toilet.

"But!..." Kath began as she took stock of the implements on a trolley beneath the bar and realised what was coming.

"But nothing. Lie down on here and do as you're told or go and get dressed, you're no good to us."

There was really no choice. She lay down and felt her ankles being cuffed and then the bar was raised and she was more exposed than she had been on that awful afternoon in the hotel.

The girl held up a vaginal dilator, smiled a slow cruel smile and ran the cold steel implement up and down the insides of Kath's thighs once or twice.

"With sluts like you it saves on lube, doing this. It gets you good and wet all on your own. I just need to make sure you're not carrying anything in there. Can't be too careful."

Kath stared at the ceiling and sighed in resignation. It was no more than the truth. Mistress had opened her up with those things before to show her off and Kath had loved it. Still she jerked in shock as the cold metal entered her and she couldn't help a strained grunt as she felt herself opened wider and wider, and then wider still and only when she was seriously frightened did the stretching stop. She craned her head up to look down the length of her body to see the black haired girl peering into her, then she inserted her gloved fingers and felt about inside her in such a dispassionate and careless way that Kath felt a rush of sluttish arousal and almost groaned as she realised that the girl was perfectly placed to detect it.

"Good! That's the response we want," the girl said and withdrew her fingers, then wound in the dilator.

Kath lay back and tried to analyse this. Hadn't Mostyn said something about her having passed the practical exam? Was submissiveness really an essential quality in Proteus recruits? And thank goodness she and Mistress had abandoned plans to smuggle in anything vaginally!

There was a cold clammy feeling suddenly at her anus and Kath realised the girl was going to check her other cavity. This time she couldn't help a gasp of pain as the dilator was opened up. She had never been very big there and almost immediately she was at the point of pain.

"Hmm! Some work needed there," the girl said before fingering her and looking up her again before finally withdrawing the machine.

"Okay, go next door and wait."

Rather shakily, Kath sat up, swung her legs off the table and stood up. What had she meant about her arse needing work? What was Proteus about if it needed its recruits to have a rectum that could take bigger things than the butt plugs Mistress used?

With her mind in turmoil she went into the next room and rejoined the others. They were sitting on wooden chairs, still naked. The chairs were in one row facing a wall on which there was a large notice saying simply; 'Silence.'

Kath took a seat next to a brunette with rather small breasts but who was ravishingly pretty, with big green eyes that anyone could drown in. She gave Kath a sympathetic smile and let her eyes travel down from Kath's face to her chest. Kath glanced down and immediately blushed and gave the girl an embarrassed grin. Her nipples were blatantly hard and erect. But so were the other girl's. They each shrugged in resignation and looked along the row, the same sympathetic smiles were in evidence all along it and Kath began to cheer up. At least she seemed to be in the company of other submissives.

Two more girls joined them, both exhibiting similar symptoms of arousal and then their number was complete. They began to look around them to see what would happen next.

A door beside the notice opened and a man entered. He was tall and broad shouldered with a boyishly handsome face. Kath felt her jaw drop open and along the row of girls there were gasps and some hastily muffled yelps of surprise. Had it been possible, Kath's jaw would have dropped further open. Not only did she know this man, at least some of the others did too. And that meant that Proteus was more far-reaching and ambitious than they had realised when they had put her undercover.

Kath's thoughts raced as she assessed all the implications that had opened up with such shocking suddenness.

"Good evening, ladies!" the man said, folding his arms and standing four square in front of them. "Any of you not know who I am?"

Kath glanced along the row and not one hand went up.

"Good! That saves a lot of time and means that the groundwork for Proteus has been done well. You know that I'm assistant trainer to Carlo Suarez at the CSL stable," the man went on.

Kath's heart was hammering now and her stomach felt achy with tension. She and Mistress had often downloaded sequences from the CSL website and watched as this man put the slaves through intensive training for the games. But what was really occupying her thoughts – and she guessed those of the other girls – were the scenes of the punishments those slaves underwent so regularly and which they had watched so eagerly as a prelude to their own play sessions.

But now that she was stark naked in front of him, the word 'play' didn't come into it.

"Be under no illusions, please." Kath forced her attention back to the man in front of her; Brian Holden. "Proteus has the full blessing of the government, and its full backing. You are here until we say otherwise, so do accustom yourself to that fact!"

"You mean we're prisoners!" To her horror the words had sprung from her own lips.

Brian Holden turned a cold gaze on her. "Yes," he said simply. "However, your personality profiles suggest that you are the sort of girls who won't find that too much of a problem." He shrugged. "Even if you do, it won't matter eventually. I have every faith in our training procedures."

"But I've got friends who'll come looking for me!" a girl at the far end shouted.

"All of you had dominant partners, it was part of our checks. And all of them were approached and their permissions obtained before you were collected."

These final words fell on Kath's ears like the footfalls of doom. Mistress knew? She agreed? Then what was all that scene at the hotel about? So it couldn't be true! But then if she had been approached of course she would have agreed. That was why Kath had been planted in Mostyn's department in the first place. But why didn't she say? She would have said something. No, it couldn't be true!

Her own turmoil was being replayed all along the line as the girls came to terms with the fact that they had been 'volunteered' by their dominants. Some of them were in tears, others were shouting.

Brain Holden was watching them carefully, she noted, and when the worst of it was over, he applied the killer blow.

"Some of them sold you to us permanently," he said.

Kath's heart skipped a beat as the image of the blonde girl from the hotel filled her mind. Tears filled her eyes and she stood up, forgetting her nudity entirely as she tried to escape, to run from the whole ghastly situation. Nothing else mattered but to get away. She made it as far as the door Brian Holden had entered by and then suddenly a man's strong arms were around her and she was carried back effortlessly, kicking and lashing out as desperately as she could but to no avail.

It was hunger that woke her. It gnawed at her as she struggled up from the depths of the only refuge she had been able to find at the end of that awful day. The mattress she was lying on was hard but at least she had a quilt to keep her warm, she looked around and vaguely remembered the tiny cell she had been brought to. The roof curved over her bed and she remembered that it was only tall enough to stand in the very centre. It was in effect a semi circle, like a barrel turned on its side and cut in half. A door of shiny new steel bars separated it from the passage outside. Careful not to bang her head she swung her legs out and stumbled upright in the middle of the floor. She went to the barred door and just for the look of the thing gripped them.

"You're awake then," a girl's voice said from the next cell.

Other memories came back. A man had carried her and the green eyed blonde down here when the chaos got too bad upstairs, the two of them had been put in neighbouring cells and after some time of fruitless shouting and screaming, they had collapsed into miserably exhausted sleep.

The corridor that ran outside their cells only ran past the green-eyed girl's one, then it stopped. At the other end, by Kath's cell was a door, and this now opened. A cheerful looking man in a simple T shirt and cargoes came in. He was built like the proverbial brick outhouse, Kath thought, his shirt strained across his pecs and the short sleeves strained around his biceps.

"Morning! I'm your trainer, Brian's the big boss, but I'll be directly responsible for your discipline. We're working the sister system, you two look after each other from now on. However rough the going gets, keep an eye out for your sister and she'll do the same for you. And believe me the going will get pretty rough!"

All this was delivered with a cheerful openness that clashed bizarrely with their circumstances and when he unlocked their doors both girls came out docile and almost curious about what was going to happen next. The man handed Kath a chain with leather cuffs at either end.

"Buckle these onto you and your sister's ankles, your right, her left. You won't need it after a few days because you won't want to leave us, but it'll save us a bit of trouble in the meantime if you get restless! Now, let's get you some breakfast and then we'll get down to work."

He walked behind them as they hobbled awkwardly along, the house was a maze of outbuildings and extensions and the cellars they were being held in were what seemed like miles away from the house proper. The stairs gave them the most problem with their chain but once they were back on ground level they made good progress towards the smell of breakfast. On their way they joined two other pairs with their guards and from the conversation, Kath gathered hers was called Mike. She stored the information away.

The breakfast was amazingly good; fresh fruit juice, coffee, croissants, jam and a soft boiled egg; all served by the guards and the back haired girl, while Brian Holden looked on carefully.

It wasn't until the meal was over that the true nature of Proteus was made clear and by then, Kath realised, the way the induction had been handled meant it was far too late for submissive girls to do anything other than accept it. But for herself there was the determination to be a good journalist and maybe win her Mistress back by filing the story of what was going on.

"You have been picked to form the nucleus of a brand new arena stable. You will be part of the very first state sponsored stable in the world." Brian told them as they sat naked at the trestle table on a bright morning with all the traumas of the previous day behind them.

"You all know that the life of an arena slave is almost non-stop sex and submission. And you're the lucky ones that Mother Nature has equipped to enjoy that lifestyle. Now, this is not a polite invitation! This is a fact. You will be subject to strict discipline from now on, and you will be subjected to a fitness regime that will test you to the limits. You do not have a choice, you have been chosen. Get over it and get on with it! Any slacking and you'll find yourself saying hello to the whipping post in the yard!"

Kath's first morning was spent at the end of a lunge rein, learning the commands from a driving whip and getting used to wearing a bridle and bit. She began to learn the dressage steps, the high-lift trot, the slow trot, she began to learn how to arch her neck and she learned that the driving whip stung like mad when you were sweating. And she also learned that Mike wielded it a lot more strongly than Clive Mostyn had. Every hour, she would be released and would shackle herself to an iron loop in the yard wall, after having freed her sister and fastened her to the rein. After an hour they would swap again. Two pairs went out running and the other two began to learn how to wrestle.

There were no rebellious scenes at all and Kath's mind wandered to the question of how to file her story. Idly she watched, once she had got her breath back, the well set up young man in front of her whipping the green eyed girl around in circles, shouting out orders and lashing her to her work. The sun was warm on her skin and the stone was hot against her back. The girl was sexy in a slender, lissom sort of way and her breasts swung and rippled deliciously, she had to admit it was enjoyable watching her getting whipped.

In the afternoon they were taken for a run. The hobble was removed and Mike accompanied them. Kath tried to keep looking around her for any clue as to where they were but it seemed as though the house was surrounded for miles by woods and fields. Mike ran easily alongside them, and when they began to flag he used a riding crop across their thighs to encourage them along. One of the hardest things Kath found was trying to get used to the way her breasts bounced as she ran, unfettered by a bra for once. But Mike pointed out that if she was a pony racer her tits would be strapped, and if she was a chariot racer, well bouncing tits was the least of her worries. He laughed but Kath couldn't. She was too surprised by the tide of warmth that swept down through her belly at the thought of being in the middle of the storm of a chariot race. She and Mistress had frequently shouted themselves hoarse watching the pell mell action from this or that arena.

In the evening they were made to stand around the whipping post and watch as the black girl and a tubby blonde were given thirty lashes with a single tail for not trying hard enough. Once she was put to bed and had heard the door to the outside world locked she immediately reached between her legs and began to rub at her clitoris urgently. It had been the tall black guard, Alex, she thought his name was, who had wielded the lash and Kath kept replaying in her mind's eye the way the two victims had spun and twisted as the lash had fallen. After all the emotional upheaval and doubts about her Mistress, it was relaxing to be back in touch with her real nature. The orgasm that eventually consumed her, freed her from all thought and she was able to recall the stinging of Mike's whip on her own skin, the delicious ripple of her sister's buttocks as they were whipped and the heavy smacking noise of the punishment whip in the yard. And as she thrust her fingers in and out while with her other hand she punished her clitoris, she wondered whether either of them had been fucked by Alex afterwards. She hoped they had been. She wished she had been.

Kath had just finished and was spinning down gently into sleep when she heard a high pitched moan from the next cell, then another and a squeak of bed springs followed by three harsh grunts with louder squeaks and then heavy breathing which gradually quieted. She smiled into the dark. She was not alone.

Sharon was alone. She had never truly been alone but in this dark cell with only a glow worm bulb lighting the passage outside her cell, she was alone and hungry. She had no idea of how long it had been since she had been brought, kicking and struggling to this place, stripped and locked in here totally on her own. All her life there had been other people, there had been shouting, fighting, brawling but never had there been silence and isolation. She had raged and screamed in fury when they left her. It wasn't supposed to be like this. 'They' had rules they had to obey. There was a system that she had learned to play. 'They' couldn't just do as they liked, that was why she and her gang and the others ruled the streets. They could do just as they liked and the system limped along behind them, ineffective and slow. It was a hindrance at worst.

And now her gang would be leaderless, they would be taken over by another leader or merge with other gangs, and when everyone learned how she had been locked up like this, she would lose all credibility and have to fight her way up again.

Somewhere outside, a door opened and then a shadow fell across the small hole cut high up in the cell door. She snarled defiance as the tall man who had brought her here held a steaming hot plate of food just outside.

"Ask nicely," he said.

She cursed him and he left.

He went so suddenly that she was left speechless and bereft; suddenly aware that with this man you got one chance - and one only. Now she was alone again and even more hungry.

CHAPTER TEN.

Angie was in a foul mood and petite blonde Sara was feeling its full effect. She was tied down to the bed in the spare room of Angie's apartment and was being cropped, hard and long. Her bottom was a raging inferno and now even her back was getting it. She had never had the crop applied there before and was finding it difficult to cope with. Her safeword kept trying to force its way out through her clenched teeth but she knew that Kath used to take the crop to her back without crying off and Sara knew she would have to take it as well if she was to stand any chance of replacing her in Angie's affections. And Angie was so deliciously dominant.

Smack!

A stroke landed square across her shoulders, the leather keeper adding a shrill descant of stinging pain to her right side, the shaft making bruising contact all across her. She couldn't help letting out a whimper, hating herself for interrupting Angie's pleasure but quite unable to find her own pleasure in this severity of beating. On her bottom, yes. She loved the crop there. She adored the heat of a well flogged arse, and a flogger to her back could make her come as well. But the crop was pure pain.

"Sorry, babe. I was miles away," Angie said, throwing the crop down onto the bed beside Sara. "It's probably a bit advanced for you."

"Sorry, Mistress. But you can carry on. I'm not at my safeword yet."

"Good girl. But I need something different anyway."

Sara felt Angie take a handful of her hair and then climb onto the bed, manoeuvring herself to sit open legged right in front of her face. For a moment, Sara was able to appreciate Angie's cunt, it was a very tidy one with the inner lips quite small and hidden between thick, pronounced outer ones. But the beating had excited her and around her vaginal entrance the inner lips now blossomed and quivered, awaiting Sara's eager lips and tongue.

Angie slid a little further down the bed and Sara's face was engulfed in the rich odour of arousal and her tongue tasted the pungent outpourings. Above her she heard Angie sigh with pleasure and she concentrated on the clitoris, lashing the hard little nubbin until she felt Angie's hands clench more tightly in her hair and she knew the climb towards orgasm had begun. And with each orgasm she was sure she was pushing the memory of Kath further into Angie's past.

When the girl had gone, Angie wrapped herself in a short bathrobe, fixed herself a drink and sat in front of the television, deep in thought. Sara was a pleasing little thing, she hadn't meant to keep her on after using her at the hotel to scare the wits out of Kath, but when Proteus had so suddenly begun and Kath had disappeared as if she had never been…well she had needs and a pretty, compliant sub like Sara was not to be sneezed at.

But now there was big trouble. Proteus had begun but that hadn't helped her at work. There was still no story. It had been a month now and there had been complete silence, so all the accounts department could see was Kath's wages still going out, the hotel sting costs and nothing to show for it all.

There was nothing else for it. She would have to face Mostyn and try and pull Kath out then cobble together what they could. It was time to cut the losses and run.

Mostyn kept her waiting, it was a studied insult but, as an investigative journalist, one that Angie was well used to and she kept calm until the smiling secretary ushered her into the impressive office. As she walked towards the desk she tried to look around, Kath had been here. Mostyn had played with her here and Angie tried to pick up some vague feeling of Kath's presence. The previous night she had slept little and now she was keenly aware of how much she missed her slave.

Mostyn rose and came to greet her with a smile and a handshake. Even Angie could feel the force of his maleness as he came close to her, no wonder Kath had responded so well to him.

"I'm delighted to meet you!" Mostyn lied glibly. "Always happy to help the press. Please, let's sit down and you can tell me how I can be of assistance."

She was deftly steered over to the sofa and easy chairs – Kath had been bent over one of these and beaten, she was sure – Mostyn sat opposite her, his body language self-confident and relaxed. Angie decided to go straight for the jugular.

"You've got some property of mine," she said.

Mostyn's eyebrows raised and he looked genuinely puzzled.

"Kath Knowles," Angie went on. "She worked for me. We put her in here to find out what this Proteus thing was all about. She told me everything – and I mean everything – about what you got up to with her, so please let's not play the puzzled innocent. Tell me where she is and what Proteus is."

Mostyn looked her squarely in the eye for a moment. His face didn't betray a flicker of embarrassment or anger and she felt some grudging admiration for the man.

Eventually he rose and walked over to the panoramic window.

"Someone once said that the first job of any elected body was to ensure it got re-elected."

"Pretty cynical."

"I prefer pragmatic. Come over here, Angie, and tell me what you see."

Angie went to stand beside him, looking down at the vast urban sprawl of London. She shrugged. "London. A city."

"Yes, but what about the people? What do they think of the modern arenas, for example?"

Angie felt a small surge of guilt as she recalled all the nights with Kath in front of the TV relaying internet films of the various games.

"I think…I think they're growing in popularity."

"Yes, I agree. And do you often walk in the streets of the city after dark on your own?"

"No, of course not. It's not safe." The answer came so fast it surprised even Angie herself.

Mostyn turned to face her. "Again, I agree. And as a government we must clean up the streets. But as a government we must also give the people what they want. The thing is that the people we must 'clean up' are also 'the people'!

"Angie, all our research shows us that we either have already lost – or very soon will lose - control of the streets. We must act swiftly and decisively and to that end we must ensure that this government is re-elected so that it can carry on its vital work. Democracy can be a bloody nuisance! So we are taking several lessons from the Romans. The arenas are more and more popular but they need slaves. We will provide them, and thus we will provide 'the people' with the spectacles they relish. A vote for us is a vote for more of what they love. Meanwhile the people from whom we recruit the slaves will enjoy having someone to look down on, thus making them more amenable and less liable to riot just so long as the government continues to provide good entertainment. 'Divide and Rule' as they say."

Angie stood looking down at the city in a daze. She didn't know where to begin, it was the most utterly cynical political manoeuvre she had ever heard of.

"Incidentally," he went on before she could reply, "I thought the Silvers were very unlucky to lose the other week. The N'Benga stable just got lucky at the end."

"What?! After the pony racing there was only ever one team in it! Those pillars nearly spoiled what should have been a well fought out finale. Okay, they were good to watch, but they nearly spoiled the sport…!" She stopped suddenly and realised she had taken the bait. She was a highly paid, respectable professional and she loved the games in the arenas, loved watching the slaves compete and suffer so erotically. It was sport to her and she had to admit she didn't care where the slaves came from.

Mostyn was looking at her with wry amusement.

"I think you see my point. In return for getting what it wants, society will get what it needs, which is the underclass divided, ruled and held where it is. And the government that can supply what society wants will be elected – another lesson from ancient Rome."

"Bread and circuses!"

"Precisely!"

"But where does Proteus fit in?"

"Have you not guessed? It's training the first batch of state-supplied gladiators."

Angie turned to face Mostyn, aghast as the final implications sank in. "But…but Kath's there! I've got to get her out!"

"Quite impossible I'm afraid, and probably too late in any case. She was a delicious creature, I actually miss her, but one has to make sacrifices and I've made alternative arrangements as I'm sure you have." He walked back to his desk and resumed his seat.

"How do you mean too late?" Angie asked, hating herself for the quaver in her voice.

"The trainer knows his business," Mostyn replied, "and she is very submissive. I don't think she'll want to leave. That's the point of Proteus really; to turn outwardly ordinary working girls into submissives so extreme they will stay loyal to their stable even if every door in the place is flung open."

"Hang on! She's not part of any underclass, why are you trying to train girls like her?"

"We envisage a stable in nearly every major city, they will need a lot of slaves! So we thought, why not push the envelope; see how far up the social scale we can spread the net."

Angie whistled in disbelief. This was far bigger than anything they had imagined. But she could see the logic behind it, the tribal loyalties that had surrounded football clubs was gone, the streets were lawless, girl gangs were proliferating and bored youths robbed and fought with impunity, although more draconian sentencing was coming in. The wealthier parts of society were so cosseted that they would grasp at anything that gave them risk, danger, sex, excitement. And if it could all be provided for them vicariously, safely on their screens, then they would most certainly vote for it, especially if the streets were safe to be walked on at night. Not that anyone would of course, not if there was a good show at an arena on the TV. She wasn't sure how she felt about Kath becoming part of it, but the journalist in her knew she was sitting on the scoop of the decade.

"Listen Mister Mostyn," she said, marching back to his desk and leaning on the front of it. "You need news management here. You need to get the public used to the idea, tease them, trail by leaks on the net. Start the debates in the pubs and clubs, then when the whole thing is really ready to get up and running, your public will be right alongside you!"

"Ah! It's not so much 'I've got to get Kath out of there,' it's more 'I've got to get my story out of there'." Mostyn smiled triumphantly.

Angie had the grace to blush. But this was much bigger than they had thought and poor Kath had just got caught in the wheels. But at least she was where she would enjoy herself and perhaps she could hire the girl and enjoy her again sometime. In the meantime she could serve her original purpose very nicely indeed.

"Yes, I admit it. This is a real scoop and you need our help!"

"You know, part of the reason we delayed starting Proteus was because we couldn't find any family or close friends for Kath, and of course I know why now. I was suspicious but in the end I thought she was so suitable, I just had to let her go. So what do you suggest?"

"What better way to get the public on-side than by serialising the diaries of a slave as she is trained for a life in the arenas. It'll be pure sex and submission and we'll spin it if necessary – but I doubt if it will be - so she's loving every minute of it. People will lap it up and flock to the games to try and identify the mystery slave!"

"And meanwhile The Journal makes a killing."

"True. But we're the only ones who can help you to take advantage of the opportunity that's dropped into both our laps."

Mostyn steepled his fingers reflectively for a moment. "Leave me your number and I'll call you tomorrow. I'll have to consult before I authorise any leaks. How had you envisaged Kath making contact?"

“Just by phone. We hadn’t envisaged Proteus involving the girls being kept naked!”

“Okay. I’ll get back to you no later than tomorrow.”

Brian re-read the e mail carefully and then took a mouthful of coffee from the mug that Caroline had placed on his desk.

“Problem, Sir?” she asked.

“Not really. It’ll just take a bit of thinking about. Bring the lads in here and get a floor plan of the house from the filing cabinet over there. We’ll need to make sure one of our little rats can find its way through the maze!”

Caroline raised an eyebrow but made no comment.

Ten minutes later, roused from their common room after a long day spent drilling their charges the trainers gathered in the estate office.

“We’re about to move onto the next phase of their training, but we’ve got to add a bit of a wrinkle to accommodate the big bosses in Whitehall. Mike, I need that brunette of yours to escape.”

There was immediate agitation that Brian allowed to run for a second before quashing.

“Only so far as the locker room. They want her to make phone contact with the outside world.”

“Why?! We’ve been told absolute secrecy is essential!” Mike protested.

“Yes, but apparently that little slut is a reporter who was planted here by her paper. The bosses want her to start filing stories…” He held up his hand to stall the storm of protest. “Don’t worry! She’s not going to finger anyone. They’ll keep a tight rein on the stories so that no one will know where this is or who anybody is. The angle will be the diary and blog of a slave girl. It’s to get Joe Public close to a slave girl so he can relate to her and take an interest as the first state arena gets set up. Makes sense.”

There were still some mutterings but he showed them the e mail and assured them that anything the brunette sent would be heavily edited back at head office.

"Now, as it happens, this sort of fits in with the next stage of training. They haven't had it for over a month, apart from wanking themselves half to death of course!"

The CCTVs in the office had afforded the men many hours of entertainment as they had watched the girls administer hand relief. Some money had changed hands on bets as to which could masturbate the most frequently and for the longest time. Steve had won by betting on both counts on the – now not so tubby – little blonde girl who had been whipped on the very first day. She had turned out to be voracious and to have remarkable powers of endurance.

"I want them used by you from now on. You too, Caroline and Helga – any of them you fancy, have them service you during the days. But it has to be random use. Don't let a pattern emerge – make it absolutely plain to them that they must serve as and when they are required to. Their wishes do not enter into it."

There was a nodding of heads in agreement.

"The only thing we need to be careful of is on those nights when Mike pays our little traitor a visit. I don't want her bumping into anyone – she needs to get to the locker room undisturbed. Now let's see which doors we need to leave unlocked and which we leave her keys to. It mustn't be too easy for her – but I don't want her wandering about lost all night. Mike, I'll tell you how I think we'll play it in a minute."

When Kath had the energy to stay awake for more than a few seconds after she was put to bed each night and had masturbated away the lusts that being naked with all the other girls had awoken during the day. And the ever-present bulges in the guards' jeans didn't help either, she had to admit that she was enjoying the life. She was fitter and stronger than she had ever been. The last time she had been weighed and measured, she had seen herself in a full length mirror and hardly recognised herself. Her hair was thicker, longer and more lustrous than it had ever been. Her waist was tight and smooth, her hips curvaceous without a trace of boxiness, her thighs were smooth skinned and tighter than they had ever been. Had she been allowed clothes, for once in her life she would have leapt at the chance of wearing a bikini. And as for her breasts! She had cupped them and stroked them proudly as they stood more proudly and more rounded than she had ever seen them. The black haired girl, who she now knew was called Caroline, had smiled at her and given her a lascivious wink before returning her to her cell.

One night, soon after, she was woken by a rattling at the door of her cell, and peering sleepily towards it she saw Mike fumbling with the lock. Eventually he unfastened it and entered, closing the padlock behind him. He was a silhouette against the dim light that was on permanently in the corridor but as he came to stand over her she caught the rich smell of spirits on his breath. He unbuttoned his shirt and pulled it off then sat heavily on the side of her bed, kicked off his shoes and then stood again to drop his pants and trousers.

Kath watched him with a strange mixture of emotions. Night after night she had lain here and felt herself pour out her juices at the thought of being taken by one of the men. But now that it was happening, she realised that it had been a long time since she had been taken by a man. And Mike was definitely all man. As he stood up she could see his physique in sharp relief and also the jutting pole of his erection. Despite the abruptness of how this was inevitably going to happen, Kath felt herself heat and melt at the sight. But at the same time she felt a pang of longing for her Mistress. The last man who had fucked her had been a slave to one of Angie's domme friends, an overweight man with a thick thatch of body hair. It had only been the pleasure she saw in Angie's face as she watched Kath open herself to someone she felt no attraction towards at all that had enabled her to moisten enough to accept his thick cock into her. And Angie had gone on laughing and joking with her friends while the man had rutted away at her. It had been that careless disposal of her body that had propelled her to orgasm under the man. And that of course had led to more amusement among the dominants.

But her thoughts were interrupted by Mike pulling aside the quilt roughly and climbing into bed with her. There was precious little room as Mike was a big man, and that meant that Kath came into contact with the whole of a man's body virtually all at once. She felt its rough hairiness and the hard muscles of his arms and thighs, and there was the iron hardness of his cock digging into her side.

"Pretty little whore, you are!" he said, slurring a little. "Need to fuck you good!"

Kath's breath came out as a tremulous sigh as she turned towards him, her back against the bricks of the cell wall and her hands began to trace the muscular contours of his body, inevitably finding their way to his groin. For his part he groped in the semi dark for her breasts, closing his massive hands in her flesh and mauling it harshly. It was just what she liked and she thrust them harder at him to encourage him. He chuckled and moved one hand down her body, cupping her vulva in it, his fingers spreading out across her bottom, his palm beginning to exert pressure on her clitoris. He began to rub at it at the same time as he slipped his other hand away from her breast and put it around her shoulders, drawing her to him. She went willingly, thrilled that at last her nudity had achieved some response. She wriggled to lie underneath him and caught her breath as he shifted his grip on her crotch and his thick fingers entered her while his thumb rubbed even more harshly at her clitoris. His erection dug into her stomach. His mouth descended over hers, redolent of whisky, demanding, hard, his tongue thrusting into her open mouth. Then with a suddenness that made her groan, he took his fingers out of her and shifted to lie between her wide-spread legs. She reached down and gripped his shaft, almost scaring herself as she tried to clasp her fingers round its thickness, but in a sudden hurry to feel it inside her, she lodged it at her entrance, he thrust, and in one smooth movement he was inside her and then further inside her and she groaned into his mouth as he thrust again and she felt him hit her cervix.

It was so good to have a man again.

She reached her arms around him to try and encompass his size. She wrapped her legs around him to open herself even more, his weight bore her down and squeezed the breath from her as he thrust for his release, then suddenly he was pounding into her, making the bed springs squeak as he drove her downwards, again and again. From deep inside her a tide of ecstasy flowered and flooded her whole body as her vagina was stimulated beyond anything it had experienced for so long. And still he thrust, now his face was beside hers and she bared her teeth into the dark as she fought for her own climax, slapping up against him as he ground down into her. Then she came, arching up off the bed, even lifting him with her as her pleasure exploded inside her. Beside her she heard Mike roar as he spent himself into her and then he slumped down on top of her, breathing heavily.

Slowly Kath recovered her own breathing and realised that she was pinned under a very heavily asleep man. She wriggled sideways as best she could and eventually managed to prop herself up against the curving wall. She looked down at him and smiled fondly at the memory of how it had felt to have him inside her, then realised that there was virtually no room for her to sleep. It was fairly warm so the thought of stripping the quilt off and wrapping it around her while she slept on the floor seemed the only alternative and she had just managed to crawl over him and was standing beside the bed when she noticed his clothes. His trousers were in a heap and on the belt, shining dully in the low light was a key ring.

Her heart stopped for a second and then pounded. But her first thought was to get to her phone, speak to Angie, resolve all the questions, put her mind at rest, the notion of escape never entered her head. She carefully manoeuvred the ring off the belt and dropping the quilt she went over to the door. At the second attempt she found the padlock key and tip-toed out, making sure that Mike was breathing deeply and steadily. The door out of the cell corridor was the next on the ring and she was in the passage that led to the bathrooms and where they ate, doors opening off it just led to the other girls' cells. Desperately she tried to remember the route they had taken the first day they had been brought there. The locker room was through the medical room and that was beyond the kitchen. The only light now was what came through the windows but with her eyes acclimatising, she crept forwards.

One door after another opened and she found herself in the kitchen. The door out was locked but she found the key eventually and was finally in the passage that led to the medical room. It was all she could do not to run. At last she could talk to Angie, find out the truth and then tell the world the truth about Proteus. The dampness trickling down her thighs embarrassed her as she remembered how eagerly she had received her jailer. But it was wrong, she told herself, she was being held against her will.

The door to the locker room opened, the bag with the keys was hanging on a hook – they must have been so confident! she thought as she hunted through it trying key after key until she found hers. Then there was a frantic fumble in the dark among her clothes – they felt strange to her, like someone else's – and then there was the comforting plastic rectangle. She turned it on and was almost blinded by the screen light, hastily she used the locker door to shield it until it was ready and then with trembling fingers she found Angie's number and called it, hoping that she would have the phone by her bed, but if not, she could leave a voice mail. Anything!

"Hello?" A sleepy voice answered after four rings.

"Oh thank God!" Kath found her voice breaking with emotion at the sound of Angie's voice.

Angie waited until the storms of emotion had abated somewhat.

"No, you silly little goose, I didn't sell you! Yes, I'm sure they told you that. Maybe some of them were, but not you! Now just calm down and tell me what's going on. Do you know where you are?"

She started to record off her mobile as Kath began to whisper her story.

"Okay, babe," she said at last when Kath's report was fully up to date – although she was sure that one of the guards would have fucked her by now, funny that she didn't mention that. "You've done brilliantly. This is dynamite! Leave it with me, we'll try and find you, I promise. In the meantime, stay safe and contact me again when you can."

She broke the connection after she had given the girl enough endearments to calm her down, then she stood up, stretched and yawned. There was still time to get some sleep. Mostyn had done well and Kath had come in pretty well dead on time. In the morning she would play it all back and begin to edit and re-write it, a lot more sex was required for public consumption. It wasn't as if Kath was ever going to read it, after all. Back in the bedroom, she slipped under the quilt and gently slid her arm over the sleeping blonde next to her.

"Please can I have some food?"

The voice was soft and lacked the defiant edge it had had for the past few days. Peter Lang grinned in the gloom outside the cell. He dipped the spoon into the broth and held it out to the slot cut in the door. There was a long silence and he could envisage the conflict raging within the slut as she debated whether to cave in after three days. But suddenly her mouth was there, opening hopefully and he began to feed her.

From here on in, it would be easy.

CHAPTER ELEVEN.

The nights were warm and Blondie enjoyed the soft breezes that blew through the gaps in her two-part stable door as dawn neared. When her breakfast was served in her trough by a young woman who always smiled and called her 'Ma Blonde', the top half of the door was left open and she could stand and look out at the yard, which stabled real horses as far as she could see, and for the few days she had been there, it seemed the weather was permanently sunny. She knew that everyone was speaking French but that knowledge had caused her some discomfort. It had been on the first morning when she had been properly awake. She had woken on her bed in her stall and there had been two people standing over her, one was a smartly dressed man in his mid forties and the other was a dark haired woman in riding clothes, complete with the sort of riding hat and gauze veil that women used to wear to ride side saddle. They had spoken to each other about her and she had recognised the words as French.

"She is a magnificent specimen when you see her close up," the woman said.

"She is indeed. We'll give her a couple of days to recover and then run her and start making arrangements," the man replied.

She had been able to speak French fluently back in the days when she used to go skiing a lot. That was back in the days before she had been...Suddenly it was as if she had been paddling in the shallows of a friendly blue sea but had taken one step too far and had found herself in cold, dark, deep waters, sinking fast. She didn't want to go back there! In an attempt to physically thrust the thought away she turned over and sat up.

"Et voila!" the man said. "Already she is well on the road to being fit and healthy once more!"

Then they had gone and she had not seen them since. Mostly she had slept and used the time to rest, the stiffness in her legs had gradually faded, the welts had been rubbed with some sort of ointment by her regular girl and were now almost gone, so far as she could see. As she padded about her stall, her chain clinking and slithering along the cobbles beneath the straw, she was aware that various strains and pulls were settling back down. At home, the vet would have checked her out and Patti and the rest of the grooms would have fussed over her but Carlo had seen fit to hire her out to these people who seemed content to let her recover at her own pace.

By the third day she was becoming restless. She was perfectly capable of earning her keep, so why was no one playing with her or using her? They must have paid plenty for her, after all. She was also feeling very horny. Having gone down so early in the finale, she had missed out on the action with the men, and it was that which made everything else worthwhile as far as she was concerned. She had always been the last, or one of the last, to go down and had always taken repeated shaggings and orgasmed time and time again for the cameras. But not on this last occasion and she was left with a nagging feeling of need in her belly.

So when at last she heard footsteps and voices approaching her stall, she was standing hopefully just inside when the woman and the man reappeared. The woman was dressed as before, in a perfectly tailored dark green jacket that hugged every contour of her spectacular figure. She wore it over a crisp white shirt and Blondie could see a fabulously expensive gold chain and locket hanging against the tanned skin of her neck. As she unbolted the door and entered, Blonde saw that this time she was wearing a calf length skirt, that matched the jacket and was cut generously, over soft, brown leather boots. The man was in immaculately pressed tan slacks and a blue sweater. Simple and elegant.

The woman came straight over to her. “Here, girl,” she said in slightly accented English, and held out her hand. In it was one of her favourite shortbread biscuits. Eagerly she bent her head and came forward as the woman held her hand up so she could take it with her teeth and crunch it up.

“That’s a good pony,” she cooed and reached out to stroke her hair. She was several inches shorter than Blondie was so she bent her head to be petted and the woman laughed in delight and patted her flank before returning to stroking her.

“She’s clear of any marks now,” the man said, walking behind her. “We’ll run her and see how she goes.”

“Okay, but I want her shod,” the woman agreed and summoned Claire, the groom. The shoes were not the clumsy hoof-like ones she was sometimes run in, but were quite feminine with three inch wedge heels, steel soled. As she stood, obediently lifting each foot behind her while Claire straddled her calf to shoe her, the woman and man fetched her tack. And it was immediately clear that they wanted a show pony. The bridle was topped with pale green and blue feathers. The girth had a beautifully worked silver coat of arms on a plate that covered her stomach, and the tail that came off the crupper, mounted on and lifted by, an upward curving silver prong, was real palomino. For her breasts there were silver cones to go over her nipples and a clever, silver filigree device that came down from the front of her high, silver collar, parted between the breasts and supported them with wire cups worked into swirling and circling patterns, so that nothing was concealed – just perfectly displayed.

Blondie relaxed, her master had sent her somewhere where they really knew about ponies.

The tack wasn't studded so it was comfortable. The crupper strap had a clitoral rasp and there was a butt plug to ensure that the prong which mounted the tail was held steady, but that was all. She was well used to the pins that pierced her nipples to hold the cones in place and merely stamped her feet irritably when they were applied. When the bridle went on, the woman spent some time admiring the heavy tongue ring she wore, before she passed the bit through it and clipped it to the rings and reins at either end. It was good to feel the straps being tightened under her chin and at her cheeks and nape again. She was back under control and her thoughts couldn't wander into dangerous territory again.

As she was led out, her sandals clip-clopping and scraping on the stone, she saw a trap very similar to the ones she was used to pulling at The Lodge. It was large wheeled and with a quilted leather seat, it was a two-seater with the shafts curved in so that her wrists could be shackled to them comfortably. The long carriage whip stood in its holder, the lash stirring lazily in the faint breeze. She was led to the front and backed between the shafts which were then lifted so she could grasp them while the karabiners were fastened to the rings in her cuffs. Then while the woman seated herself and Blondie adjusted her grip as the weight shifted behind her, the man clipped blinkers onto her bridle.

With the taste of the steel bit in her mouth, the tight strapping about her head and body, her vision restricted and her hair, gathered into a pony tail, bouncing on her shoulders, her tail swishing against her thighs, she felt alive again. The whip lightly touched the centre of her back and she immediately leaned into her work. Within a few paces she was able to break into a trot and the reins were dragged hard to her right as she was made to turn the rig and head out of the yard. Once the rattling of the wheels over the cobbles had stopped and the trap was running on the hard- packed, red earth track that stretched in front of it, Blondie felt the whip flicked backwards and forwards across her back and shoulders a few times. She picked up the pace.

"Good girl!" the man's voice called. "Trot on now!"

The whip rested lightly on her back again to tell her to keep it up and feeling content and happy, Blondie headed out into the parkland which was all she could see dead ahead of her. Gradually the track bent to her left and eventually, still trotting easily, she saw the house from between her blinkers.

It was the most beautiful château that she had ever seen. The panes in the tall windows sparkled in the morning sun and the blue tiled turrets and steep roofs reached high into the sky above the dormer windows of the third storey. It was surrounded by a mill pond smooth moat and the track was leading towards a bridge that spanned it. She was whipped up as they approached it to help her trot up the upward slope and then they were coasting down and around to the front door.

"Whoa!" the man called, hauling back on the reins and making the bit slide back into her mouth, dragging her tongue ring with it. She reared her head and leaned back, bringing the trap to a smooth halt at the foot of the stairs that led to the front door which opened and a woman dressed in an old fashioned serving maid's dress came down the steps carrying a hamper. There was a slight alteration in the weight distribution behind her and she knew the hamper was being stowed behind the seat. Then she was whipped up again and they headed out into acres of secluded pasture and woodland.

She was trotted and walked until the heat of the sun was making sweat run down between her breasts and her crupper was beginning to chafe between her labia. The couple driving her seemed content to meander along tracks that were sometimes in the shade and sometimes out in the full glare of the sun, but weren't too hard on her. Nevertheless, after an hour or so her breathing was loud in her ears, saliva was hanging in strings from the corners of her open mouth and dripping onto her breasts and she could feel sweat running down her back and stinging as it found the stripes from the whip. Then whoever was driving decided that nothing would do except a full gallop. The whip began to land with real venom for the first time, and also for the first time, it was expertly wrapped to bite and sting her breasts, so conveniently held out-thrust by the filigree cups. Instantly all thoughts of discomfort were banished. More effort was needed and her master had taught her that her only reason for existing was to provide it for those who required it from her.

Joyfully she flung herself forwards and lost herself in the sweet sensations of physical exertion under the pleasure and pain of the lash. She was running almost blind from sweat and tears by the time she was reined in, gasping around her bit and slathering down her chest. The couple dismounted and thoughtfully the woman came round and wiped the sweat from her eyes and stopped them stinging, and as her breathing calmed down, Blondie settled down to wait. She knew she was in the hands of competent slave handlers who knew how to get the best from her. Her master had known best all along – as always.

Marie unpacked the terrines and the bread whilst Marcel opened the Krug and the pair settled down to enjoy the day, the food, the drink and the slave. Marcel had left Blondie with her hands raised and tied to a branch of the spreading chestnut they sat beneath. The pair sipped their ice cold champagne from the cooler and surveyed Marcel's prize. He smiled in amusement as he noted how Marie feasted her eyes on the slave's magnificent physique. His step sister had always been an avid collector of submissives – male and female - and here she was at last, alone with the most famous one in the world. He noted her breasts begin to heave as she took in the flesh and blood reality of Blondie's naked breasts, she began to fidget her own thighs beneath her skirt as she surveyed the blonde's long and graceful thighs.

"Make her dance for me, mon cher," she said at last, sitting up straighter and unzipping her riding boots to wriggle her toes in the grass beside their picnic cloth.

"As you wish," Marcel said, draining his glass and standing up.

He unscrewed the prong her tail was mounted on so that it wouldn't hamper the lash and laid it carefully aside, then unshipped the driving whip. The big blonde watched him from over one shoulder calmly as he looked her over and measured his distance before beginning the beating. Whipping up a pony was always enjoyable, but was restricted to what would make her run better and keep her focussed on her work. But here, he was free to enjoy a full body whipping purely for the pleasure of it. And afterwards there would be all the considerable pleasures that Marie could provide him with – and had been providing him with for many years. Blondie offered a flagellator a superb body, the back strong, the shoulders broad. The waist was slender, flaring out to broad hips with buttocks that cried out to be lashed. And as for the breasts and the delta at the top of the powerful thighs! With her girth protecting her stomach, there was no reason to hold back.

He didn't.

The blonde spun and writhed at the end of the rope as the lash smacked home, the long tail wrapping her and the weighted end thudding onto her. Occasionally a muffled grunt escaped her as a particularly spiteful lash bit at the fronts of her thighs or dug in between them. After about fifty he stopped for a break and strolled back to refill his glass. Marie had shed her skirt, jacket and shirt, and was wearing only the exquisitely embroidered corset she wore beneath them. She was kneeling up, her thighs well apart, one hand idly stroking between them. She smiled at him as he resumed his seat, her eyes bright and eager.

"She can soak it up alright! When can we play with her properly?"

"We've got guests in a couple of weeks and I thought it might be a good opportunity to begin to advertise – and to play of course."

He watched the blonde whose breathing had now eased down once more. But her writhings under the lash had inflamed Marie and she flung herself onto her step brother, who lay back and shed his light sweater as she kissed him lightly and then began to make her way down his body. He knew that he was the only man in the world to whom she offered fellation and it made the experience all the sweeter. He lifted his hips to help her strip him of his trousers and pants, then she knelt up and urgently fumbled them down to his ankles, almost ripping his shoes off in her haste, then with a sigh of satisfaction she lay forwards between his spread thighs and began to lick her way up from his balls, her fingers gently looped around the rapidly hardening shaft of his cock. Marcel lay back and absorbed the pleasure of Marie's industrious tongue as it foraged deep behind his balls and slowly worked its way back up, then there was the delight of feeling her soft lips furled carefully over her teeth as his glans was taken deep into the tight little cave of her mouth. Now her tongue worked its magic properly, flicking and licking delicately, exciting, teasing. He held on to his self control though – she would gladly swallow him if he chose to spend in her mouth, but he rather fancied the humid tunnel of her vagina. The sight of the blonde's well-whipped body was driving him on, but he never fucked a pony slave while she was in harness; he felt it sent out the wrong message to her. So he would fuck his step-sister instead.

Roughly he grasped her head and pulled her off him, rolling her onto her back and following so that now he lay between her wide spread thighs, her plump breasts spilling from the basque's quarter cups. He lowered his head and nipped sharply at both deliciously rubbery nubs. Then he clasped one hand harshly around the softness of the breastflesh itself and manoeuvred his hips until her felt his helm come to rest at her entrance. Eagerly she reached down between them and as he thrust, she guided him safely into her welcoming warmth. He looked down into her large, dark eyes, watching them close as she savoured the delights of his long, slow surges into her body, he smiled at how well he could control this woman who herself was a professional controller of submissives. And as he began to increase his tempo and his pelvis slapped against hers and she bucked up against him fiercely, her eyes snapping open as her orgasm rushed towards her, he knew that their next gathering would not be short of slaveflesh. Between them they would see to that. They always did. Marie's mouth opened in a silent O and then she began to utter cry after cry as her step-brother rammed into her, before he too roared his release and with final, tremulous, convulsions, they collapsed and lay still.

Later on they lay companionably, side by side, propped up on their elbows and looked at the blonde slave, standing patient and impassive by the trap.

"Suarez will do all he can to stop you," Marie said eventually.

"I know. I'm rather counting on it," Marcel replied.

Blondie could not sleep. It had been a long afternoon and it had not helped having to listen to and watch the man and woman repeatedly fucking only a few yards away from her. After their first bout, the woman had sat astride the man's impressive cock and then after a further interlude, during which she had been whipped again, this time by the woman, the man had taken the woman doggy style, right beside Blondie's feet, right there on the grass. Then they had caressed her between their naked bodies, she had felt the man's hardness at her back, the woman's breasts had rubbed her chest just below her own. She had cruelly squeezed and twisted her pierced nipples. Then they had laughed at the sticky outpourings of her cunt as they squeezed past the crupper strap. Just a touch of a finger on the clitoral rasper would have brought her off. But they would not give her even that and she had had to endure watching yet another rut. Then the woman had taken the whip on the drive home and been much harsher than the man – which came as no surprise to Blondie.

The aching need between her legs that had been there since the last games had become a raging inferno but she couldn't find any way to assuage it. She tossed and turned on her straw, trying to rub her thighs together, she even turned onto her face and brutally rubbed her sore nipples against her sheet to try and garner some shards of pleasure, and it was probably the noise of her doing that which alerted the groom on his nightly patrol. Her stall was suddenly lit by moonlight and the figure of a man was in the doorway. She lay with her legs spread, her torso half twisted towards him, and waited to see what he would do. He looked both ways to make sure he was unobserved and then slipped inside and closed the door.

In the sudden dark she smiled as she heard the rustle of clothes being discarded, then the straw moved and he was kneeling beside her, his fingers groping roughly for the slit of her vulva. He had no problem locating her wide open entrance and sank them into her, twisting and flexing them, fetching groans of relieved pleasure from her. He muttered something about 'to hell with leaving her untouched until the party,' and she felt his fingers leave her before his full weight came down onto her, the hard shaft of his cock spearing up in one smoothly accepted lunge that had her gasping as her tunnel was stimulated for its full length. He was as urgent as she was and for a few minutes the darkened stall reverberated to the sound of a purely animal rutting as the two bodies slammed and slapped against each other, each one pursuing their own pleasure. At last, they both froze at their peaks, Blondie's body bowed upwards under the man, her strong legs almost lifting him bodily off the bed of straw. Slowly they subsided, and almost as an afterthought he kissed and twisted her nipples, making her grimace in the dark.

Then he was gone and she sank into a deep sleep.

The next night he returned with some friends and they took her in all her holes until they were fully sated but none of them dared whip her. Claire gave a secretive little smile when she saw the state of the semen stained sheet the following morning. Back at the CSL stable an illicit orgasm would earn the slave a beating at the whipping post in the yard, but Claire seemed content to keep her secret and there was no retribution. However there were no further nocturnal visits either and Blondie wondered if Claire was exacting a price from the men for her silence.

A few days later, when Blondie was kicking the walls of her stall in frustration and boredom, Claire came for her in the middle of the day. She had a leash in her hands and Blondie looked at her hopefully.

"Now, ma blonde," she said, clipping the leash to her tongue ring. "You're joining Monsieur's zoo. Won't that be fun?"

CHAPTER TWELVE

"I've never felt so sore! I mean the guys here are just so fit! They shag you over the table at lunch, they shag you in the middle of training and yesterday Mike, our guard, stopped me when we were out on a run and had me give him a blow job right out in the open. Like it was in the middle of a field! But what a cock! He's massive and when it comes in your mouth you're like; 'OMG! I'm gonna drown before I get this lot down me.' But you do anyway. Lol! And at least I'm getting fit too. They work us hard but there's no way I've got any fat on me that I shouldn't have. I've got a real flat tummy for once and the last time I was weighed I'd lost about ten pounds since I arrived. Mind you the girl who does the measuring and weighing likes to be looked after too – if you know what I mean. She's got really nice legs and she tastes good anyway so why not. Specially if it means a whipping if you don't. Not that that's too bad with some of the hunks we got here.

"Training's getting harder now! When you do press ups, they put spiked pads on the floor under your boobs, it's amazing how many I can do now before I give up. And the rowing machines have got dildos on the seats. Honestly a girl doesn't know if she's coming or going! Lol!"

Angie sat back and stretched then re-read Kath's – now edited - blog before sending it off to Mostyn. He insisted on vetting every word but so far was satisfied with the response from the public. 'K; the diary of an Arena slavegirl' was pulling hits by the tens of thousands and the transcripts in the paper were being discussed and leched over in pubs and clubs up and down the country.

On the sofa opposite her Sara was curled up and watching some soap or other, her short wrap left her pale and smooth thighs bare. Tomorrow was a club night and they would celebrate. After all payment for Kath had just landed in Angie's account from Mostyn's department and she was feeling flush. She was also feeling randy. Putting the laptop aside she stood up, Sara immediately looked at her for orders. Angie clicked her fingers and headed for the bedroom, behind her she heard the TV being switched off and bare feet padding after her. She smiled, subs were so damn easy! They deserved everything they got. In this case it was going to be the heavy leather flogger –the one with the studs.

'Lol!' she thought.

Their training had entered a new phase. They were much fitter than when they had arrived and, as if they recognised that fact, the men began to use them sexually much more frequently so that they were kept exhausted at each day's end. Mike now frequently went into the cell next to hers and screwed her 'sister', whose name she still didn't know. Kath could lie and listen to the noises, and frequently masturbate as she did so. But she was smugly aware that he only ever slept with her and she was able to continue to sneak out and phone her reports through. They weren't regular of course, but Angie seemed happy.

The harsh discipline was becoming second nature and punishments were now dealt out each evening after supper. With no concessions to the weather the naked girls lined up by the whipping post and listened as 'The Boss' read out any punishments. The girl concerned would step forward and stretch her arms out along the bars of the T shaped whipping post to have her wrists shackled and then a cold, measured beating would ensue. But increasingly the girls would be hauled out of their cells quite late at night and taken to a sort of common room where the trainers relaxed, and there the sex would be hard and steamy and if there were any beatings, they were of the hot and lusty type that Kath was used to. For the first time she was acquainted with needle play and finding herself lying, tied down to a medical couch, squirming under the masterful gazes of her guards and trainers, Kath found a rich source of pride and pleasure, swiftly followed by ecstasy as one or other – or more – of the men took their pleasure with her afterwards.

The work outs in the gym, now that the men had adapted some of the equipment were proving extremely effective and she was aware that when she was set to wrestle another of the girls, the bouts were harder and longer. She was also insanely proud of her new-look body, even despite the spiked pads on the gym floor, her breasts were higher and firmer and so were her buttocks. Caroline said the same and always had her kneel and lick her out when she was weighed, it turned out that her first suspicions had been right. Beneath her crisp white coat, Caroline was always naked.

One night, Mike altered his routine. To start with it was the same though, Kath was roused by his coming through the door from the passage into their little enclave. He paused, deciding which of the two morsels he would choose and plumped for the green eyed girl on this occasion. Kath heard him enter the next cell and soon there was the sound of bed springs creaking. As usual she spread her own legs, imagining the blonde next door, splayed out for taking beneath Mike's muscular body, and began to rub at herself as she heard the girl begin to cry out and the bed springs creak more and more rapidly. The climax came quickly; too quickly for Kath and she was still rubbing, her fingers swirling urgently, as she heard the cell door swing open and then clang closed. With a stifled groan she lay still, not wanting the humiliation of being found masturbating by Mike. But instead of him passing her cell and leaving, she looked up as she heard her own door being unlocked. Mike was pushing the blonde girl into her cell. She sat up as Mike followed her in.

"It's time you two got properly acquainted," he told them. "The going gets tough from here on in and you'll need each other." Then he left.

Kath swung her legs off the bed and padded over to the other girl. They looked at each other in the dim light for a long moment. Speech had been forbidden for so long that they didn't dare break the rule. But, Kath thought, if Mike had specifically told them to get to know each other…Well, if it meant another visit to the whipping post, so be it. She had had several and they had been pretty fair beatings, but nothing she couldn't handle.

She went towards the girl who was standing in a slightly awkward, huddled way and Kath realised the poor girl had been yanked unceremoniously straight out of bed after a good shag, and now she looked, she could see gleaming snail trails of spunk running down her thighs. She put a companionable arm round her shoulders.

"What's your name?" she asked in a voice that came out as a whisper at first.

"Annie," the blonde replied. "Yours?"

"Kath. Come on, let's get into bed and we can make the most of being allowed to gossip!"

Annie smiled but stayed where she was.

"You never been with another girl?" Kath asked, taken aback. Annie shook her head, mute with embarrassment.

"Well, look at it like this," Kath said. "You're standing stark naked in a prison cell with your jailer's spunk running down your legs. Climbing into bed with me can't really make it much worse, can it?"

Annie managed a rueful grin and slid in next to Kath as she got back into bed. For Kath it was heavenly to feel a girl's body, soft, warm and sensuously curvaceous next to hers again. But she took things slowly, given Annie's inexperience and simply lay on her side, an arm under the girl's neck.

"I'll tell you about me, then it's your turn," she said and told her about her Mistress and how dominant she had been and how she, Kath, had been a submissive for some ten years and Angie's slave for two.

Annie confided that although she had always had intensely submissive feelings, it had only been in the last couple of years that she had had the courage to explore them and had found a dominant boyfriend. She had loved submitting to him and was no stranger to the whip, but he had never wanted her to play with other submissive women.

"It's not so bad here, not now they just take us when they want. I really like that," Annie said. "It's just that I can't believe I was sold!"

Kath looked down at the girl as her bottom lip quivered and tears threatened to well up in those bewitching eyes. She leaned down and very gently kissed her soft lips.

"Even that cloud could have a silver lining," she murmured.

She felt Annie freeze for a second at the touch of her lips and then slowly her mouth opened and her tongue flicked out. Kath deepened the kiss, feeling her breasts brush Annie's as she bent further over her. Annie must have felt it too because she gave a throaty little moan and suddenly Kath felt her hand on her right breast, gently and nervously stroking it at first but as Kath pushed her tongue more passionately between Annie's lips, she felt the girl's fingers close over her nipple and begin to squeeze. In her turn she moaned her pleasure and moved her left arm so her hand rested on Annie's delta. With no hesitation she parted her legs and Kath's fingers began to explore the sodden pubes and engorged lips of the recently used vulva. She gave it a good stirring up with her fingers and then withdrew them, breaking the kiss and holding them up so Annie could see as she sucked them, smacking her lips at the rich blend of tastes.

"Mmm," she said. "Want some?"

Annie giggled and bit her lip excitedly as she nodded. Kath foraged with her fingers again and Annie began to melt with pleasure before Kath raised her fingers again and let the girl lick the mixture of her own juices and Mike's sperm off them. Then Kath bent her head and took Annie's right nipple into her mouth, gently tonguing the deliciously rubbery little nub until she felt it harden and then she nipped it with her teeth, fetching another groan of pleasure from the girl. She lifted her head and grinned at her new lover, then began to slide down her body.

"Oh god," she heard Annie whisper as she realised what Kath was about to do but she made no move to close her legs and Kath was able to settle her face just above the girl's vulva. She had a pungently fragrant odour to her excitement and Kath breathed it in and savoured it before lowering herself and probing with her tongue. Burying her face as deep as she could she took one long, luxurious lick up the full length of Annie's slit, tasting once again the thrilling mixture of juices that characterised a recently vacated vagina – it was a taste that held many fond memories for Kath. Eagerly she stuck her tongue out and foraged deep inside her for any more. Annie began to buck her hips at her as she did so.

Her clitoris proved to be a wonderfully sensitive and prominent button that only took a few licks and flicks of the tongue to have its owner's juices flooding over Kath's face. In the dark she heard Annie climax in a series of low growls that were very different from the cries she made when Mike took her. When Kath resurfaced, Annie covered her face in passionate kisses and murmured her thanks before she wriggled her way down and returned the favour. She worked so hard and delved so deep with her tongue that her enthusiasm made up for any lacks in her technique and Kath orgasmed massively before the two lovers entwined sleepily and happily. Kath's last thought was of Annie's prominent little clit and what a treat it would be for the men to play with when they had her with her legs raised and spread in their recreation room. But maybe they already had.

At breakfast the next morning, the Boss announced that all the girls would now be kept clean shaven and Kath breathed a sigh of relief, she had resented the growth of unruly dark curls at her groin, she was used to being smooth down there and although Caroline and Helga had kept armpits and legs smooth, up until now they hadn't touched the pubes. She wondered if it heralded some new development in their training and was soon proved right.

The Boss stood behind her and lightly ran his riding crop down her spine. Mike stood opposite him, over Annie.

"I think you're over optimistic, Mike," he said when he'd finished telling him they were going to be kept shaven from now on. "They've come on well, but not that well."

"Sorry, Boss, I disagree and I stand by what I said last night." He went to stand behind a brunette who was one of the pair of girls that the Boss himself guarded. Mike reached down and grabbed a breast. The girl gave a strangled yelp of shock as his hand clenched, two fingers trapping and squeezing the nipple.

"There, you see!" he said. "Still a bit raw. I reckon mine can take them, no problem."

"Twenty says they can't." Behind her, Kath heard a crisp note crinkle and locked nervous gazes with Annie as they realised a bet was being made.

"You're on and I'll raise you another twenty, Boss!" Mike said gleefully. The girls all looked anxiously at the grinning male faces, they all understood that when men made bets concerning naked girls, whoever won, it was unlikely to the be the girls. But if anyone was going to pay the price for losing, it was most certainly going to be the girls.

"Okay, then are you agreeable to a wrestling bout in the gym in half an hour using a proper ring?" Mr Holden asked.

"Yep, that's fine by me!" Mike said and returned to stand behind Annie.

"Steve, go and set it up please. In the meantime Mike, I suggest we take our respective pupils for shaving and then give them some last minute guidance. Alex and John, you take the others for shaving in a while then to the gym."

Kath propped herself up on her elbows and watched Caroline working on her. The black haired girl had put her on her back on the couch and cuffed her ankles to a spreader bar before raising it, very much as she had on the first evening. Now she was using a cutthroat to slice away the troublesome growth from between her legs. It was a soothing feeling as she was using plenty of foam. She knew that a gladiator could have nothing on her body that could give an opponent a handhold, and a thicket of pubes would be a very tempting target. As she watched, Caroline daintily held up and stretched a labial lip while stroking it with the blade. Kath watched the expression of deep concentration on her face, it was similar to the one Mistress' face had worn when she had been pegging or piercing her down there. There was something very seductive about being a slave at an arena stable, she thought. True they were kept almost as some sort of livestock, but at the same time care was lavished on them that most girls could only dream of. Their hands were kept clipped together behind them for almost every waking minute so that the grooms and trainers brushed their hair, made sure their bowels were in good order, cut their nails and performed almost every function a normal girl would do for herself. But, she thought as Caroline finished up and wiped her groin clean of foam, now was the time when she began to earn her keep.

When Annie's blonde fuzz had been dealt with, Mike led them on their leashes back to the little passage outside their cells.

"Now, don't forget, it's not just about winning, it's about putting on a show!" he told them.

Kath couldn't help feeling a hot surge at her belly at the thought that soon she would be competing and suffering naked for the amusement of decadent crowds; people just like she had been, people who were happy to turn on their screens and watch and enjoy the erotic cruelty. Now all the practice and training would start to pay off. They had spent weeks learning how to fall without hurting themselves.

"You'll get hurt in plenty of other ways! Believe me!" the Boss had told them. "So there's no point in getting hurt when you don't need to!"

They had learned how to grip a nipple so that the recipient of the hold would find it hard to break it. They also learned how to register the pain so that the crowds could see how much it hurt and how to follow the girl applying the hold around the ring, begging for mercy.

They had learned the dreaded crotch hold, which was usually applied towards the end of a bout, when the girl who was on top wanted to move towards finishing her opponent off. When applied from in front, it meant turning the hand upwards, and inserting the thumb into the vagina and the first two fingers into the anus, then hoisting the unfortunate girl high into the air. The first time that Kath had applied it in practice to Annie when they were sparring, she had been amazed at her new found strength as she had held the blonde, teetering in the air, her mouth a horrified 'O' as she had desperately clung onto Kath's wrist to keep herself upright. Then at the command, Kath had clenched her fingers and withdrawn. Annie – and the others who were being hoisted by their sparring sisters – collapsed wailing and curled around their crotches on the ground. It had been some time before they had recovered enough to reverse roles.

Kath had been doubly penetrated by a large variety of objects in her time. But the sensation of having her body hoisted up by the penetration of both passages was as unsettling as finding that unless she clung on to Annie's wrist between her legs, the prospect of falling forwards or, worse, backwards, from that height and with the hand still in those passages, was terrifying. Then came the clench and snatch and Kath's yelps joined the others as they all fell in heaps on the gym floor.

Then they had practised the hold from behind, the thumb in the anus and the fingers in the vagina.

The Boss had smiled grimly when he told them; "You will notice that the vaginas are always open and easy to penetrate! That's because you're hopeless slavesluts who can't get enough pain and degradation!" And Kath hadn't been able to disagree. The whole experience had been wonderfully painful and humiliating.

Now they were going to get a chance to apply those holds – and others – in anger. It wasn't until much later that she realised that the thought of having them applied to her in anger, hadn't even occurred to her.

"Now, understand this," Mike told them. "I've got forty quid riding on you. If you lose, you'll take forty at the post. Win and you can enjoy the Boss's tarts getting the same!" Then he placed a hand on each of their shoulders and looked them both in the eye. "I meant what I said to the Boss. You can take them! Make me proud of you! And always remember to give 'em a show!" He smiled, gathered their leashes up and led them back. As Kath followed behind him meekly, watching his broad shoulders, trim waist and muscular, tight buttocks, her mind kept replaying that smile and those words; 'make me proud'. She was suddenly utterly determined that that was what she would do. For the first time since she had arrived at Proteus, she felt that she hadn't lost a mistress but gained a master instead. And she wasn't going to let him down. Beside her she could feel the same stiffening of resolve coming off Annie. They belonged to him and they were going to make him proud.

A proper ring had been set up in the gym. Its floor was about four feet above the gym's floor, there were three ropes slung between the four posts. The posts themselves had some padding around them but Kath knew from practice that if you were flung against them, it could hurt if you weren't able to take the impact properly.

Practice. That was all it had been up until now. Gym mats had been spread out around a padded post and moves had been choreographed then rehearsed, each girl working with her sparring sister. Now those moves had to be strung together to avoid a heavy price being paid at the whipping post, but most importantly to avoid the look of disappointment that would inevitably be on Mike's face.

The rest of the girls had been ranged, kneeling along one wall, their trainers standing guard over them. Mr Holden and their two opponents – the tall black girl and the brunette who was about Kath's height were waiting for them beside the ring.

"Rules?" Mike said as he brought them to a halt beside the group.

"Nah! No point where they're going," Mr Holden said. "All four into the ring from the start. Only knockouts count, once one's down for ten she's out. The contest ends when two girls from one team are down. No holds barred and anything goes until then."

Mike nodded. "Sounds fair enough," he said.

Their leashes, collars and cuffs were taken off and they were given a hearty smack on the rump to encourage them to clamber up and into the ring. Kath couldn't help rubbing her neck, it felt very odd not to be collared, just when she had felt like securely owned property once more, her collar was removed! But one look down at Mike, who gave her a knowing wink before he retreated and she knew whose property she was.

She brought her mind to bear on the job in hand and tested the ropes to see how springy they were and prodded the post padding, then jumped up and down on the floor to test its spring. All four of them did the same and the men cheered as their breasts bounced appealingly.

From beside the ring Mr Holden raised a whistle to his lips and blew it. Immediately all four girls advanced. Kath found herself up against the black girl. They tested each other with interlocking finger holds and Kath was surprised that she seemed to be about as strong as the taller girl, she broke the hold and dived for the girl's ankles, yanking them up towards her and sending her sprawling backwards. Faintly she heard cheering as she launched herself full length onto her opponent. The girl's body felt delicious beneath her but there was no time to appreciate it as Annie and her foe toppled over on top of them and all four girls squirmed on the canvas, trying to regain their feet. Kath and the brunette were first up and Kath took a forearm to her cheek that sent her back down and then the black girl was onto her, twisting her arm up her back and then reaching over her to grab her nipple and twist it. She yelled in pain and twisted violently, managing to dig an elbow into the girl's stomach and making her release the hold. Kath scrambled up and grabbed the black girl's hair, pulled her up, yelling in her turn and thrust her headfirst into a post. Then she spun and delivered a joined fist blow to the back of the brunette's neck, dropping her in front of Annie, who screamed in joy as she dropped onto the prone body on her knees. Kath was grabbed by the hair from behind, whirled round and found herself thrown clean through the ropes. The hammered-in lessons saved her and she rolled safely as she landed on the wooden floor but was still dazed for a second as she staggered up and found that the black girl had followed her out and now delivered a forearm blow right across both breasts and before Kath could fall backwards, grabbed her hair again and threw her back under the bottom rope. She got onto all fours as soon as she could but the black girl vaulted over the ropes behind her and delivered a kick that landed squarely between her legs. It was no worse than a heavy lash with a single tail whip but they had rehearsed this. Mr Holden had told them that it was arena crowd's favourite move.

Kath threw herself forward, curled around her crotch and sure enough the girl came for her, forgetting their training. Kath rolled onto her back and lifted both feet as the girl leapt, taking her in the stomach and hoisting her clear over the top rope. Then she was up on her feet and diving after her prey. The girl's breasts were not as big as Kath's but the nipples were deep red and invitingly long. Kath got both of them and pulled the girl up, twisting them hard and lifting so that it was difficult to break the hold. The girl screamed and waved her hands, begging for mercy as Kath relentlessly pulled her back towards the ring. Clearly now she could hear male and female voices cheering her on and her blood sang through her entire body. For the first time she experienced the joy of fighting naked for others' pleasure, being the crowd's plaything, and she knew with cunt-wetting excitement that it didn't matter to the crowd whether she dealt out the suffering or was on the receiving end. But it mattered to her master.

Greatly daring, she released the right nipple and dropped her hand, then brought it up between the girl's spread-open legs. Kath laughed in delight as the girl's eyes opened wide in horror as she felt the double penetration; thumb in the wide open and so moist vagina, finger in the rectum. Then, keeping the nipple hold she hoisted with all her strength and lifted the wailing girl over her head and threw her back towards the ring. For a moment the effort unbalanced her and she took a second before leaping back up to find her opponent had fallen face down across the ropes and hadn't untangled herself, leaving her delicious buttocks high in the air in front of her when she sprang back onto the apron. Kath got in three or four satisfyingly hard smacks before the girl managed to wriggle back into the ring and turn on Kath, who ducked through the ropes, intent on finishing the job. But disaster struck as Annie's opponent threw her bodily across the ring and straight into Kath. Both girls landed in a heap in one corner, Annie's body between Kath's legs making her head hit the post hard. Dazed, they tried to untangle themselves and get up but Annie was still groggy and the brunette closed in, putting one arm between her straddled legs and lifting, to body slam her onto the canvas. Almost in slow motion, Kath watched Annie crash down, shock waves making her buttocks and breasts ripple. But then everything speeded up again as reality returned and she felt her hair grabbed again. This time she was in her turn thrust head first into the post, twice and then spun round, making her stagger giddily. A forearm hit her across her face. She reeled again. Her arm was grabbed and twisted. Something hit her between her legs again, but now she was genuinely dazed and didn't make any show apart from a shocked yelp. Then she was tripped and the canvas was suddenly under her face as the black girl landed full on her back, pressing both her shoulders down. From somewhere outside the ring, she heard Mr Holden begin to count.

No!

From deep inside her a furious denial bubbled up and with all her strength she managed to twist and throw the girl off. But as she staggered back to her feet, the, metallic taste of blood in her mouth, her opponent was straight back on her. This time it was Kath's turn to suffer the nipple hold. It stung unbearably but as she dimly heard the cheering, she knew exactly where the lancing pains were earthing themselves. With a shocking suddenness that left her gasping, the hold was released, then another forearm smash caught her, she fell backwards but was caught by the ropes and bounced back into a crotch hold. She screamed in genuine fear as she was lofted high up and her whole weight bore down on both her passages. Then she felt the fingers clench and snatch away. She yelled as she fell, instinctively trying to curl forwards and crashed onto the canvas with no pretence of any science. Once again her hair was pulled and this time her face was slapped back and forth. The girl was playing with her! But Kath knew she had nothing left and had to take it. Then she was pulled up, an arm went between her legs and she was hurled out over the top rope. She just had enough wits left to remember how to fall and then as she lay face down, gasping for breath, she felt the black girl's foot on her neck and heard Mr Holden counting again. This time there was nothing she could do.

When the count finished, she was turned over and the girl settled herself on her knees above her face and then settled down onto her face. Kath knew what was required and happily pushed her tongue up into the hot, wet sheath of the girl's cunt, knowing she herself was spreadeagled on her back in complete submission, showing everything to an eager and appreciative audience.

Somewhere above her she heard some thumping and shouting and then there was more counting. When the black girl stood up and acknowledged the applause, Kath could see Annie, the top half of her torso lying over the edge of the apron, her bedraggled blonde hair hanging down. All she could do was brace herself for Mike's wrath. But instead of fury, he knelt beside her with a towel and wiped the blood from her lip then towelled her down briskly as she staggered upright again.

"That was a good show! You lost, but you lost well. That's ok. You'll take them next time."

Then while she braced her arms against the apron and bent to get her breath back he tended to the dazed Annie, whose left eye was nearly closed. They grinned sheepishly at each other. Their opponents slapped their backs as they went back to Mr Holden and from over by the wall, the trainers and the slave girls all applauded.

"Now, as you know," Mr Holden announced as the noise subsided, "in an arena when you lose, the ref. will count upwards until the tally of lashes to be taken gets the thumbs up. But on this occasion the tally was set at forty. Sentence to be carried out immediately!"

Outside, it was a fine late summer day, Kath and Annie were tied to either side of the T bar, facing each other. Mike delivered Annie's lashes and Mr Holden attended to Kath. Kath felt a deep affinity with Annie now. They had been through something together and she could see from the girl's one good eye that she felt the same. They looked steadily at each other as they jerked under each lash, refusing to make so much as a moan. The two flagellators stepped forwards when the sentence had been carried out and both reached between their respective girl's legs. Kath had to bite her already swollen lip to stifle the groan of pleasure she so wanted to give when she felt Mr Holden's fingers enter her with complete ease. She knew she was on the edge of orgasm and was now, battered and bruised but unbowed, an arena slavegirl.

Later that night, Brian sat back in his armchair in the Rest and Recreation Room. Steve was flogging one of his girls on the X cross against the opposite wall. John was working on one of his on the medical couch, Alex had one of his over a whipping bench and was caning her. The air was filled with the snap and thud of the cane and whip, the girl on the bench was whimpering softly and writhing prettily as she came.

In the chair beside him, Mike was leaning back and holding Helga's head firmly down as he came in her mouth and just behind him, Caroline cracked a bottle of champagne.

It had been a good day. Tomorrow they would stencil numbers on the girls and they would move further down the road to their destinies.

When they heard the cork pop, the men gathered by Brian as he stood up, leaving their girls securely hooded so they could talk without being heard.

"Gentlemen – and ladies!" he began, getting an ironic cheer as Helga was still licking an errant drop of Mike's sperm off her finger. "I believe we really have the makings of a stable here. All we need do now is nurture and direct their own natures. Tomorrow I suggest that Alex should challenge John's girls to a boxing match. The day after we'll have a pony race and after that it'll be log pulling. In due course my two will be ready for a return bout with Mike's. This time I think boxing."

"Fine with me, Boss," Mike agreed.

"A toast! To Proteus!" he proposed.

Glasses clinked and were then emptied, Caroline refilled them and the men returned to their fun. Brian waited until she had finished and then ran the back of one hand down over her left breast, making her draw in her breath sharply with pleasure. "You, upstairs now and wait for me. Lay out the kangaroo hide whip."

"Yes, sir."

Brian stayed long enough to socialise and congratulate his men and then went up to his room where Caroline was waiting, collared, cuffed and naked.

Angie stared balefully at her mobile phone, lying mute on the coffee table. She had sent Sara to bed in order to get some time to herself and was considering the implications of the fact that she hadn't heard from Kath in over a fortnight. She might have to continue the blog herself if the wretched slut didn't get in touch. She poured herself another scotch and nurtured her resentment. Just because she had been sold didn't give the slut the right to turn her back on her mistress.

She hated to admit it but she didn't want to lose Kath. Yes, the money she had got for selling her had been welcome but somewhere deep inside, she had always thought that she would get her back. But now something was telling her that even if she hadn't sold her, Kath had been lost the minute she had been picked by Proteus.

In the small hours of the morning, Carlo fell asleep over his laptop. Once again he had been trawling every chat room he could find that had any connection at all to the arenas. Somewhere, he told himself, there would have to be a whisper, a shadow of a rumour about Blondie. Surely no one could find themselves owning the tall blonde and keep utterly quiet about it. But there wasn't a murmur anywhere. The only scrap of comfort he could glean from the current situation was that at least the Owner's Council seemed to be watertight and rumours about CSL having lost Blondie weren't circulating – yet.

Sharon finished her food and licked her fingers to make sure she had got every last morsel. Then she carefully replaced the plate on the shelf outside the slot in her cell door. For a couple of weeks now she had been allowed to feed herself. But tonight she had got extra rations because she had won a fight. It was that simple. 'That Man' as she was coming to label the lean and wiry man who had brought her here and who had fed her from his hand and who had bested her at everything, who had given her orders to obey, had punished her for disobeying and rewarded her for obedience – That Man had set her to wrestle naked with another girl. It had been fun! She had never been close to another naked girl, let alone held her and grappled with her. It had felt good because That Man had told her she was doing well. She had held the other girl down and had been given more food. The other girl had been whipped.

They seemed to do that a lot here. It had come as a bit of a shock when she had discovered that there were more girls being held here, and she resented any of them getting even a second's worth of attention from That Man. The fact that the girls were whipped didn't bother her – it just seemed an extension of how the world had functioned anyway. It was a bit more crude but still it was strong preying on weak. But this time she knew she was weak – and she knew where the strength lay. She wanted as much of That Man as she could get.

She had been whipped a few times herself and it hadn't bothered her – she had had worse – but she hadn't liked That Man not coming to her cell, not talking to her afterwards. When he had whipped her she had looked over her shoulder at him as he flogged her, determined not to miss a second of him concentrating entirely on her. No one had ever done that before; spent time and trouble on her, let alone a man who could command her. As she had done well that day, she dared hope he might come to her cell and let her kneel before him and suck his cock. She smiled in the darkness as she heard a door open down the corridor and his measured footsteps approach. She knelt down, ready to please him.

CHAPTER THIRTEEN.

Kath sat up slowly on her cot, careful not to disturb Mike. She climbed over him and squatted down by his discarded trousers, carefully removing the key ring without making it jangle. She checked he was sleeping deeply as she slipped out of the cell and began to make her way towards the locker room once more. It had been some time since she had last had the opportunity to report to Angie, and it was only some odd sort of lingering journalistic professionalism that drove her now. She referred to Angie in her mind as just that – Angie – she was no longer Mistress. Mike was Master as far as she was concerned and since the wrestling bout, he had taken to sleeping with both her and Annie together. The narrow cots meant that most often he would stand by the bed and watch Annie and her make love before joining in by fucking one of them as they entangled with the other.

After the punishment beating for losing the wrestling match, Kath had not expected him to come to their cells but he had turned up, seeming quite cheerful and had taken her into Annie's cell. He had made them perform a sixty-nine while he undressed, standing over them and when they were approaching their climax, Kath had felt her hindquarters grabbed and he had lifted her bottom up. She had stayed where she was, with Annie's fragrant juices seeping over face, envying Annie for lying where she could look up and see Mike kneeling over her. Then she felt him sink into the hole that Annie had so lovingly prepared and as he fucked her he had sunk down enough so that Annie could lick his balls. Kath tried to keep on licking her as she was driven into the heavens by her master's cock and ended up bringing Annie off by crying out as she came, her mouth pressed passionately against Annie's cunt and her tongue rasping at her clit.

He had spurted most of his jism up her but had left some so that he could withdraw and push his cock downwards so that Annie could get some too. Then he had made them change position and continue until he had recovered enough to shaft Annie and Kath had been able to lick him while he fucked her. Then while they lay happy and exhausted he had told them that the boss was pleased at the show they had put on.

"You stood up to a fair bit of punishment, you took your falls well and you didn't go down too easily. You'll get plenty of chances to get your own back."

He had left them to sleep together then, but hadn't been back since, until that evening.

Kath tip toed along the empty corridors until she came to the locker room and found her phone. She screwed her eyes up against the glare of the screen and waited until it was ready, then she found Angie's number and called it, for the first time realising that the voice at the end was her editor and no longer her mistress.

"Hello?" Angie sounded understandably sleepy.

"It's me," Kath said. "Are you ready to record?"

"What? Kath? Is that you, babe? Hang on!"

Kath listened to the rustling and visualised Angie disentangling herself from the duvet and trying to gather her wits. Suddenly she was hit by a bolt of homesickness. How could she have mentally deserted her mistress so easily? She recalled the scent of Angie's body in the warm bed beside her, the feeling of curling up, spoon-like next to her on cold mornings while her hand slowly found its way to Kath's breast and then her delta. And all the while she had been having these wonderful adventures with hunks like

Mike and gorgeous girls like Annie, her mistress had been patiently waiting for a phone call.

She heard Angie grumbling as she fumbled for her gown and smiled to herself in the dark as she envisaged the room and the hallway outside.

"What's going on Mistress? Is everything ok?"

Kath froze at the sound of a female voice.

"Shut up!" she heard Angie hiss. "Right fire away, Kath, I'm here!"

Kath took the phone from her ear and gazed at the screen stupidly. An insect-like chittering coming from the speaker as Angie called her, trying to get her back.

Stupid! Stupid! Kath fumed at herself, how could she have thought for one second that Angie would deny herself any pleasure in her absence? It was probably that daft little blonde tart she had used in the hotel room.

Well then, her thoughts raced on, should she not report in as a journalist anyway? After all she did want her employers to get her out of here. Didn't she? Well didn't she?

After a second more hesitation she hit the off button, stored the phone and left the room. She wasn't tip toeing anymore.

Kath closed the cell door quietly and stood looking at Mike. He was fast asleep on his back, his deep chest rising and falling with his breathing, his thick, muscular thighs spread carelessly wide. Now, once again moving stealthily she approached and knelt beside the cot. Mike's cock lay against one thigh, the dark ball sac hanging temptingly just below it. She leaned across one thigh, stuck out her tongue and began to lick it, then she moved upwards and began to lick at the soft shaft of the cock itself. She felt him stir as the cock began to pulse into life. She gently held the helm in one hand and just dabbed at it with her tongue. He moaned and his hand found its way down to her head where it pressed her down. She smiled and ducked her head obediently, opening her mouth wide and taking in the smooth roundness of the glans, her tongue tracing the slit that traversed it. When he was fully lodged and her mouth was stuffed deliciously full of him, she began a slow, nodding motion, letting him into her relaxed throat as much as she could. He moaned again and his fingers clasped harder in her hair, he began to buck his hips up towards her face and then she felt the tell-tale thickening of his shaft. She cupped his balls respectfully in one hand and used the other in a gentle milking motion up and down the shaft, then relaxed and let him pump himself into the narrow confines of her mouth and throat. Splash after splash spurted into her and she swallowed each one gratefully. He sighed in release and propped himself up on his elbows as she continued to hold him in her mouth, licking him and encouraging every last morsel from him, and fetching the final spasms of pleasure from him.

When he was finally finished, she released him, licked her lips and sat back on her heels.

"Sir, there's something I need to confess to you," she said.

Later that day Brian and Mike faced each other across Brian's desk. They had had a video conference with Mostyn, who had had a call from the woman who had sold the girl who now bore the number seven, to them.

The blog was massive now and she would just have to ghost write it as best she could. But what were they to do with the miscreant herself?

"Well she's got to be really punished," Mike said.

"She thinks she deserves it and if she doesn't get it, she'll smell a rat! She must've started out thinking she was going to bring us down," Brian said.

"Boss, just imagine if there really had been a leak – one we really didn't know about and control – and then we rumbled it. What would we have done to that girl?"

Brian sat back and pursed his lips in thought, it was exactly what he had been thinking too.

"I think I'd have rung Carlo to start with." He sat forward and picked up the phone.

It was a cold, crisp day and the slaves all wore the woollen ruanas they used until they warmed up on days like these- the simple blanket-like garments slipping over the head and then the ends being tied with a leather belt at the waist. Their hands were clipped neatly behind their backs and they stood in a line to witness the start of Number Seven's week of punishment.

"…her intention was simply to bring down this stable and destroy everything we have built up. Everything you have striven for, fought for and achieved would have been thrown away! You would have been released back into the world to face those who sold you!" Brian told them. "All the lies and the double dealing that make life so difficult out there, you would have had to deal with again! But here, you are safe! Here you know what you are! You know what you are for!" He paused. "And you know what we are! In the ring, between the shafts, hauling logs – and of course, under the lash, there is no room for dishonesty! Together we can make a great stable, but first we must show Number Seven that we will not tolerate deception and disloyalty. To her credit she has admitted her crime and submitted herself to her due punishment – a punishment that you will all share in administering!"

Brian had been walking slowly up and down the line of girls and now stopped to examine the expressions on their faces. To a girl they were shocked and angry. They had been cast adrift suddenly when they had been taken by Proteus but had found the certainties in their lives that their submissive natures longed for and now one of their own number had been plotting to disrupt everything again.

He turned away and smiled grimly towards his team who flanked the frame on which the hooded figure of Number Seven now hung by her wrists which were enclosed in thick suspension cuffs. Otherwise she was naked, occasionally she shivered, but whether that was from the cold or from apprehension, Brian neither knew nor cared. Mostyn's manoeuvrings with the girl had been a nuisance and with a few decent beatings, he could get his little squad sorted out properly, so he was eager to get started and get it over with.

"Step forward Number One!" he called.

The black girl stepped out from the line and he handed her the coiled single tail. It was the standard disciplinary tool, well worn and soft, so it wrapped lovingly around its victim but still with a core of venom when swung hard.

"Five lashes anywhere on the bitch's body. Remember what she was going to do to all of us, and if I think you're holding back, you'll get the same as she's going to get!" he told her, then stood back.

He was impressed by how well the girls had learned their craft. Each one swung the lash hard and accurately. The suspended girl, unable to hear the lashes coming, twisted and swung – her feet a clear twelve inches off the ground. He watched the grim determination on the faces of the girls as they worked on their comrade. He was delighted with how they changed their stance so that sometimes they wrapped her body completely and sometimes they let the tip of the whip bite deeply at the middle of her back. It was just as well that the hood's stopple had been applied at the start of proceedings, Brian thought as he watched Number Eight, the girl's own sparring sister, throw the whip deliberately hard at her hips, making her try and draw up her thighs to protect herself.

By the end of the forty-five lashes she was striped from shoulders to knees, but still with enough spaces to allow Helga and Caroline to add their contributions. Then Mike lowered her, freed her wrists, slung her over his shoulder and took her off to solitary confinement. He and the other men would make their contributions later.

As her head bumped and bounced against the back of the man carrying her, Kath slowly eased her teeth out of the dents they had made in the rubber, penis shaped stopple. It had been the best and worst of beatings. The best because it had been so painful. The worst because it had been done with no pleasure; no emotion save that of anger. And she deserved it. She deserved all that they were undoubtedly going to do to her. Dimly she heard a door close, she was picked up and dumped unceremoniously on a rough blanket that immediately chafed at her weals. For a moment nothing happened and then she felt the full weight of a man on top of her, barging between her legs, thrusting for her vagina with a rock hard erection. But of course, what else could she expect after such a thrashing? And what else would he expect but that she be open and wet for him in the wake of that thrashing. He slid smoothly into her and began to thrust hard and fast, seeking only his pleasure. Kath was rasped against the blanket as the man on top of her rocked her in his quest for release. She clenched her teeth against the stopple once more and tried to control her breathing through the nostril holes as his rough handling ignited the masochistic fires inside her. She felt him straighten and freeze for a second and then he was pounding into her, harder than ever and still careless of her pain, sending her toppling out of control and into orgasm, her breath snorting through her nose as she came, her teeth aching with the pressure of her bite on the stopple.

Then his weight vanished and she was left to snort and snuffle her way back to normality. After a minute or so she felt the laces at the back of the hood being undone and suddenly she was back in the world of light as it was pulled off and she saw Mike looking down at her.

"You've got a lot more of that to come," he told her, his voice cold and threatening. "Better rest!"

He padlocked a steel cuff round her ankle and then left her. Slowly and stiffly she climbed to her feet and looked around. She was in a chilly stone room with one frosted glass window set high up in a wall. The floor was stone flagged and cold to her bare feet. There was a simple bed with a duvet on a thin mattress, a toilet and a sink. Mike slammed and locked the door behind him. Kath curled up on the bed and let her fingers trail across the welts that criss crossed her body and thighs. She was strangely satisfied and even smiled as she felt Mike's sperm begin to ooze out of her. This was a price she had chosen to pay. She had to pay it, until it was paid she could not be a full member of the stable. And that was what she wanted; more than anything.

When it was all over, Annie told her that she was a week in solitary but she lost count of the days. The men kept her in a constant state of confused arousal and pain. It seemed almost every hour, one or other of them would take her into the room next to her cell and beat her. It was another plain stone cube, but was equipped with an X cross, a whipping bench and a caning stool. It had long ledges either side of its raised central bench, which sloped downwards. She was made to kneel on the ledges and bend forwards, the central bench supporting her chest and knees but leaving her bottom raised. She had been caned plenty of times in the past but never the way she was caned on what turned out to be her final morning. During her week she had taken a couple of good whacks with a crop and a particularly whippy cane which she instantly named The Bitch – after the way it stung. But as a finale Mike administered what he called a judicial caning. It was a punishment caning; pure and simple. He took a step back once she was mounted and then strode forwards, Kath heard him coming just before the stroke exploded across her buttocks – and there was no other word for it. It flashed a brilliant light of pain across her mind and she was still trying to scream when the next detonated – and the next. She was vaguely aware of gaping like a landed fish as the merciless assault went on and on until finally she found her voice and shrieked. And for a few minutes the small room was an inferno of noise as Mike swung the cane at full strength and Kath screamed until the last part of the price she had to pay had been extracted from her quivering body.

During the week, the other girls had repeated the whipping she had initially received, sometimes it was at a cross set up in the yard, once she was ankle suspended in a frame with her legs spread wide apart. The girls were given a long tailed flogger and eagerly set about punishing those parts of her body that were their shared female inheritance. And of course they were much harder on her than the men would have been. They left her swinging from the cross beam, her eyes watering so much she could hardly see, a burning and stinging fire raging between her legs and across her breasts. Steve had overseen that punishment and inevitably had presented his cock to her mouth in its aftermath. As her wrists were tied together and hanging below her head, all she could do was open her mouth as wide as it would go and take him in. She had to leave it up to him to steady her against his thrusts. He could have held her by her hips or chest. Instead he just grabbed her head and crudely face-fucked her. As she was upside down, she wasn't able to use her tongue to stimulate the sensitive underside of his helm and so he lasted considerably longer than normal and as a result she was able to achieve a small climax as he took her with such arrogant carelessness. Fortunately he was too involved in his own pleasure to notice and she escaped further punishment. Alex treated her to the harshest breast whipping she had ever taken while she was tied face outwards against the cross. The Boss himself contributed a fierce back lashing about halfway through her week, when her first tranche of welts had faded a bit, and followed it up with a pin wheel.

By the time Mike led her back into the main body of the house, with her hands clipped together behind her and her bottom ablaze with colour, she knew she was back where she belonged. Most importantly she knew that Mike had really put his stamp on her. But so had the arenas. She had no illusions about the fact that he and the Boss might sell her on. It was a prospect that filled her with excitement as well as fear. She wouldn't want to leave this stable but there were plenty of other knowledgeable owners and trainers out there who might make her life even more interesting.

She rejoined the slaves as they were having their evening meal. She was led in and then turned around so that they could all see the devastation that had been wrought on her buttocks, as well as the fading traces of all the previous punishments. Kath felt a surge of pride as she heard a collective indrawing of breath from the girls.

"She's paid the price for what she did and that's an end of it," the Boss told them. "She's back now and will take her place as before. Is that clear?"

There was a subdued chorus of assent and then, wincing, Kath sat on the wooden bench beside Annie.

Later on, Annie did her best to kiss away the hurt from her bottom, then Mike joined them and Kath felt her old life finally slough away completely. Angie, the paper and everything were gone. All that mattered was the stable and her performance.

CHAPTER FOURTEEN.

On the evening of the Baron Sagemont's next grand dinner, the slaves were paraded before the guests as they sat at table and were tethered in front of them so that they could be observed and considered. The guests were sexual gourmands and pored over the dishes that were on offer for later in the evening as a greedy diner would hesitate and change his mind over a menu – unable to choose because what he wanted was everything.

The dining tables were set out in a U shape in one of the ballrooms, beneath chandeliers that built towers of glittering light towards the distant ceiling. The polished floors rang to the sounds of footsteps as Marcel's house staff served course after course of light, savoury dishes that would inflame the carnal appetites rather than dampen them. And all along the tables the lights reflected off the crystal glass of the wine goblets that were constantly being refilled. Conversation was loud and cheerful among the guests as they discussed and assessed the slaveflesh before them. The slaves themselves were tethered to rails that ran along the fronts of the various tables. The females – and they were by far the majority – had their leashes running from where their hands were clipped together behind their backs, between their legs and then to the rail. The few males likewise had their hands clipped behind them but their leashes ran from the various piercings their mistresses had had put into their cocks and balls.

All the slaves were masked with animal heads. It was a tradition of these gatherings that the slaves contributed by the guests should be anonymous and should be shared out amongst all the guests. The masks were almost hoods in that they covered the upper faces completely and the heads, leaving the women only a hole for their hair to show at the back, gathered into pony tails. Just their mouths and eyes showed, wide, apprehensive and excited. Some owners had added ball gags if they felt that their property might disgrace them by making a noise during dinner. Each slave wore a floor length cloak fastened at the neck but as they had been paraded to their places, the heavy material had pulled back and now simply framed the vulnerable nudity each slave presented.

Marcel was well pleased with the display, there were some succulent pieces there, ready to be played with down in the château's cellars later on. Beside him, Marie squirmed in her seat with excitement. The guests had all dressed in eighteenth century costume and the neck line of her embroidered gown barely contained the rippling and trembling mounds of her breasts. She had contributed two well-muscled young men and three girls to the evening. Her male slaves were both proudly priapic – as she had trained them to be – as she pointed them out to Marcel.

"You can hood their heads, but you can't disguise a cock!" she giggled as she and a friend considered what they were going to do to them later on.

Marcel listened fondly while his eyes remained on the tall figure in front of him, her breasts riding high and proud on her chest, her freshly shaven delta just showing the start of her labial split and her long thighs parted enough to allow her leash to pass between them. The fox mask she wore allowed the mane of blonde hair to escape onto her shoulders. He had cheated a little and ensured that Blondie was stationed directly in front of his place. She was magnificent, standing taller and more proudly than any of the other females, occasionally allowing the tip of her tongue with its sombre steel piercing, to wet her full lips.

Marcel let his thoughts wander towards the end of the night when he would take this princess amongst slaves to his bed with Marie or any of the other free women and sample those lips at their most intimate and submissive but he was interrupted by the guest sitting on his other side.

"Got anything special lined up tonight?" he asked.

"We've got a punishment coming up and a branding later on."

As he finished speaking, Guillaume, resplendent in breeches, brocade jacket and wig, strode up to the head table and begged permission to introduce a punishment that had been requested by Madame de Brunaille. Her slave had been less than enthusiastic when she had been lent to a friend and Madame wanted the slut to be taught that she was available to anyone Madame gave her to. To that end she wanted the girl beaten round the tables. It was another tradition amongst Marcel's group and the news was greeted with applause and feet drumming on the floor as the stocks were wheeled in.

They were the bench variety, where a body can be strapped down along the bench, whilst the head and hands are trapped in the stock boards at the head. This one had simply had small castors added to make it mobile. A girl was already strapped tightly to the machine, face down when she was entered. One of the stewards that Marcel employed pushed her until she was in front of her Mistress' place. She was a tall woman in a pale blue silk gown, she held lorgnettes up to her eyes to survey the naked wretch before her.

"Well, you slut? Do you confess that you thoroughly deserve this punishment?"

"Yes, Mistress. I…I won't ever be disobedient again!"

"You're right, you won't! Beat her round the tables please, M'sieur!" She waved a languid hand at the steward, also in costume who was joined by another. They stripped off their blouson tops and there were murmurings of female approval of the muscular physiques thus displayed.

The girl was quite plump and as she lay along the top of the bench, displayed a pleasingly deep amount of buttock meat. Her back was quite broad and her thighs long enough to take plenty of work from the heavy straps the men now took down from the ends of the stock board, where the girl had been able to see them. She whimpered just before the punishment began.

As soon as the men started, throwing the lashes down with enough energy and passion to fetch some applause from the onlookers, the conversations and laughter began again. The loud smacks of the straps landing from right and left of the slave echoed in the high room and after only a few, the sound was joined by high pitched, fluting cries. Some of the tethered slaves became restless when they heard the punishment begin but Guillaume and some of the others, Claire among them calmed them down with a word or a stroke. Marcel noted that Claire seemed to find calming the male slaves with a squeeze and a stroke of hard cock, the more appealing and made a note to see to her downstairs if the chance arose. He noticed the tall blonde in front of him made no reaction whatever, even when the stocks were brought to a stop right beside her and another twenty lashes were delivered before the stocks moved on. The wailing was almost constant now and the buttocks jiggled up and down frantically under the relentless fusillade of strikes from both sides.

"Stop!" Madame called. "The slut's coming! Wheel her away into a corner and we'll finish her later."

The wailing was replaced by sobbing as the slave was pushed into a corner.

Towards the end of the meal she was taken out again and beaten along the rest of the top table and all along the length of the left leg of the U. This time the girl managed to hold her orgasm at bay and got through to the end.

Her mistress rose and took a bow as the stocks were wheeled away. The girl's cries and the whips striping her had inflamed the diners nicely, and the way the three bodies involved in the display had gleamed with sweat under the lights had lit the fuse that would lead to the explosions of pleasure in the cellars. Marcel rose and held up his hands. There was instant silence.

"My friends, it is time to make our way downstairs! Please make free use of any slaves – including my household ones for whom there wasn't sufficient room at the table. We will be pleased to witness the branding of our dear friend Gerhardt Buerger's lovely slave Agnetha – a lady I know many of you have enjoyed in the past! Now, may I suggest we move along and meet after disrobing!"

Marcel watched as his friends drifted away and his staff began to gather up the slaves' leashes and lead them away too, then he made his way downstairs to the stone-pillared cellars. At the foot of the stairs were the two disrobing rooms. To the left was the women's one where they helped one another out of their gowns, ready to face the night's pleasures in basques, stockings and heels. To the right was the men's room where shirts were removed and the buttoned panel at the front of the breeches was removed so that the cocks hung free. But with what was on the menu, they would not be hanging for long.

Marcel contented himself with observing for the first hour or so. He wasn't surprised to see that an Englishman, Sir Willoughby Gore claimed the blonde first off, and with the help of Guillaume, now naked to the waist, looking very un-butlerish and sporting an impressive erection, stretched her out face down between four chains anchored in the low ceiling. Between them they hauled her arms up first and then her legs until she hung at waist height, spreadeagled, her body bowing downwards but under enough tension to hold her reasonably level. He took a stock whip to her back and she took it for a good thirty lashes before she started bucking and twisting in her bonds. He stopped and added weights attached to screw clamps to her nipples and labia, then started in again. He kept working on her back, Marcel noted approvingly until she was making the weights swing and clonk together beneath her and then he moved to her backside. Almost immediately her pelvis began to move up and down and the buttocks clenched as she began to orgasm. He kept up an impressively regular rhythm as he flogged her upwards until she roared her release and then hung limply, a long trail of ejaculate elongating slowly towards the floor from her cunt. Several people had seen and noticed the tongue ring.

"Marcel found her in the Middle East, he tells me," Sir Willoughby said as he stood between her spread thighs and inserted himself easily into her vagina.. "By God, you can tell arena stock by the way they grip you!" he crowed and landed several hefty hand spanks to the buttocks. "Come on, my beauty!"

Someone else availed themselves of her mouth and Marcel moved on, well pleased. They would play with her all night and nor recognise her – because it simply couldn't possibly be Blondie herself. But tomorrow!

He watched Marie do something terrible with needles to the cock of one of her young men, but perversely the thing only grew even more massive as the scrotum became a pin cushion and an injection of saline turned the foreskin into a sort of rubbery tube around the base of the glans. At last the body, arched out from a stone pillar by the tether Marie held that was attached to the ring through the helm itself, could take no more and spurted several splashes of thick, creamy spunk at its Mistress' feet. Marie gave a cruel little smile and told the unfortunate youth that he would pay for his incontinence and, still holding the deflating cock by its ring, she took up a thin whippy cane and began to belabour the shaft.

Marcel smiled and shook his head, even as he moved off, his ears ringing with the youth's yelps, he could see the cock hardening again.

He found a return to what he felt comfortable with when he found one of his own slaves, with a blackbird mask on, bent over a whipping bench and being flogged by an old Dutch friend of his. The girl was just about to orgasm and so he stuck his cock straight into her mouth and she made a fair job of sucking him and screaming her release at the same time – until he came and she spluttered helplessly. Her flagellator laughed as her cunt spurted and Marcel left her draped over the bench, wrung out, being fucked and with sperm dripping from her face.

He moved from suspension to suspension – from wrists and ankles – and from beating to beating with canes and single tails, he helped apply the flesh rakes to freshly flogged skin, he enjoyed the abandoned shrieks of climaxing slaves and the satisfied roars and sighs of the dominants as they came. Then finally

Guillaume announced that it was time for the branding and Agnetha was led in.

She was a fine figure of a woman in her forties. The exigencies and discipline of a slave's life had kept her stomach flat and her breasts, although heavy, reasonably prominent. Her buttocks too were still smooth and her thighs shapely enough. The major part of her attractiveness however, as she was led in on her collar and lead, was that she was easily five feet ten tall and all her curves were on a scale rarely seen in the ranks of the slaves. Added to this was the fact that it was known she could exhaust several flagellators during the course of an evening and still orgasm into the small hours under needle play and waxing.

Her owner stepped forwards and requested that she be flogged hard before accepting his brand, as an orgasm would help her endure the brand, and it was a mark of the affection in which she was held that she was allowed this favour. Marcel himself administered the thrashing which Agnetha took standing unbound in the middle of the great cellar's floor, her hands clasped behind her neck, her back hollowed obediently. The other slaves had to wait for their treatments until after Agnetha's was complete. And everyone gathered around. Once she had come with her characteristic jiggling and oddly – given her size – bird-like cries. She was put face first against a stout wooden door that the men had brought down earlier and propped against a pillar. She was spreadeagled against it and bound at wrists and ankles, waist, chest, thighs and upper arms. Then Guillaume brought in the brazier and placed it behind her where she would be able to feel the heat. The iron was already in and one of the stewards began to use bellows to bring it up to white heat. Gerhardt stood forwards.

"Do you willingly accept the mark that is about to be put on you?" he asked.

From where he stood, Marcel could see the look of devotion on the woman's face as she stated her willingness clearly and steadily.

Gerhardt bent and picked the branding iron out of the fire, he examined it critically and replaced it for a few more seconds. Like the other dominants in the group, Marcel was fond of Agnetha's strength and durability and was pleased for her that she was to be marked, but what especially pleased him was that Gerhardt had chosen not to brand the buttocks. They were of a size and width that would be a travesty to compromise with a permanent mark, much better to keep them so that they could be re-marked afresh each time she was used. Her brand would be her Master's initials on her right shoulder. The letters would be two inches high and seared into her where any summer dress would leave them in plain view, which was Gerhardt's intention.

He bent again, examined the iron again and decided it was just right, tapped it gently on the brazier's edge, then in one smooth and decisive movement, turned and applied it to Agnetha's pale skin. But apart from her head snapping back, which was all the movement she could make, she held her peace while Guillaume counted and the cellar filled with the smell of roast flesh, then at the signal he pulled it clear and the woman slumped forwards. Most of the crowd clapped, but some of the women waved their hands in front of their faces and complained about the smoke and smell. Gerhardt laughed and said she would be punished as soon as she was recovered.

Time and again during the evening Marcel returned to the blonde. She was in constant demand and served calmly and well at all times. The men were entranced by the strength of her pelvic floor muscles, the women loved her length of tongue and both sexes adored her stoical endurance under whatever was done to her. A stoicism that was only occasionally interrupted by orgasms that produced squirts of thick ejaculate and which entertained the company greatly.

At last he retired to bed with a sleepy and replete Marie. The final act of the evening was to fuck his step-sister while Blondie lay behind him and licked his balls.

The following afternoon he showed those of his guests who hadn't had to leave or who were still asleep, around his zoo.

There were some twenty or so, some who had seen it before and some newer friends who had yet to see it.

Marcel led them along a stone tunnel that came off the back of the cellar they had occupied so enjoyably the previous evening and which was being cleaned as they passed through. It had once been an escape route during the Revolution but now led to an outbuilding that he had converted for his own very special purposes. The group emerged into a low and spacious building that had a very odd layout. Chairs and tables were laid out on the huge floor area and there was a bar in one corner. But the main part of the floor was filled by elongated glass cubes, enormous ones, they stretched into the room from the left hand wall. And within the cubes there were people. To be more precise there were girls and women. As the group approached the enclosures the new guests dropped their voices until Marcel put them at their ease.

"It is a revolutionary new glass that is completely one way visually and which is impervious to everything up to a direct hit by a shell. Let me show you."

He picked up a wrought iron chair and approached the nearest glass cube. Within it was a room furnished with a bed, beyond that room but still within the glass was a bathroom and toilet and beyond that was a day room with an array of gym equipment as well as chairs and a TV set. The suite was occupied by a tall black haired girl who was naked and who was currently lying back in one of the chairs with one leg cocked over the arm and with one hand idly rubbing her clitoris. Marcel approached and swung the chair with all his might. It hit the glass with a dead, thunk sound and rebounded, almost taking him off his feet. The girl never stirred.

"You see, inside the walls are dark and solid looking. They have no idea that we are here or that we can see them. No noise or vision penetrates from the outside. In a minute you will see…ah!"

There was a door into the day room and this now opened to admit Guillaume. He closed and locked the door behind him. The girl sat up and grinned lasciviously at him. The onlookers saw his mouth open and close, and the girl's, but no sound escaped. They watched as he put her up against the wall right in front of their faces, her breasts flattening and going white against the glass, her face looking straight into theirs, seeing nothing. Some of the first time female guests stifled excited yelps as she was restrained, spreadeagled in front of them and behind her Guillaume shook out his favourite single tail.

"She has thirty lashes twice a day," Marcel explained. "Even after last night there are no allowances made."

He moved on as the whip began to fall and the girl's body flinched and twisted alluringly against the glass. "Let's have a look in the other cages and you'll notice that you can walk down the sides, so there is nowhere that you cannot see. You'll notice the daylight tubes from the roof? I believe a slave flourishes best in near-natural conditions. The cage doors lead into a corridor that leads down the outside of the building. No clue about this observation lounge can be garnered from the front. We can observe their behaviour in complete privacy from here."

"She's a new addition isn't she?" Sir Willoughby asked, reluctantly tearing himself away from the beating.

"She is, and she's another arena purchase. But a rather special one!" Marcel replied. "Now our next exhibit you didn't meet last night, they were given to me by the Prince of Bakhtar in payment for some small service I rendered him."

The next cage was much bigger and housed six, beautiful, olive skinned girls who were currently in their bedroom, which they shared, they were combing each other's hair as each emerged from the shower and helping each other to put on make up and to dress in filmy and sparkly costumes.

"They will entertain us tonight with dancing. After that they may be taken to bedrooms but I'm afraid I don't want them beaten or used hard at all, they're promised to a friend of mine for a week or so." He paused awhile as some members of the party went along the sides of the cage and one drew their attention to the fact that one girl had her hand working deep between another girl's legs. Marcel smiled and joined the group who began to relax and laugh openly as they watched the two girls entwine and recline back on a bed, the few garments they wore were soon removed and in front of their invisible audience the two smooth and lissom bodies wove together. A third girl went a bedside cabinet and took out a strap-on, to much enthusiastic encouragement from outside her cage she knelt behind the girl who was on top on the bed and with a bit of effort managed to sink it into her cunt.

"Can you get sound on this, Marcel?" one guest asked.

"We can, but may I suggest you return this afternoon and you can enjoy a pre-dinner drink and watch their antics at your leisure. You can also have one or two exhibits introduced into another cage and see what ensues. Alternatively you can have an exhibit beaten, or pierced for your pleasure. But for now, I really just want to show you something that I had intended to keep secret but simply cannot resist telling you, my dear friends, about!"

He led them past several more of the hi-tech cages, each of them containing a slave from various parts of the world, all of whom had served the previous night and who were recovering now.

"We will allow them to play later for your entertainment, but now, come to the last cage!"

The party, attracted by the eagerness in Marcel's voice, scurried after him and arrived at the final cage. In it was a tall, voluptuous blonde who had obviously been recently severely whipped and was on her knees thanking her flagellator. There was an awed silence as they watched the woman finish swallowing then stand up as the man left her. Her hands were clipped together behind her back and she was facing away from them but as the door closed, she flicked her blonde hair back and turned to face them. There were gasps and shrieks as they recognised Blondie.

"You were playing with her all last night!" Marcel told them delightedly, and allowed himself to be persuaded to recount the true story of how he had got hold of her.

"But what will you do with her?" Sir Willoughby asked. "She's priceless! Undefeated! A legend!"

Marcel stood close to the glass as the blonde approached looking moody and bored, alone of all the cages her dayroom consisted of a straw bed with a sheet thrown over it and some gym items. There was not one item of comfort.

The blonde came right up to the glass and stared out as Marcel came close to the other side and caressed her face through the two inch thick wall.

"Undefeated? They all say that about the great Blondie, don't they? But it's not really true. Not really. She has been beaten in single combat just once."

His audience looked at him blankly.

"Does anyone remember a then-unknown gladiator being beaten in a cage fight and being spirited away from Conor Brien's stable, only to re-appear at The Lodge in England under the care of Carlo Suarez?"

"But that was ages ago! Since then she's…"

"She's gone on to be the invincible Blondie," Marcel finished for Sir Willoughby.

"She threw that fight! Everyone says!" he responded.

"Has she ever said as much?" Marcel asked. There was a shaking of heads. "Then we don't know for sure."

"But look here, the girl who beat her's long gone, Marcel."

He took a deep breath, savouring the moment. "No she hasn't. Come with me!"

He strode back along the cages until they came back to the first cage. There he presented his newest acquisition with a flourish. "This is none other than the long lost fighter who was in the cage that night with Blondie. Ladies and gentlemen, in a few weeks I intend to find out, once and for all, whether Blondie really deserves her reputation for being 'undefeated' in single combat. I will put her in a cage with this one and let them fight it out all over again!"

There was immediate uproar, mostly of joyful exuberance at the prospect of finding out the answer to the question that everyone had debated or glossed over for so long.

They watched as the dark haired girl was taken down and mounted on a dildo set in the seat of a rowing machine and put to work.

"She was out of the arenas for a while and is just getting back into form, but will be ready very soon, so Guillaume informs me. Tickets will go on sale shortly to a carefully picked audience, and you, my good friends will be at the head of the queue. Of course I was reluctant to kidnap such a piece of work as Blondie, but could you see Carlo Suarez risking his precious prize possession on a single fight? No! Of course not! So as a sportsman I had to act once I found – or once I was able to buy - this one. Now it must remain a closely guarded secret of course, otherwise Mr Suarez will be sure to try and spoil the fun!"

He offered to show them all the provenance they wanted to confirm the dark haired girl's identity and led his guests back into the house.

Blondie wandered around her quarters, impatient for the man to return and release her hands so that she could work out on the machines. Or maybe she would be run in harness, she needed to be active! The previous night had been good, these people had got their money's worth out of her, the breast suspension and whipping at the end had been exceptionally good. She glanced down proudly at the lines still engraved in the roots of her breasts from where the ropes had held her. Pretty soon now her travelling crate would arrive and she would be flown home to her own stall, where she would know all the other slaves and grooms and where her Master could always find her and take his pleasure with her. This had been the longest hiring out she could remember and she wanted to go home.

She looked around her at the strange, smooth, dark walls. It just didn't feel right. No one had assessed her welts and marks for recovery time before transporting her home, and in her experience that always happened the morning after a party. The hirers were always anxious not to run up too big a bill! A nasty little kernel of unease was beginning to unfurl in the pit of her stomach. Blondie wanted to go home.

CHAPTER FIFTEEN

Kath squinted down at her breasts and tried to settle them a bit more comfortably within the corset. Comfort, however, she reflected grimly, was not what the things had been designed for – quite the reverse in fact. This was an arena boxing corset. It was made out of leather and considered purely as an article of female apparel, it did the superb job of accentuating the female form that all basques did. It nipped in the waist, supported the bust and drew the beholder's eye to the flare of the hips. However, the outside of it was covered in small round metal plates at regular intervals and on the inside of the garment each metal plate became a sharpened stud. They were not needle sharp, but they were pointed enough.

Kath could feel them just warming to her skin, they nuzzled her cosily, pressing against her stomach and sides and the undersides of her breasts, where they rested on them. Now she was trying to get her nipples positioned between them so that a jab wouldn't dig a stud into her tender nubs. Eventually she was satisfied and Helga pulled on the lacing at the back, drawing the metal even closer to her flesh and making the corset almost a second skin. Then the groom moved round to stand in front of her and held up the leather thong. Kath swallowed nervously and nodded, reaching for the groom's shoulder to steady herself as she lifted one leg.

They had practised boxing, of course they had. They had had the Velcro straps wrapped around their fists and Mike and the others had drilled them on jabbing and hooking and combination punching on hanging bags in one of the barns. They had tried on the corsets, but as the boss had said; there was no way to practise beyond that, you just had to do it. And today she was going to do it. So was Annie. It was their chance to get revenge on One and Two for the wrestling match.

Because of the severity of Kath's punishment, this bout had been delayed and in the fortnight it had taken for all her welts and bruises to fade, she realised she had assumed some kind of celebrity in the eyes of the other girls. She alone amongst them had faced the full fury of the stable's discipline and had come through it. None of the others wanted to go there and respected her having done it. Whatever her crime had been didn't matter any more, she was one of them. For a couple of days she and Annie had been left in a cell on their own and had slept and made love and Annie had tended her various hurts.

Kath was ecstatically happy she realised as she lifted her other leg and stepped into her boxing thong and Helga eased it up her thighs.

This was the bit that she was both dreading and looking forward to. The thong itself had the same studs on the inside. The triangle at the front of the scrap of leather was arrayed with potential torment for the girl wearing it. For a masochist it could provide instant orgasm, and therefore defeat, if struck. Helga pulled the thong up, made sure the thin strap sat comfortably along the perineum and up between the buttocks and then returned to the business end. She pulled the front away from Kath's pubic mound and reached in, using her fingers to part the labia and then gently allowing the leather to settle back.

Kath could feel the cold metal kiss her sexflesh, there was even one of the evil little studs nestling right up against her clitoris. A solid jab there and she would be helpless. But it was the same for their opponents. She glanced across at Annie and they exchanged smiles.

They would fight in adjacent rings and Kath had drawn the brunette.

Helga wrapped her fists in the weighted straps and she was ready.

Out in the gym the other slaves knelt along the length of one wall again, and again Mike and the boss led out their teams to stand by the rings.

"Rules?" Mike asked.

"Nah! Except body shots only, head shots mean a whipping on the spot," the boss replied again, much as Kath had expected. "Apart from that, knockdowns to the count of ten."

"One or two?" Mike asked.

The boss made a show of inspecting the girls in front of him. "They look strong enough, let's make it two."

Kath smiled inwardly at the helpless masochist she was. It meant that the loser would take a real pounding, being put down and counted out twice before the contest ended, but she couldn't wait to see how she took what the ring would throw at her as she ducked in and began to limber up.

There was no bell, just a blast from the boss's whistle and then the brunette was coming for her. Kath's first reaction was that the girl looked fabulous. The corset suited her so well that all Kath wanted to do was rip it off her and have her, but fortunately the sight of the weighted straps across the knuckles that wove threateningly in front of her, calmed her libido and she got down to work. Any girl knew that breast shots and uppercuts were contest winners so both girls kept their elbows in and crouched forwards. The brunette made the first swing, trying to club a punch into Kath's ribs but Kath saw it coming and swerved away in time. She jabbed in return and managed a blow low down on the girl's stomach before she could get her guard up again. The brunette gave out a gasp as the punch drove home and Kath's spirits soared.

She feinted a jab to the girl's right side, she swivelled and covered up allowing Kath to get a straight right hand into her exposed left side. Again there was the gasp and Kath felt the impact this time. The weights made the punches slow, but they made them telling. The girl tried to dive in on Kath, unleashing hooks to right and left. But Kath covered up and gritted her teeth, preparing to take the punches to her sides. The girl collided with her, face to face and with Kath's fists gathered at her chest. Kath watched her face as she rammed her own tits onto Kath's fists. Her punches landed almost painlessly behind the studs on the sides of Kath's corset and her mouth opened in a silent gasp of pain and then Kath pushed her away, she staggered, helplessly absorbed in the pain and pleasure at her breasts and Kath went straight in for the kill, almost laughing with pleasure at how easy it had been. Two straight jabs landed squidgily, one on each tit and the girl reeled back even farther and into the ropes. Kath lowered her fists and hooked from left and right. The girl covered up and bent forwards, twisting to left and right as the blows landed. While she was distracted, Kath let loose a straight jab that drove in to the breasts. The girl went down onto one knee and Mike started counting. Kath stood at the regulation distance of three feet and waited. The arenas believed in punishing failure and the crowds wanted spectacle not fair play. At five the girl staggered up and immediately had to cover up in the face of Kath's joyful onslaught. She bent so low that she had to be careful not to earn herself a whipping by hitting above the shoulders. But she hooked up into the girl's midriff, mainly hitting her arms and fists but digging them into the studs nonetheless. The girl began to totter and Kath remembered her training, she looked again and saw the girl's legs were splayed. Almost laughing aloud, Kath dug a final left towards her opponent's breasts and then immediately swung a right hook between her legs from behind. She felt her fist sink into the plump cushion of the brunette's cunt and she toppled forwards onto her face, crying out and curling up, cradling the hurt. Or was she coming? Kath stood over her as Mike counted, it was hard to tell. She rocked about and moaned and as the count got to ten and stopped she grabbed a rope and hauled herself up again. Her hair was dishevelled and hung over her eyes but Kath could see the light that burned there and realised that whether she had come or not, she knew the only way to avoid her master's wrath was to go down fighting.

Kath smiled fiercely and allowed the girl to come away from the ropes – always put on a show! For her part, the brunette did well. She knew that the game was almost certainly up and so threw caution to the wind and went for Kath with both fists swinging in wide and slow arcs that would have put her down if they had connected, but Kath was floating on adrenalin by then and ducked and bobbed fluently until she got another straight jab in to the breasts. The girl staggered but came on again. Again she took a jab and again she came back for more, her fists by now were hanging by her sides, the weights having taken their toll. Kath realised that her opponent was almost at the point of orgasm and began to put on a show herself. She started fending her off with little powder puff pushes to the breasts and actually saw the disappointment on her face when they weren't real blows. But it allowed her to make one more rally and come at Kath again – who knew that Mike would have seen that and would have liked it. Kath danced back, making her miss time and again, exhausting herself until finally Kath was able to grab the girl's hair with one hand and with the other wind up an uppercut. She telegraphed it outrageously, windmilling her fist before the dazed girl's half-closed eyes. Vaguely she heard rising cheers from the audience as they saw the brunette's widely straddled legs and then Kath swung in the final blow. The brunette played her part well and took the full impact but jumped into the air as if she had been lifted bodily by the punch, then she crashed down and was counted out again.

Kath looked across to see Annie back her opponent into a corner and begin to pummel her. It looked like that was going well too. She turned back to the brunette, sprawled on the canvas on her back, her breast heaving as she panted for breath, and she stood over her face then carefully sank to her knees, parting them wider and wider until she felt her fallen foe's mouth begin to pay tribute to her, kissing her gently either side of the thong, just at the apex of her thighs, her labia feeling the soft pressure of the kisses and her cunt aching for more.

Outside the ring, money was changing hands as the boss counted the black girl out for the second time and Kath and Annie had their revenge.

When the flogging had been completed and the girls had gone on to sparring and log pulling outside, Brian picked up the phone in his office.

"Mr Mostyn, I think we're ready now." He listened for a moment. "Yes, two weeks is fine. See you there."

Sharon couldn't believe the joy of feeling her blood pounding through her veins, keeping the rain and mist at bay even though she was cunt naked. She was learning more about herself and about this new life every day now. She was toiling uphill, her bare feet squelching through puddles of brown water that lurked between tufts of coarse grass. Behind her was a log, chained to a yoke that passed across her shoulders. Her arms were outstretched and her wrists clipped to the yoke. Her right hand touched the left one of some white girl they had shackled to the same yoke. And That Man was driving them at the end of a whip up a steep hillside, out in the wilds somewhere. She dug in hard, desperate to please him, cursing the stubborn piece of timber that lurched behind them, catching in everything, sinking into every mire they waded across. It was a nightmare, except that with this special man's voice urging them on as if they were a team of horses and flinging blazing hot lashes down onto their sweating backs and across their flanks, it was where she wanted to be.

"Whoa! You lazy bitches!" he called eventually and they were allowed to stop, their breath and sweat enveloping them in clouds of steam.

"Okay, not too bad!" he said, rubbing both girls lightly with one hand, across their shoulders and running the now-coiled whip across the upper swells of their breasts with the other. Sharon's heart swelled with pride and she glanced across at the other girl who returned the smile. The man broke out a bar of chocolate and fed both of them a small piece.

"Right. We're going to leave the log here, jog down and then we're going to get another one and bring it back up here."

Neither girl could restrain a groan.

"Shut that!" he snapped. "You're still two seconds slower than the best team. I've got fifty quid that says I can lash you two tarts up here faster. If you can't do it, I've got four stakes here that say I'll stake you out and give you each fifty lashes! Now let's go!"

Sharon considered what it would be like to be staked out on the freezing, wet grass for beating and decided she had something left in reserve after all, she looked across at the other girl and hoped that the bitch did too.

A quarter of an hour later they lay at the top of the hill. Sharon could feel her heart pounding fit to burst from her chest, her legs trembled and her arms were numb from pulling at the yoke. In front of her face the man's boots squelched to a stop.

"Just goes to show what a lazy bunch of sluts you are. That was three seconds inside the best time. All it takes is a bit of encouragement!"

He bent down and she felt his strong arms lift her and set her back on her feet, then he helped her partner up and again produced a bit of chocolate. Then he left them to go and sit on a rock and enjoy the view for a while.

Sharon heard his mobile ring and watched as he took the call.

"Yes, two weeks is fine, Mr Mostyn! We've got a stable here!"

The man strolled back with a rare smile on his face and his hand hovering at his flies.

"Now which of you is going to get this, eh?" he asked, pulling his erect cock out of his trousers. Both girls were far too well trained by then to attempt any answer to the rhetorical question and waited quietly as he pushed them both down onto their knees. In the end, Sharon got first suck as he said he liked her mouth and lips. The other girl got second suck and when he came he shared it out between them, spraying their faces and making them hang their tongues out shamelessly as they sought to catch every drop they could.

Steve and Alex finished lashing their teams over the line and the squealing, jiggling onlookers quietened down as it became clear that Steve's pair had won by a nose. It had been a good log pulling race, plenty of whipping and a close finish as well. Kath was coming to realise that an arena slave had a lot in common with an arena spectator. They both liked what was done in the arenas!

The pull had been over rough terrain in one of the fields some distance from the house and as the two teams knelt and recovered, the boss gathered them all round in a close ring with himself at the centre. He made sure that each girl was split up from her sister and Kath found herself between Number One and Number Nine.

"Now I've got something important to tell you!" he said. "You've got used to working with your sister as a team against whichever pair we've allocated to you. And you've done well!"

Kath felt his praise as if it was meant for her personally. The boss didn't give out praise very much, and it was a welcome surprise when he did.

"But now we've got to move on. This isn't a holiday camp!" he went on. "We're building a stable here and now you're going to come up against another squad!"

He strode over to Kath and pulled her a little way into the circle then turned her around to face the other girls. "Your enemies aren't Number Nine or Number One! Or Number Seven here! From now on every girl here is your sister. If she's in trouble you help her. If you're in trouble she'll help you. You know each other well now, you know you all fight well. From now on you all fight together!"

There was an excited stir in the circle of naked girls but the boss had one more surprise.

"From now on you all sleep together too!"

At the end of the day's training they were taken to a dormitory in a wing of the house they hadn't been in before and left unhobbled and unshackled to shower and wash and relax for an hour before lights out. And even when the lights did go out, they were left free and took full advantage. Kath finally found Annie in the small hours and crept into bed beside her having tried out every other girl in the room. Annie's goodnight kiss tasted as richly of girl as Kath's own mouth did.

Carlo's phone went when he was walking back to the CSL yard from the main house. He was skirting the dark bulk of the training arena guiding his steps by the security lights that came on to mark his passage as he walked. It had been a passably entertaining evening in the Common Room, the place where The Lodge's Housegirls could be played with by any guest, even if she wore a disk at her collar that marked her down as booked for the night. But the truth was that he was falling out of love with the whole slave/domination/submission culture. He could still appreciate how beautiful a girl looked when tied ready for her discipline. He could still appreciate the eroticism of knowing that she genuinely wanted what was about to happen to her, and of course the way her body spun and quivered under the lash and the way her buttocks swayed when struck and her breasts rippled was superb. But somehow, since Blondie had gone, it was as if he was watching everything from a distance. He didn't feel involved any more.

In fact he was composing a speech he intended to make to John Carpenter in the morning. It was time he retired. Brian and Tony could carry on CSL perfectly well.

He stopped for a moment and cancelled out all his prepared words in his mind. He took a deep breath and framed the thought that had been skirting his mind all evening. He was tired.

The phone vibrated quietly in his jacket pocket. He sighed and took it out. It was Johnson N'Benga. No doubt it would be a 'nothing to report' call, but we're doing all we can, Carlo old buddy.

"Carlo!" Johnson's rich voice immediately grabbed Carlo's attention, it sounded more animated than usual. "I think I've got something!"

Carlo held his breath. "It's just a whisper, but I've had an e mail from an old friend who says a friend of a friend is cock a hoop because they've been able to buy a ticket for the event of the century."

"What the hell's that?"

"I don't know, my friend. Not yet. But I've asked my contact to try and find out. It's definitely to do with the arenas and it's being held in Europe."

Carlo breathed out and began thinking out loud, furiously hard. "Why so secret? If it's that big, why not publicise it? It's got to be her! It's got to be! They're scared of losing her! If she can be stolen once, she can be stolen again! But what are they planning?"

"Carlo, I admit it looks promising, but that's all it is at the moment. Please try and be patient. I'll call you again tomorrow."

Carlo looked up at the clear night sky and tried to calm himself, but how could he? Blondie was out there somewhere and she would be wanting him! How could he have been so selfish and stupid, his Blondie wouldn't give up on him, she would be believing he would come for her. Well he would! He didn't have time to be tired, he had work to do!"

He strode forwards, determined to spend the night in every chat room and forum around the world that might have a whisper about a special event being held.

Marcel was worried, although he wouldn't dream of showing it. He drove Blondie out around the estate three days after the party and there was clearly something wrong with her. He stared moodily at the strong back as it flexed, pulling the trap on a clear morning that had just a hint of autumn chill about it so that her breath still steamed. He flicked at her again with the whip, this time across those delectable buttocks and for a moment there was a slight acceleration but then she settled back into a lethargic trot.

Guillaume had told him that she had refused to work out in the gym that morning. He had lashed her as hard as he had whipped any slave, he said, and she hadn't even moved from where she was standing. And now he had the feeling that she was running purely because she wanted to, and if she stopped wanting to, she would just stop. There would be nothing he could do about it.

He had thought there would be some sort of reaction to the absence of Carlo, but he hadn't expected anything this dramatic. His plans now depended on the carefully sown hints he had planted in the rumour mill that was the world of the arena followers. The trouble was that he couldn't check how well the rumours were spreading. He just had to hope that Carlo would come running.

In the meantime the girl he had bought in America continued to train and develop well. She had taken Guillaume for a very brisk few circuits of the racing track that very morning, trimming seconds off the times she was clocking when she first arrived.

Marcel seriously considered, for the first time, what it would mean if Blondie actually lost this fight.

Back in her cell, the slave everyone knew as Blondie, slumped against the wall behind her bed and closed her eyes. The run had been good, the whip pleasant enough. The beating she had taken for not exercising had been energising but she had no intention of doing any exercise other than running, which she enjoyed.

She was beginning to realise that she was in deep trouble and far away from her Master, who might not even know where she was. In her mind she replayed the journey from the last arena she had fought in, to the plane. It seemed more and more likely that she had been kidnapped. She was also becoming aware that she couldn't hold out as Blondie if her Master wasn't there. It was Carlo who had invented Blondie, had shaped her and made her his. Alone, it was ridiculous to pretend that she was Blondie. She was just plain – she veered away from the thought of reclaiming her real name, as if striking out back into shallow water – mentally she got her feet back under her and succeeded in shutting out the thoughts.

But she was left alone all that day and the next. And by the end of that day she knew she was no longer Blondie. She couldn't keep the unwelcome thoughts at bay if she was on her own. She had to think of a way out of this mess and Blondie didn't do thinking – at least not outside an arena. To do that she needed the girl she had once been. She needed to be Tara.

She had sobbed all through the night as she released the memories and thought of how much Tara had lost by becoming Blondie, but now she was over it and ready to fight. She might be naked and handcuffed but at least she knew she was nobody's obedient little slaveslut anymore. If she was alone; then she was Tara.

Guillaume got a kick in the balls that left him retching on the floor when he brought her food and she had bolted before he knew what was happening. She pounded along a corridor looking for somewhere she could find something to press against the karabiners in her cuffs so she could slip them apart. However, all she achieved was running straight into the man who seemed to be in charge of this place. They collided at a corner and sent each other flying but Tara was faster back to her feet, however the man just managed to grab an ankle and start yelling for help. In a minute she was caught and was bundled, kicking and biting back into her cell.

"You must do something, M'sieur. It will be a walkover and they will want their money back!" A still-pale Guillaume and Marcel were watching the girl who had once beaten Blondie work out in the stableyard, she was sparring with one of the stable hands who was holding a big block of foam filled plastic. She landed a roundhouse kick and followed it up with a dazzlingly fast combination of punches. She looked in superb condition, her hair was thick and glossy and her body was toned, the flesh firm and gleaming in the sun as she sweated.

"I think you are right," Marcel said thoughtfully. At this rate Blondie wouldn't last a minute and the kind of people who were paying the kind of money he was asking would not be happy. And as for the websites and some pay per view TV channels that were bidding for the rights….their owners would not stop at writing angry letters if the spectacle turned out to be a damp squib. He pulled himself together.

"Work her for another half an hour, then give her her morning beating – fifty lashes from now on, twice a day." He walked away heading for Blondie's cell.

She was sitting up on her bed, back against the wall, her hair tousled, livid marks on her thighs and arms from the struggle to get her back in there. She glared up at him, sullen and defiant. Marcel stood and looked down at her for a moment, reviewing his strategy. There didn't seem to be any alternatives.

"I mean you no harm," he began. "I am purely a sportsman who is consumed by curiosity. There are tens of thousands of people out there who also want to know whether you threw that final fight before you were taken from Conor Brien's stable."

At the mention of Conor Brien's name her head snapped up again and the blue eyes blazed with fury.

"It's alright, I have no plans that involve him!" Marcel assured her. "But I have found the girl you fought that night and I want to re-stage the fight. Your master would not have let you risk your reputation. But it is essential to the reconstruction that he is here when the fight takes place – just as he was the first time. He will be here! I am making every effort to lure him here..."

The blonde was on her feet in an instant and Marcel had to whirl around behind her to avoid the kick. Then he held her close against him as he finished.

"To lure him here so that he can be with you! I want him here so that we can reconstruct the match as accurately as we can and you will be free to leave with him afterwards! I swear it! You know your master, think about it. How else could I get him here?"

He felt the tension drain out of her as his words sank in and she thought of her master. Of course he would come for her, Marcel could almost feel the thoughts running through her mind. She turned her head and nodded just slightly. He released her.

"Now," he said, "do you want to see who you're up against?"

Again there was the slight nod and Marcel led her out, not on a leash but gently guiding her by an elbow, as if she was a timid creature that might take flight at any time. And he could still feel there was some tension there. If he could just get some indication of activity from CSL, it would seal the deal with her, he thought.

He made a mental note to make the paper trail he had put in place, just in case it was needed, a bit more plain. Maybe everyone was being just too discreet this one time. One phone call to someone in the accounts department of a big local firm was all it would take. The man had already had his palm greased.

Out in the yard, Annette, the ex-Lithuanian schoolteacher, was pulling a log at a fast walking pace across the cobbles, her arms stretched out on a yoke. The stable hand was encouraging her by pulling hard on her nipples. As they watched, she reached the end of her run. The hand uncoupled her chains and had her stand up straight, still yoked. Guillaume then stood forward and began to deliver her morning ration of lashes. They watched her stand impassively as the single tail snaked out and caressed her back with its harsh kisses. After twenty-five had been counted, he went to stand in front of her. She re-settled her feet to withstand the lashes coming from a new direction but took them in silence.

Beside him, Marcel could feel the blonde begin to stir as she responded to the sight of the fine body taking its discipline so readily. He risked a sidelong glance and saw her nipples standing hard and proud.

Later that day he went online and saw that the chats about what was going on in France were getting more specific but still, that call might be worth it. Carlo couldn't fail to pick up on the trail then. He looked in on Blondie and found that she had cleaned her trough and was prowling her cell impatiently.

"He will be here!" he told her.

She tossed her hair back and gave him a fierce smile that said; 'I'm back!'.

Marcel couldn't help striding forwards, there was something so challenging and so proud in that smile.

He grabbed her hair and wrenched her head back, then kissed her briefly before bending his head to suckle at the nipples that swelled and hardened almost instantly. He dug his hand roughly between her thighs which parted eagerly for him and he bore her down onto the straw bed. It took him only a few seconds to fumble his trousers open and push them down his thighs, and then he was on her, his cock nudging urgently at her entrance which opened smoothly for him.

He rode her to a shattering orgasm and as he came down he felt her arch rigid beneath him and her belly fluttered and spasmed around his cock as she too came.

CHAPTER SIXTEEN.

Carlo was infuriated, he replayed the video for the umpteenth time that day, still finding it hard to believe that they were actually putting film of Blondie in training on the net. She was shown with weighted boxing straps pummelling a punchbag. She was shown log pulling under the lash of someone whose face was carefully blurred out, she was shown weight lifting and she was shown under the whip for purely training purposes as far as he could see. It didn't appear to be a punishment. In fact it was pretty much the same regime as he would have imposed if he had had her under his control. And then there was the other girl. He couldn't remember too much about the night they were aiming to reconstruct, it had been a hectic dash for freedom with the unconscious Blondie over his shoulder. But he could remember watching in dismay as his star pupil was beaten down in the cage. Now he was asking himself if she really had thrown the match. He watched the other girl training and had to admit she was fast and fit.

In vain he and Tony and John had tried to find out the whereabouts of the venue but maddeningly there was no word. People seemed happy to chat online about the event, discussing which girl might win, but no one was letting on where the fight would take place.

They had used every single contact they had inside and out of the arena world but come up with nothing.

Until with only forty eight hours to go, John Carpenter got a call from The Lodge's sister club in France. One of their members owned an industrial plant hire and builders' supply company and the manager of one of its branches had drawn his boss's attention to the hire of a crane, scaffolding and bench seating to the Baron Sagemont. The baron was a well known aficionado of the arenas and when Carlo saw the word 'crane' he felt the hackles on the back of his neck rise.

On that fateful night the cage in which the girls had fought had been hoisted up into the night sky on the end of a crane's arm. It had been swung around the arena so that even those in the topmost tier of the terraces could get a close up view of the action. It also meant that the cage itself was continually swaying and swinging, making the contest more unpredictable.

Had it been that factor which had defeated Blondie? Well there was no time to ponder that question now. John had a helicopter pick him up from The Lodge and by dawn of the day of the fight, he was cruising around the perimeter of the baron's estate in a hired car, looking for the way in. He and Tony had googled it before he left and he had come equipped with pitons, a rope and a thick blanket. Already there was some traffic arriving at the main gate and being ushered in by men who looked as though they meant business. Carlo had decided that he would wait until early evening before trying to scale the wall, by then people would be streaming in and security would be stretched, if he could just get in and join the crowd, he was certain that no one would recognise him in the dusk and amid all the excitement.

Eventually he found the part of the wall that Tony and he had reckoned to be the easiest to scale and he settled down to wait. He had to admit that he had no idea how he was going to free Blondie once he was inside, but he just felt that if he got in, some opportunity would present itself. It wasn't much of a plan but it was all he had.

Blondie looked up hopefully as her cell door opened but it was only the Frenchman who was in charge. As hard as she had tried over these last few weeks, she hadn't entirely been able to put Tara back in her place so that she could relax and be Blondie again until Carlo came for her. A treacherous voice kept whispering that the Frenchman was lying; Carlo wasn't coming for her; she was on her own. During training she had heard and seen the preparations for the fight and knew that it was imminent but still there was no Carlo.

There had been no training for a whole day and she knew that the fight was to be now. The Frenchman held a bright blue satin cloak for her and a be-jewelled leash.

"Don't worry," he told her. "I made sure he couldn't fail to find out where we are. He'll be here."

With her mind still clouded, Blondie couldn't relax and concentrate. She felt ill at ease still and knew that until Carlo was there, she wouldn't feel properly whole. But there was nothing else to do other than to play along and hope. She stood up and allowed the cloak to be fastened at her neck and the leash to be run forwards between her legs.

The stadium had been constructed on a level field about a quarter of a mile from the house. It was nowhere near the size of a proper arena but it did well enough for the crowd which now occupied every single seat. They had been warmed up by the spectacle of the baron's zoo being paraded and then the compere had claimed that the baron had deliberately postponed discipline until that night so that the slaves could provide entertainment. Each girl had a charge sheet read out against her and was dealt with for the crowd's entertainment. The whole thing was lit garishly by floodlights as Blondie was led to wait her turn, she saw one of the Bakhtar girls suspended upside down and thrashed by two men, one working exclusively between her legs. As she was tethered to one of the scaffold poles that held the terraces up, she saw that the beating had stopped and now a vibrator was being plied in the girl's vagina – or rather it wasn't. It was just being introduced a few inches, allowed to buzz away for a few seconds and then it was withdrawn. The girl was begging dementedly for release and the compere was referring to the crowd, asking for the thumbs up or down. Of course the thumbs were all down, the evening was young and the crowd wanted a lot more entertainment yet. The familiar atmosphere of decadent cruelty and sexual arousal flooded through Blondie and for a moment she forgot about the fact that her master still hadn't appeared.

Above her head feet drummed on the boarding and out in the pitilessly lit arena, some more of the zoo's inmates and some slaves lent by the baron's friends were tied out on tables, their legs raised and spread. Ticket numbers were drawn at random and if the winners were male they were invited down to sample them and mark them out of ten. Other winners were invited to wind a handle as hard as they could for a set number of seconds in order to build up an electrical charge. When the time was up, the current was released and passed through electrodes clamped to a girl's labia, the idea was to see if anyone could make her come with one single charge. Cries of orgasm floated up on the night air in amongst the laughter and cheers of the crowd.

Quietly, from out of the shadows under the opposite bank of seats, two figures appeared. One was Guillaume and he was leading the dark haired girl who wore a green cloak and was tethered as she was. The two surveyed each other, weighing up the possible strengths and weaknesses. She looked fit and strong, Blondie had to admit, but then so was she. Her problem was that she just couldn't focus down on the business in hand properly.

At last the warm up slaves were exhausted and the compere announced the evening's main event. The crowd settled down into that hungry silence that Blondie recognised so well as he outlined the reason for the re-match. It still came as something of a shock to her that people all over the world had been wondering about that original fight. Carlo had kept her cocooned from her fame to some extent and now she could appreciate why. But where was he?

"So with no further delay, bring on the contestants!" The compere reached his peak and the crowd rose applauding thunderously as Marcel led her in and Guillaume brought in the dark haired girl.

And still there was no Carlo.

Carlo waited until the light had nearly gone altogether before he finally opened the boot of the car, took a quick look around and hammered in pitons between the stones of the wall up as far as he could reach. He replaced the hammer and slung a loop of rope round his neck and one shoulder, took the thick blanket out, locked the car and climbed up the improvised stairs. He threw the blanket across the razor wire on top and after a few tries lassooed the branch of a tree that came near the wall at this point. Then he swung himself in without putting too much weight on the blanket covering the razor wire and let himself down.. There was no time to bother about covering his tracks, so he just marched straight off towards where he could see car headlights moving slowly along a drive inside the estate.

After several minutes of walking, he realised he had left things rather too late. The cars were becoming fewer and the noise from behind some trees in the distance was growing louder. He broke into a trot.

The road was deserted when he finally reached it. He began to feel the first stirrings of real unease. He was too late. He picked up his pace and began to run away from the direction of the wall and towards the noise, which was now reaching a crescendo. He had to find out what was going on. He felt the sweat grow clammy on his body as he neared the source of the noise and heard a voice announce her name over the PA. He accelerated and never saw the guard step out from behind a shrub on his right, trip him and twist his arm high up his back as he fell forwards.

"Good evening, Mr Suarez," a voice said in his ear. "We've been expecting you."

Blondie could not honestly say she remembered the girl from the fight so long ago but she remembered the cage. There was a door cut in one side that could be locked, a cage stayed shut until only one girl could walk out. The sides were too high to be climbed over but the top was open. Ropes led up from the four corners of the top to a central hook hanging from the crane's jib. That meant there was plenty of play for it to tip and tilt as the girls moved about inside. The open top meant that a weapon could be thrown in from time to time – but only one of any sort, and it was up to each girl to get it and use it.

The applause was deafening as the two gladiators were led out. Even the noise of the crane's engine starting was drowned out and only a rising cloud of grey smoke betrayed the fact that it was ready.

The compere kept stoking up the atmosphere as they followed their leashes towards the cage but once there, with the crowd now baying for action, the cloaks were unfastened, the leashes, collars and cuffs all removed and the two naked women shoved in with surprising speed. Blondie stumbled as she entered a few steps behind the other girl and before she could recover her balance, the cage was lifted high into the air and swung around so that it passed in front of one bank of seats, throwing her onto her back.

"That's not a good omen f you've got your money on Blondie!" the compere cried.

She sat up but the other girl was on her with no hesitation and had her in a headlock before she fully knew what was going on. For a second all thoughts about Carlo vanished and she was pure fighter again, going face down onto the mesh floor of the cage and then wriggling backwards to escape the hold, before throwing herself onto her opponent's back. The girl was fast and ducked her head so that Blondie went flying over it and was turned head over heels as she stood up under her flying body.

The mesh floor with the bars underneath hurt her back as she landed and she was caught flat on it by the other girl who landed with her elbow in her stomach. Blondie doubled over, nearly winded completely, only her ring rusty instincts saving her from being completely immobilised.by making her tense her stomach and half roll away. Even so she found herself dragged up before she had got her breath back and Irish Whipped. The world spun crazily as she somersaulted in mid air and crashed back down on her back. But this time she was quicker and rolled away before the follow up arrived. Only then was she able to keep her feet for a second and re-gather her senses. The dark haired girl was advancing in a half crouch, looking fierce and determined. Blondie backed away, playing for recovery time and found herself backed up against the side; she feinted to the left and danced away as the girl fell for it. Then it was her turn to charge but again the girl was quick and she found herself face first against the wire, one arm up her back and her breasts painfully rasping on the wire. The faces of the crowd seemed to hurtle past as the cage swung, up above her on the screens she could see her face twisted in anguish as her nipples were pinched in the mesh. Behind her the dark girl was grinning. Blondie dug her free elbow backwards and was rewarded by a sharp grunt of pain. She spun round but was flung to the floor again as the cage suddenly dropped and a riding crop was flung in by a guard who was standing in the arena beside a table of implements. Blondie scrabbled forwards desperately but was pulled back by an ankle, the dark girl scrambled over her, Blondie rolled over and flung her away, then lunged but was held again. Once more the dark girl scrambled bodily over Blondie and this time they embraced like lovers, face to face. Blondie managed to pinch and scratch at the girl's nipples and she screamed and rolled away, but one out-flung hand grabbed the crop. They scrambled up and the girl charged in lashing wildly with the crop while Blondie covered up as best she could. The braided shaft landed with bruising force on her back and ribs and thighs but she could take that all day. She made a grab for the girl's leg when she came too close but the dark girl was agile enough to dance back without being overbalanced and slashed wildly across Blondie's chest, catching both nipples hard. She yelled and turned away, taking yet more stinging slashes across her buttocks and reeling back against the cage's side, facing the crowd. The crop continued to slash down on her and somehow she just knew that she didn't have the reserves to beat this foe. She was too good for her to take on in her current state of uncertainty.

The cage lurched and swung and the crop sliced down and cracked across her back and she began to sink down to her knees. Then the crane swung the cage once more and the owner's box came into view.

In this temporary arena it was no more than a canvas roofed balcony affair set high up at one end of the oval. But as Blondie's dazed eyes took it in, she saw a figure slowly climb into sight from the stairs which led up to the back of the terraced seating. For a moment, standing right at the top the man paused. He was picked out by the floodlights against the ink-black sky.

He looked directly at her.

It was Carlo.

Blondie let out a scream of joy as she saw him take in her predicament and form a fist with his right hand and mouth some words. She knew what he was saying. He was telling her to fight!

It was all she needed. Her Master was back.

With a roar of defiance she turned and whipped the crop out of the astonished girl's hand and sent it flying out into the night sky.

Then she grabbed the girl between her legs with one hand, got a handful of hair with the other and hoisted her high into the air before flinging her bodily against the opposite side of the cage. As she did so a short and whippy cane was lobbed in and Blondie picked it up as she advanced on the girl. She played with her for the crowd, flicking at her thighs and breasts as the targets appeared as she feinted and danced around her victim. But still the girl didn't give in and although heavily welted, she managed to grab the boxing strap that was next in. She waded through some hard strikes and cornered Blondie before landing some heavy, roundhouse blows to her stomach and breasts.

Blondie covered up again and crouched down as if beaten. The girl lifted her fist high to smash down on her back but Blondie came back up minus the cane.

This time she went for a crotch hold and got it. The dark girl was lifted high and then toppled, wailing, backwards as she snatched her clenched fingers out of the rectum and vagina. The boxing strap was no help from then on. Blondie picked her up long enough to swing her around to dizzy her and then swing her full force into the corner. The cage juddered but the girl tottered up and staggered forwards. Blondie bent and picked her up across her shoulders to spin her again. This time her despairing scream stilled the arena as she crashed into the side and hit the floor.

Blondie strode across and grabbed her by the hair, hauling her up to her knees. The girl was dazed and only came to life when Blondie twisted a nipple savagely. The crowd's thumbs were out and all pointing down. The tall blonde looked around and saw them. This was her realm. She was the queen of the arenas and no one in the stadium that night or who saw the fight on screen, would forget it. She bent once more and picked the girl up easily, holding her horizontally above her, then she stretched her arms high above her head, the dark girl now too terrified to wriggle.

Cameras flashed all around and in the months to come, this was the iconic image of Blondie in action. Legs braced, arms aloft, a struggling and vanquished girl held above her.

In his seat next to the baron, Carlo grinned fiercely, counting under his breath. He knew she would milk the moment and finish it with impeccable timing.

"Now!" he whispered.

Blondie pushed the wretched girl a little higher and then simply stepped backwards. The girl barely had time to scream before she hit the floor and Blondie came down on top of her back.

The crowd's thumbs came out pointing upwards. There was no point in going on. The question had been answered and the makeshift arena shook to the applause.

EPILOGUE.

Peter Lang and Brian Holden leaned happily on the wooden fence which surrounded the pen in which the girls were fighting. A hosepipe had been played on the earth floor within the fence and to start with twenty naked furies had battled it out inside. A small invited audience had watched raptly, cheering and clapping occasionally as some slippery bit of girlflesh was grabbed long enough to fetch a cry from the victim, or, even more occasionally, a body was thrown hard enough to make the thick ooze splash. The girls had raced, fought, boxed and lashed each other over two days and both men were well pleased. Currently there were only three pairs still staggering back into conflict, the rest had been pulled out by their trainers as exhaustion had claimed them. Neither man was bothered about which team had won. They knew that by fighting so grimly, both teams had justified the Proteus project.

The first official gladiator stable would be established in a few months, and these twenty girls would be the core of its stock.

"We'll put 'em in the same barracks tonight and they'll sort out their own pecking order by the morning," Peter said.

"Well worth watching the CCTV!" Brian suggested.

Peter laughed. "Oh, yes! They'll get all the fight out of themselves and by the morning we'll have a team, once all the bruises and scratches have healed!"

Out in the mud the last pair had struggled up one last time and were flinging filth at each other as they knelt up, unable to stand up any more. Brian was sure that one of them was their journalist and he pointed her out to Peter.

"Talented lass!" he said. "You obviously punished her well. That one she's got in the headlock went by the name of Sharon, I believe. A right hard case when I got her, but a reformed and useful member of society now!"

The reformed and useful member of society yelped as Kath got a crotch hold on her but had no strength to lift, so the two bodies fell back into the mire, locked together like the lovers they might very well become.

As the men stepped in to haul the exhausted bodies out of the pit, Angie got up and left. She wasn't sorry for Kath, why should she be, the girl was as happy as a pig in…well she was happy. Angie realised she felt sorry for herself and that made her bad tempered. But Sara would help her bear her loss, and of course she now had the money for a cruise in the Med for a month.

Carlo had yet to announce Blondie's retirement but when she came downstairs from Carlo's room at the CSL stable wearing the clothes that Patti had been out to buy before their return, it was clear that Tara was back. She looked stunning in a flared beige skirt and crisp, grey shirt with a high collared jacket over it. She had travelled back from France in some of Claire's cast offs; Carlo having decided that her retirement started immediately. She wasn't ready for underwear yet and her breasts pushed firmly against the silk of the shirt. Her legs looked even longer as they were in to-die-for heels that Patti had spent a small fortune on in London.

Carlo was actually nervous. Her tongue ring had come off only that morning and he was very well aware that although he had tamed and trained Blondie, he now had to get to know Tara. However, he was reassured to see that she too was blushing and nervous.

He scolded Patti and everyone out of the office and threatened them with dire punishments if they even peeked out of the stable windows when they left. He offered her his arm and grinning, she accepted.

"We are going for a turn around the grounds, then we are lunching with John Carpenter and his wife in the private dining room," he told her. She nodded, still reluctant to use her voice.

"And after that....well let's start thinking about where we'd like to live."

"The... We... West Country's nice," she managed in a hoarse whisper.

They stepped out into bright, cold sunlight.

"Well money's no problem, and with the first official arena opening down that way, could be a good investment."

Tara's heels clicked and scraped on the cobbles as the couple walked side by side, trying to wear away the strangeness. Suddenly, Tara stopped and looked up at the clear sky.

"Do you know what the last thing I did was before I was enslaved?" she asked, her voice becoming a rather sensual growl.

"No," Carlo said, looking at her anxiously. This was still sensitive territory but she was adapting quickly and coming to terms with everything. She could now accept that as Blondie, she had had pretty good times and she had freely chosen to retain her CSL brand. So she was no longer grieving for Tara's lost years

"I went sky diving," she said. "Have you ever done that, Sir?"

"No," Carlo replied, suddenly very sure that he would be doing it very shortly if Tara had any say in it. "Come on, we've got a ride waiting for us up at the main stable."

Blackie had been warmed up for them on the treadmill and was waiting in full dressage tack between the shafts of a two-seater.

Carlo wasn't sure how she would react but he needn't have worried, she was thrilled to be able to appreciate a pony slave in her full finery and gleefully inspected the crupper strap to make sure it was tight enough, and did the same with the tit straps. She would need to be run in harness herself from time to time, he was sure of it.

He courteously handed her into her seat then took his own and picked up the driving whip. On a whim he held it out for her and she slowly ran a hand up the shaft and then touched the lash which was just stirring in the breeze.

"It belongs in your hands, Sir," she whispered. "And always will."

Carlo smiled at her as her hand caressed his, holding the handle of the whip firmly and expertly.

"You know you're an honorary Housegirl? And I'm an honorary member, so we can come back whenever we want."

"I always wanted one of their dresses!" she said with a broad grin.

"I always wanted to see you in one of those dresses!" he replied and whipped Blackie up. "Mind you," he added as they passed under the arch and Blackie trotted out into the parkland. "I always wanted to see you out of one of those dresses too!"

Tara laughed and leaned against her adored Master.

"Please can we see how fast she goes? I've never driven in one of these before!"

"For you my lady? Anything!"

The whip hissed and smacked on the pony slave's back and she leaned further forward, opening her stride and making the wheels rumble over the tarmac.

As Carlo encouraged her and the lash sang in the clear air, Tara laughed for the sheer joy of the wind in her hair and a future that looked as bright as the autumn sky overhead. With her Master beside her, Blondie would never be far away but now Tara was back and both were content.

The Arena Series:

Each novel can be read as a self-contained and complete story in its own right, but together they build into a tapestry of vividly portrayed characters whose actions are played out against the erotic backdrop of the modern arenas.
These are the most talked-about and sought after books we've ever published.

Into the Arena

A beautiful, thrill seeking blonde meets an intimidating stranger and finds herself enslaved and taken on a long voyage of self-discovery.

The Gladiator.

Tara's progress in the arenas as she struggles to escape from the tyranny of her owner. Struggles for possession of the beautiful 'Blondie' go from arena to arena.

The Prize.

Ayesha is a seductive and treacherously deceitful girl who becomes the subject of a bet between two powerful players in the arena world. As her treachery is revealed, so more people are drawn into the arenas.

Slave's Honour.

Follow the fortunes of a new slave trainer learning his craft from the man who tamed 'Blondie' and enter the world of the girls who work in the stables where they are kept. Some of the best pony slave writing ever!

Last Slave Standing.

Once again the blonde 'Queen of the Arenas' is centre stage as powerful men fight over her. But out on the arena floor there is also the challenge of the ultimate contest for her to contend with.

Girl Squad.

The only female owned and trained squad of gladiators takes on the might of the men. But they have a secret weapon.

Naked Ambition.

The destinies of two beauties, Angel and Ayesha are intertwined and the ending packs a punch!

Seed of Submission and Fruit of Submission
By Robin Ballantyne.

The first two novels by a talented newcomer. The books follow the adventures of the female side of a family as they find their true calling at the hands of the men in their lives.
Original and highly-charged! Watch out for the third novel in 2011!

Subduing Jacqueline and Mastering Jacqueline
By Jordan Church.

From inside a psychiatric institution, Wayne Jones masterminds a hierarchy of dominant men and submissive women. But will he be able to make Jacqueline, smart, professional and clever fall under his spell?
The concluding part of this absorbing struggle will be released n 2011.

High Heath Academy and Hard Lessons
By Alan Raison.

For lovers of CP this is an unmissable treat as girl after girl has to bare and bend! There is a non-stop supply of inventive girl on girl action and Headmaster on girl action too, as the High Heath Academy seeks to control its unruly pupils!

Tormented Passage
By Robert Carradine.

Beautifully illustrated by 'Loki', this is a sci-fi take on SM as female passengers pay a heavy price to voyage on the ships of the future. A real must for connoisseurs of Silver Moon.

The Reins of Power
By Elizabeth Johns

Another impressive debut! Elizabeth Johns' tale of a spoiled celebrity getting her comeuppance is told in sensual detail. A glimpse into the bedrooms of the rich and depraved, and finally into their stables too.

Write to, or phone, Silver Moon Readers' Services to find out about our ever-expanding range of high quality erotica. You'll also find that there are titles which you can buy that you can't get in the book shops and there are always bargains available to our members. And membership is free!

The Whipmaster series
By Francine Whittaker

The Whipmaster
Pleasure Control
Bridled and Bound

Francine has consistently been one of Silver Moon's best selling writers and the Whipmaster is one of her most popular creations. Tyler Morrison is the sullen and resentful gypsy lad with a big chip on his shoulder. And when he unexpectedly inherits a fortune and a stately pile as well, it's payback time as far as he's concerned. Which is bad news for some women who crossed his path in the past.

Duty Bound
By Francine Whittaker

The most recent Francine title and one of her best. Rusty is a fiery and sassy redhead who is footloose and fiancé free until she meets her nemesis! Then all of a sudden the sultry heat of Africa, the darkest of continents, and a mysterious island all feature largely in her immediate future.